GIFT FROM THE SEA

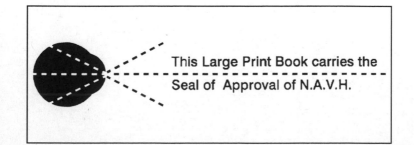

This Large Print Book carries the
Seal of Approval of N.A.V.H.

GIFT FROM THE SEA

ANNA SCHMIDT

THORNDIKE PRESS

A part of Gale, Cengage Learning

GALE
CENGAGE Learning·

Farmington Hills, Mich • San Francisco • New York • Waterville, Maine
Meriden, Conn • Mason, Ohio • Chicago

GALE
CENGAGE Learning

LIBRARY OF CONGRESS CATALOGING-IN-PUBLICATION DATA

Schmidt, Anna, 1943–
   Gift from the sea / by Anna Schmidt. — Large print edition.
      pages ; cm. — (Thorndike Press large print gentle romance)
   ISBN 978-1-4104-7660-9 (hardcover) — ISBN 1-4104-7660-X (hardcover)
      1. Nurses—Fiction. 2. World War, 1914-1918—Fiction. 3. Large type books.
   I. Title.
PS3569.C51527G54 2015
813'.54—dc23
                                                    2014041088

Published in 2015 by arrangement with Harlequin Books S.A.

Printed in Mexico
1 2 3 4 5 6 7 19 18 17 16 15

He will rule from sea to sea
And from the river to the ends
of the earth.

— *Psalms* 72:8

To all who serve in war and peace

In Flanders fields the poppies blow
Between the crosses, row on row,
That mark our place; and in the sky
The larks, still bravely singing, fly
Scarce heard amid the guns below.

We are the Dead. Short days ago
We lived, felt dawn, saw sunset glow,
Loved and were loved, and now we lie
In Flanders fields.

Take up our quarrel with the foe:
To you from failing hands we throw
The torch; be yours to hold it high.
If ye break faith with us who die
We shall not sleep, though poppies grow
In Flanders fields.
— "In Flanders Fields"
Lt. Col. John McCrae, M.D.

CHAPTER ONE

Nantucket Island
  January 1918

Maggie Hunter gazed out the windows that encased the cupola at the top of her family's inn. She rocked slightly from side to side, her arms folded tightly across her body, as the cold, sleety rain lashed at the glass like a whip. She came here often now in spite of the gray and blustery January weather that promised a long and especially harsh winter.

She came to wait for the tears she had not yet shed in the long months since she'd received the news of her fiancé's death. It was here in this cupola where she and Dr. Michael Williams had spent some of their happiest hours. Here they had played as children, dreamed the dreams of teenagers and planned a life together. It was here that Michael had proposed marriage. And here Michael had scanned the waters of the Atlantic, gazing through her father's telescope every day in search of any sign of the German U-boat that might be lurking offshore. And it was here, in this glass-enclosed room on a clear, warm April day less than a year earlier, that Michael had announced his intention to volunteer as a medic. America had finally entered the Great War, and he was determined to do his part.

Every day, just after completing her shift as a nurse at the Nantucket Cottage Hospital, Maggie made this pilgrimage. The inn was her home and her family's business. She stood at the windows replaying the events of the summer day just three months later when Michael's father, Dr. Thomas Williams, had pulled his carriage up to the inn's entrance and slowly climbed down. His stooped shoulders seemed to bear a heavy load. The pounding of the sea against the shore and the high winds that foretold a summer electrical storm drowned out most of her father's deep voice as he came out to greet the doctor. But she had caught snatches of their conversation — "just come . . . his mother . . . devastated . . . Michael . . . gone . . ." — before Tom Williams broke down completely, sobbing against her father's shoulder.

Maggie had not cried that terrible day,

even when her mother held her tight, murmuring words of consolation, assuring her that in time she would come to understand God's will in all of this. And hearing those words, Maggie felt the icy fingers of rage grip her heart and freeze her unborn tears. God? What kind of God took fine young men in the prime of their lives, when they were on the verge of greatness, of doing good work, of making a better world for others?

Why?

Through the weeks and months that followed she buried herself in work, often volunteering for extra shifts and private duty so that she was exhausted enough to assure a dreamless sleep.

Now Maggie pulled her coat closer and buried her fingers inside the cuffs. The cupola was unheated, and even with the protection of being enclosed, the wind and cold found every crevice. Still she stayed, her heart and mind focused on the past and the dreams of what might have been that had died with Michael.

"Maggie?"

Maggie turned at the faint sound of her name. Her mother's voice, once strong and commanding, had become so weakened by her exhaustion after a recent bout of influenza as to be almost unrecognizable.

Maggie stepped to the doorway. "Up here," she called. "I'll be down in a minute."

"It's so raw out. Can you see your father coming?"

Maggie stepped back to the window and peered out into the gathering gloom of the late afternoon. Far in the distance she could just make out the comforting silhouettes of the lightships that guarded the coast. Her father was part of a volunteer group that patrolled assigned sections of the beaches at dawn and dusk. Maggie tried to see through the sleet streaking the window and the patchy fog. A figure — no, two — carrying something between them.

"Someone's coming," she called back, "but I don't think it's Papa." Even as he approached his fiftieth year, Gabe Hunter still moved with the elegant grace and purposeful stride of a man years younger. Although he had taken the death of every Nantucket son to heart and stayed up nights worried about finances and his beloved wife's health, he refused to abandon his faith.

"Are they coming here?" her mother asked.

"Yes. I'll be right down," she said and took a long, steadying breath before entering the narrow entry at the top of the spiral stairway and latching the trapdoor behind her.

"I'll stir the fire," her mother said, already on her way down the back stairs.

Maggie removed her coat and hung it on an upstairs hall tree. She was wearing her nurse's uniform. Her shift had been as long and exhausting as ever. So many new patients to attend to as new cases of the suspected influenza spread across the island like the omnipresent fog. Everyone on staff at the hospital had been given a dose of the vaccine developed by a doctor in Pittsburgh to prevent the flu virus, and so far it had been effective. In fact, it had been so effective that Doc Williams had insisted that anyone dealing with the public be vaccinated. That had included her parents, and although her mother had contracted the disease after receiving the vaccine, her case was far milder than some Maggie had seen in the hospital.

She pressed her palms over the white apron that had been pristine and starched earlier in the day and was now limp and soiled. She fumbled with tying a fresh bow as she ran down the wide circular stairway that ended in the large, welcoming and deserted lobby of the inn. The flames of the fire flared as her mother poked at the top log; then she crossed the hall to perform a

13

similar prodding on the fire laid in the large dining room. Maggie straightened the guest register and other items on the front desk. Any visitor to the inn held the promise of a paying customer — always a rarity in winter and even more so now because of the war.

Not a minute too soon, Maggie positioned herself behind the desk and plastered a smile on her face as the wide front door crashed open, rattling the etched-glass panes. In an instant the lobby was filled with the full force of the storm as well as the figures of two men, completely soaked and carrying between them a third.

"Papa!" Maggie cried as she rushed forward to shut the door and attend to her father. He and their neighbor, Sean Chadwick, were bent nearly double under the weight of a man who appeared to be quite unconscious. Or perhaps the man was dead.

The one thing that was sure to bring Lucie Hunter on the run was any indication that her beloved Gabriel might need her. The minute she heard Maggie's cry of alarm, she ran to the lobby. At the same instant their housekeeper, Sarah Chadwick, burst through the curtain that separated the front desk area from the kitchen and family quarters.

"Sean, what is it?" Sarah's eyes were wide

with fear and panic as she glanced from her fisherman husband to the inert form he and Gabe carried.

They eased the man onto one of the long wooden benches near the entrance; then Sean stood upright as he stretched his back in relief of having put down the heavy load. The five of them stood in a semicircle staring at the bedraggled body dressed in a black rubber diving suit.

"Sean found him on the beach," Maggie's father explained to her mother.

"He was barely moving when I spotted him," Sean added. "It's a wonder I saw him at all."

"No diving shoes," Papa noted. Instead the man wore two pairs of heavy wool socks tucked securely under the legs of the diving suit. The socks were covered in ice. "I suspect he was attempting to swim ashore."

"War or not, you know better than to go out in a storm like this," Sarah said, fussing over her husband as she helped him remove his rain slicker and shook it out before hanging it on the hall tree.

"You've lost your hat," Lucie added as she, too, relieved her husband of his coat.

"It's along the road," Gabe replied absently, his eyes returning to the young man.

Maggie took a step closer and studied the

stranger. "Is he dead?" she asked. At the moment, he seemed more sea creature than human. Nevertheless, he could bring questions from islanders already hyper-paranoid about the possibility of an imminent invasion.

The young man twitched and muttered something incomprehensible but clearly not English. All three women gave a little yelp of surprise and took a step backward.

"He's not dead," Gabe confirmed.

Sarah carefully pulled back the tight hood that covered much of the man's face and all of his hair, and her eyes teared. "Oh, Sean, he's no older than our own George," she whispered as she dropped to her knees next to the inert body.

Sarah Chadwick had worked at the inn from the day it had opened. She and her husband, Sean, a native Nantucket fisherman, had lost their only son to the war. George, who had been like a brother to Maggie, had volunteered with Michael that same April day and had died in battle just a week before they'd received the news of Michael's death. The family had lived in the smaller cottage overlooking the harbor where Maggie's grandparents had lived when they were alive. Since George's death, the cottage had been closed and Sarah and

16

Sean had taken a small room on the third floor of the inn.

"What are you going to do?" Lucie asked her husband.

"Oh, we must care for him," Sarah exclaimed before Gabe could form a reply.

"We don't even know him," Maggie pointed out. He was wet and filthy and she should have felt repulsed. Yet there was something about him that made it impossible for her to turn away. Maybe it was the golden hair that reminded her of summer days and hay drying in the fields and Michael stealing a kiss as they crossed the dunes.

"Sarah's right," Sean said with quiet determination. "We have to attend to him. He's almost surely suffering from frostbite and who knows what else."

"But look at him — he doesn't look like anyone we've ever seen on the island. And who goes swimming or diving in such weather? He could be working for the enemy," Maggie said, amazed at the need to state the obvious.

"Whatever his purpose, he is a young man in trouble. God makes no distinction between His children when they are in need," Lucie reminded her.

Maggie turned to her father. "Surely, the

17

authorities must be notified."

"Excellent point," Gabe replied. "Lucie, love, would you ring for Thomas?"

Maggie's relief was short-lived. Although Dr. Williams and her father were in charge of security on this east side of the island, she knew by her father's tone that the doctor was to be called to treat a patient — not as an authority. "I meant the coast guard — that authority."

Her father nodded. "The storm's got to run its course. There's a full-scale freeze-up in the harbor with no steamboat service for the last two days, so there's no hope for a transfer until the ice starts to break up," he said. "For now this young man is hardly a threat, and when he comes to, we may well be able to glean more information."

"Besides," Lucie added, "we are surmising that he is not one of our own. It's unfair to assume anything just because —"

The young man moaned as one hand dropped off the edge of the sofa and his fingers fell open, revealing a small gold cross.

"He's a Christian," Sarah said, smiling as if that alone solved everything.

Maggie's father moved to the man's head as Sean prepared to take his legs. "Maggie, go up ahead of us and turn down the bed

18

there in number three."

"But number three is —"

One look from her father was all it took for Maggie to head for the stairs. Number three was their largest guest room, occupying the premier corner of the inn and offering a panoramic view of the Atlantic as well as Nantucket Sound. It hardly seemed the right place to take a complete stranger who was almost certainly the enemy.

"I'll call Dr. Williams," Sarah volunteered. Her leather soles made clicking sounds on the wide-planked floor as she headed down the hallway to the alcove where the telephone sat on a small side table. They had placed it there for the convenience and privacy of their guests as well as the family.

"Let me cover the bed with a rubber sheet," Maggie's mother said as she rushed up the stairs ahead of the men.

By the time her father and Sean had made it up the stairway and maneuvered the man to the high four-poster bed, Gabe was perspiring and his breath came in irregular huffs. "Heavy," he commented as they heaved the man onto the bed — diving suit and thawing, dripping socks and all.

"Who could he be?" Mama wondered aloud.

Gabe stepped closer and considered the

stranger's matted mass of blond hair, which matched his dirty, close-cropped beard. "I have no idea," Gabe replied. "Maggie has a point. He's not from around here — that's certain."

Sarah entered the room and went immediately to the bedside. "The doctor is on a call. I left word for him to come when he could." She brushed the stranger's hair away from his forehead with two fingers. "He can't stay in these wet clothes," she said to Mama.

Gabe nodded. "Maggie, go get a pair of my pajamas and some fresh linens. We'll need to change this bed once we've cleaned him up."

"Go on," her mother instructed, shooing her toward the open door.

"But —" Maggie protested as her mother closed the door. "What if he's a spy?" she muttered, finishing her thought as she stood alone in the hallway. It had not escaped her notice that even the man's socks were not the kind normally seen in Nantucket — or in America for that matter. Her grandmother had been an expert seamstress and quilter. Her mother's knitting and needlework were legendary on the island. Maggie knew the difference between American and foreign-made goods. Even the cut of the diving suit was unique. And what if he were only one of many who had come ashore? Had anyone else considered the idea that enemy invaders might even now be plotting the occupation of Nantucket Island?

Am I the only person in this household who thinks this man's sudden arrival is more than a little strange? She rummaged through her father's bureau until she unearthed his oldest pair of pajamas.

Dr. Williams arrived an hour later with the news that the lines of communication between the island and the mainland were not operating. "Looks like a real nor'easter," he surmised. "Could be a couple more days before the harbor can open," he added as he followed Maggie's father and Sean up the stairs to the guest room. While the three men conferred behind the closed door of number three, the women gathered in the sitting room just off the lobby to await the doctor's diagnosis. Maggie's mother tended to some mending while Sarah paced and Maggie sat on the edge of her chair, her eyes glued to the closed door at the top of the stairs.

Another hour passed and the only sounds were the ticking of the grandfather clock by the front door and the howling wind and drizzle turned icy sleet that was tapping at

21

the windows. Finally the door at the top of the stairs opened, and the low murmur of male voices drifted down to the women. Mama's fingers stilled even though she kept her eyes on her handiwork. Sarah stopped her pacing and waited, while Maggie leaped to her feet and rushed to the foot of the stairs to meet her father. "Well?" she asked.

"Sit down, everyone," Gabe said quietly as he descended the stairs with Sean and the doctor, the gravity of the situation clear in their expressions.

Maggie could almost taste the tension that seemed to permeate the room. "Has the man passed?" she asked. These were turbulent times that made normally sane people act out of panic and fear. Would they be hailed as patriots or arrested for harboring the enemy? She gulped back the bile of anxiety that had formed at the back of her throat as her father placed a sodden leather wallet on the table and carefully removed one of the papers.

"Our guest is Stefan Witte of Düsseldorf. That's in Germany," he added, as if they didn't already know that. "According to these papers we found under his diving suit, he is twenty-six years old. If Tom's German can be trusted, his papers identify him as a communications officer assigned to the German Naval Command."

Sarah and Lucie gasped, and Maggie moved in for a closer look at the document her father had spread across the front desk. Same age as Michael.

"He is beginning to regain consciousness," Dr. Williams reported, "although it is difficult to tell if his ramblings are the result of delirium or he is attempting to tell us something. He appears to be in a great deal of pain, though he takes it well. I expect that's the frostbite starting to thaw."

"Did he say anything that made sense?" Mama asked.

"A couple of words," Gabe replied. "We believe that he was aboard a German vessel — probably a U-boat — that made it past the lightships keeping watch."

"In any case, he appears quite agitated, which is dangerous given that we cannot know the extent of the tissue damage the frostbite has caused," the doctor added. "In addition to the frostbite, there is also the potential he'll develop pneumonia." He turned his attention to Maggie. "The frostbite seems limited to his toes and fingers. I expect the hood protected his ears and much of his face, but we'll need to keep a watch on his nose and cheeks."

"Yes, doctor," Maggie replied, automatically dropping into her role as charge nurse for the patient.

"Keep his hands and feet elevated and splint the fingers and toes between regular massages of those exposed areas with snow through the night." He continued to speak to Maggie as a colleague.

"Is he suffering?" Sarah asked, wringing her hands.

"Tom has sedated him, and that should help him make it through the night," Sean assured her.

"And tomorrow?" Lucie asked.

Dr. Williams cleared his throat, then glanced at Sean and Gabe before answering. "We've decided that in light of the storm and the fact that the island is virtually cut off from the mainland, the best course is to keep his presence here to ourselves for the time being. At least until we can find out who he is, how he got here and whether there are others. If we raise an alarm, it's likely any cohorts he might have will panic and go into hiding. We might never learn their true purpose."

"Isn't that a job for the military?" Maggie asked, increasingly aware that everyone but her thought this was a good plan.

"Oh, Maggie," Sarah said, "he's a young man and he needs our help. What if he were one of our boys over there and some family had found him half-drowned?"

"He is German," Maggie replied. "He is our enemy." Have you forgotten? Forgiven?

Sarah turned away, and Lucie stared at Maggie for a long moment. "My darling daughter, what has this war done to you?"

"This man is not Michael — or George, Mama," Maggie protested.

"Margaret," her father said sternly, but Mama held up her hand as she looked deep into her daughter's eyes.

"No, but like George and Michael, he is a young man in a foreign land. You have always been the one to remind us that there has already been enough loss of young lives on both sides of this horrible war." Her voice caught and Gabe moved to her side, but she waved him away as she fought to control her emotions. "Stefan Witte is our guest," she continued in the firm voice she had always used when Maggie was in need of a reprimand. "He is ill and injured. Before we ask any questions or bring others into this, we will do our Christian duty. We will nurse him, feed him and show him that although our governments may be at war, he has nothing to fear while in our care." She paused for a moment and then added, "Am I making myself clear, Maggie?"

"Yes, ma'am." It had been weeks since Maggie had seen her mother so strong, so in command of the situation. On the one hand, it was a welcome change. On the other, there was a German seaman under their roof and it was naive to think that the milk of human kindness might be enough to defend them.

After Dr. Williams gave Maggie the medications she would need to administer for the pain and more detailed instructions for tending to the man, he promised to return the following morning at first light. He shook hands with Gabe and Sean, nodded to the women and left. Once he was gone, Maggie's mother took charge.

"Sarah, if you would see to some clear broth now — our guest has to have nourishment."

Sarah nodded and Sean followed her to the kitchen.

"I'm going to sit with him," Gabe said, and Lucie touched his cheek gently before he started up the stairs.

Maggie waited until she was sure her father was gone and then said, "Mama?"

Mama turned, her expression softened by her moment with her husband. But when she saw Maggie's face, she frowned. "What is it?"

"I can't do this."

"Do what?"

"Mama, he's German."

"And I'm Irish and you're American. Oh, Maggie, you have always been the first to stand alongside anyone in need. When others on the island shunned the Schulers even before America became involved in this horrible war, it was you who called on them, brought them back to church and made clear to all that these were Americans who happened to have a German surname."

"Yes, but —"

"And isn't that the very reason why you became a nurse? So that you could help others?"

"I know, but —"

"Now this young man comes to us and you want us to turn our backs? He's a child of God."

Maggie swallowed hard as she stared at her mother. "You speak of him as if you know him. We know nothing about him except that he is German — not American with German ancestors like the Schulers. What if he's a spy? What if even now his commander is sitting out there under the sea, waiting for some signal?"

Mama blinked and then released a sigh of pure exasperation. "I simply do not understand what has happened to your sense of charity."

The war happened, Maggie thought, but her mother was as aware of that as she was. Sarah returned from the kitchen bearing a tray with a bowl of steaming broth, a spoon and a linen napkin. She started for the stairs.

"Maggie will take that, Sarah," Mama said, her eyes never leaving her daughter's.

The challenge was clear. Without a word Maggie accepted the tray and climbed the stairs. The door to room three was slightly open, and she could hear her father's low voice repeating two words.

"Stefan Witte," he said several times, then added, "Can you hear me, son?"

"Do you think he can understand you?" Maggie said as she set the tray on the bedside table. She busied herself with stirring the broth and then unfolding the napkin, refusing to look at the man on the bed.

"Perhaps not, but keep talking to him," Papa instructed. "He's moving around more now, and Doc says that's a good sign. If we can get him through tonight and tomorrow, Tom says he just might have a chance."

A chance for what? To spend the rest of his days in a military prison? To face a firing squad? Maggie thought as she spread the napkin over the man's chest, keeping her eyes glued to his fingers resting on extra pillows, their tips as white as the snow outside. Her parents had indeed gotten him out of the wet clothes, and he was dressed in her father's pajamas, the covers tucked tightly across his chest. The bed also had been changed, and Maggie noticed a pile of dirty linens in the corner near the door with the man's now lifeless diving suit flopped over the top like some rag doll.

"I'll take these down so they can be washed and hopefully salvaged," Maggie's father said as if reading her thoughts. He picked up the pile and opened the door wide. "I'll have Sean bring you a bucket of snow for massaging his fingers and toes. If you need help, just call out."

"He seems harmless," Maggie said, more to reassure her father than because she had made any observation of the man beyond the fact that he was wearing dry clothing and covered by clean linens.

Gabe smiled at her. For an instant he looked like a far younger man, and Maggie saw that he was excited by the events of the evening. When America had finally declared war, she remembered how her father had anguished over his inability to go to the front. She recalled how both he and Sean had seemed to envy Michael and George their youth and the chance to fight for their country. And now perhaps the front had come to him.

Men.

She waited until she heard Papa's footsteps descending the stairs and then took a deep breath and turned to face the enemy.

CHAPTER TWO

Maggie's first impression was one she would never have expected. Cleaned up after his obvious battle with the sea and the elements, Stefan Witte was strikingly handsome. His face, relaxed now by the drug the doctor had given him, was pale except for a faint sprinkle of freckles across his nose. His blond beard and mustache highlighted full lips and cheekbones that might have been chiseled out of stone.

Judging by the way his feet — elevated along with his fingers — pressed against the footboard of the bed, Maggie surmised that he was easily as tall as her father, and possibly an inch or so taller. His forearms were exposed, the sleeves of her father's pajama top pushed back. She could not resist noticing how they were roped with muscle, tanned and covered by a fine pelt of golden hair. His fingers were long with a yellowish, waxy cast to the skin that had been exposed

31

to the elements. If his frostbite was mild, the skin would eventually turn pink and blisters filled with clear liquid would need to be drained. If the frostbite proved more severe, the blisters would be black and there was every possibility that Dr. Williams would need to amputate one or more of the digits.

Maggie shuddered at the thought and turned her attention to the task of getting him to swallow some of the broth. Papa and Sean had positioned him on a stack of pillows so that he was half sitting up in the large four-poster bed. Maggie pulled the napkin higher under his chin, and in the process her knuckles grazed the softness of his beard — in need of a trim.

"Nein!" he cried out and Maggie jumped back. As suddenly as he cried out, he settled back into sleep, but his dry, cracked lips under the moustache continued to move as if searching for words.

She waited to be sure there would be no further outbursts. His deep-set eyes were closed now, the pale lashes and thick brows softening the chiseled planes of his cheeks and forehead. His hair, like his beard, was still matted with debris in spite of the hood of the diving suit and Mama's attempt to wash him. Maggie suspected that once washed, it would be thick and curly. There wasn't one thing about him that reminded her of Michael — or even George — and yet as she gazed at him, she could think only of her fiancé and her dear friend.

Here was the enemy in the flesh. A man like this one had shot George and dispensed the torpedo that had sent Michael to his grave in the sea he had always loved. What could her parents be thinking in taking such a creature into their home?

"Well, Stefan Witte," she muttered, "let's see if we can get some of this broth down — though with you unconscious, I can't see how."

She picked up the bowl and spoon and perched on the side of the bed. She dipped the spoon and then blew on it to cool the broth. "Open," she commanded as she guided the liquid to his mouth. Without a moment's thought, she made the transition from horrified civilian to professional nurse. She had been given her instructions — instructions as always aimed at getting a patient to the place where he or she could leave the sickroom or hospital. It occurred to her that she should ask the doctor to teach her a few words of German so that she could communicate those instructions to the man. Surely the sooner he got his strength back, the sooner he could be transferred to the mainland to face his punishment and the sooner her family would be rid of him.

Broth dribbled off the sides of his mouth and ran down into his beard, but his lips parted slightly and at least some went into his mouth.

"Let's try that once more," she said, more to keep herself on track than for the hope of any conversation with him. "Open," she said again, and this time because his lips parted slightly, perhaps by instinct, less spilled.

Maggie set down the bowl and looked away as she reached for the napkin to wipe his mouth. Without warning he grasped her wrist and just as quickly released her.

Her first instinct was to cry out for help, but she saw that his eyes were still closed and realized that his action had been no more than a reflex. "Stop that," she ordered as she carefully examined the splints and bandages the doctor had applied to be sure there was no damage. The next time she looked up, his eyes were open.

Her heart hammered as she stared into twin pools of emerald, like the calm waters of Nantucket Sound on an autumn day. She knew she should call for her father, but her voice seemed momentarily frozen and she refused to let the man see that she was afraid of him.

"So, Stefan Witte. You are awake." She pronounced his surname with a *V* for the *W* and in two syllables, as Doc had done when he had corrected Sean earlier. *Vit-ta.*

The man's eyes widened in surprise that she knew his name; then he looked around the room, taking in his surroundings as well as the change of clothing. Sheer panic brought him to a full sitting position for just an instant before he cried out and collapsed back onto the pillows, his face shiny with beads of perspiration, his entire body convulsed by a fit of coughing and obvious pain. When the attack passed, he stared at her, his eyes narrowed with fear and suspicion.

"You have reached the island of Nantucket, off the shore of Massachusetts in the United States," she told him while she ran cold water in the small sink behind the door and soaked a washcloth, then wiped his brow. "My father brought you here to our inn on the island." She soaked the cloth again, wrung it out and folded it to place on his forehead. "And you don't understand a word of this, do you?"

He pushed the cloth away and struggled

to sit up. "I know English," he said. His voice was weak, but other than a slight German accent his diction was perfect — almost too perfect. "Who also knows of me?"

Maggie bristled at his abrupt manner and rudeness. "Well, you are quite welcome. I imagine you are overcome with gratitude that we have rescued you and — at some danger to ourselves, I might add — taken you in. We could have called in the military, you know. There are ships anchored all over the place."

"Who also knows?" he repeated, his eyes demanding her answer.

Maggie sighed. "My parents, our cook and her husband, who found you, and the doctor, of course."

An expression of utter defeat crossed the man's face as he sank further into the pillows. He murmured something in German and then closed his eyes again, but Maggie knew he wasn't sleeping.

"You need sustenance. Here, eat this." She placed the tray with the soup bowl on the bed beside him, then stood by to see what he would do. She half expected him to send the tray and its contents crashing to the floor with a swipe of his bandaged hand.

Instead he stared at the broth, then up at

her. Eyeing her with suspicion, he secured the spoon with his thumb against the juncture of his forefinger. His four fingers stuck out like a salute. He could not hide the pain that shot through his damaged fingertips with the effort, but stubbornly he filled the spoon and stared at its contents.

"It isn't poisoned or drugged, if that's what you're thinking," Maggie said, irritated that this German would doubt her or her family. When he continued to hesitate, she pried the spoon from his grasp and took a sip of the soup. "See? Perfectly fine."

She was tempted to make him watch while she devoured the rest herself, but Doc had mentioned possible dehydration and the need to push warm liquids into the man's system through the night. It had been one thing to hand-feed him with the man unconscious. It was quite something else to have him watching her. Casting about for a solution, she poured a little of the contents into a water glass and held it to his lips. He grasped the sides of the glass with his palms and using this method he quickly finished the broth.

"Vielen Dank," he murmured as she removed the tray.

"You are welcome," she replied, assuming by his tone that he had just thanked her.

"How much English do you know?"

"*Ich bin* — I am a translator," he said.

"For the Germans?"

His eyes narrowed again and he did not answer.

"Are you a spy for your country?" she asked, deciding that they may as well find out what they were up against now while the man could barely raise a soupspoon to his lips much less murder them all in their beds.

"Translator," he insisted, his voice weak and raspy.

"On a German U-boat?" Again she saw a flicker of acknowledgment that she'd guessed right before his eyes shuttered again. "Is that how you came to be on our beach? Your ship dropped you there so you could what? Spy on us? Make your way to the mainland and send back information?"

"You talk too much and foolishly," he muttered, and then he started to cough and choke, gasping for air as he looked at her with alarm.

Maggie was tempted to let him believe that she had indeed poisoned him, but instead she pushed him forward and started pounding his back with the flat of her hand as she called out for help.

"Mama!" Instinctively she knew that calling out to her mother rather than her father would prevent setting off waves of panic through the household. Nevertheless the response was the sound of multiple footsteps coming up the stairs. Meanwhile she eased Stefan forward, balancing his weight against her shoulder in order to give his lungs more room to function properly.

"What is it?" her father asked, reaching the room ahead of the others and rushing to the opposite side of the bed.

"Shall I call the doctor back?" Sarah asked, clutching her elbows as she stared at the young man who was still coughing and gasping for breath. Sean set down the bucket of snow the doctor had ordered.

"He'll be fine," Mama said, and something about her calm assurance caused everyone including Stefan to breathe easier. Gabe moved aside to allow his wife to attend their patient. "Breathe deeply and slowly," she advised, making exaggerated hand gestures and breathing sounds to demonstrate.

"He speaks English," Maggie said, resisting the urge to point out the obvious fact that this supported her theory that he was a spy.

"Translator," Stefan gasped, his eyes on Gabe.

"Well, whatever languages you speak,

you've done enough talking for tonight," Mama instructed as she helped Maggie ease him back onto the pillows. "What you need is rest." Stefan shivered and Mama pulled the covers up to his chin as if tending to a child. "Why, you're burning up," she said after placing the back of her hand on each of his cheeks and then his forehead. "Sean, please hand me that bucket of snow so Maggie can start the massage of his fingers and toes that Tom ordered. And the rest of you, leave the man in peace." She pulled a chair close to the bed. "I'll sit with him awhile."

"Lucie," Gabe said, and it was both a warning and a plea. "You haven't been well yourself. Perhaps —"

"I'll sit with him," Sarah offered.

"I am perfectly well — just a bit tired. No, Maggie and I can take the night in turns," Lucie decided. "You heard Tom. He's not nearly out of danger yet."

"I'll bring an extra pillow and blanket from the linen closet," Sarah said. "One of you can get some sleep on the chaise while the other keeps watch."

Maggie tamped down her innate alarm that their patient who had seemed almost robust while gulping down the broth looked quite frail now. Not that she wished his

40

health to worsen, but he was the enemy and surely she ought not to care so much. Yet when she saw how pale he'd become and how he shivered violently, Maggie could do no less than follow her training. She removed the soft bandages and splints on his left hand, then plunged her hands into the bucket of snow and began slowly massaging his frostbitten fingers.

Her mother shooed her father and Sarah from the room, assuring them that all would be well. Sean set a second bucket packed with fresh snow at the foot of the bed, and Sarah brought the blanket and pillow. After shutting the door, Mama dropped the bedding onto the chaise, then returned to the bedside, where she stroked dirty blond curls away from the man's forehead. "Sh-h-h," she whispered soothingly. "God has brought you to this safe place."

As she gently wiped perspiration from the man's cheeks and neck, Mama hummed a lullaby that had always been Maggie's favorite. "Show me how to use the snow on his toes," she said, watching Maggie's rhythmic stroking of the man's fingers.

Maggie pulled the covers free at the foot of the bed just enough to reveal their patient's feet. She had seen cases of frostbite before, and as such things went, Stefan

Witte appeared to have a relatively mild case in spite of his ordeal. With practiced efficiency she folded a towel and placed it under his heels. He winced and his feet twitched spasmodically. "Take away the cotton separating his toes," Maggie instructed.

Next she scooped up a handful of the snow and divided it evenly in her hands. "The snow numbs the shocks of pain," she explained as she slowly began massaging the snow against his heel and then the arch and then the toes.

"Let me try it." Mama scooped up snow and started on the other foot. "I think he's starting to relax," she whispered.

And Maggie saw that it was true. His face was less tense, his limbs less rigid. "While you do that, I'll work on the fingers of his other hand," she said, taking another handful of snow and lifting Stefan's right hand in hers.

"How long?" Mama asked.

"Until . . . until it melts." Maggie's voice cracked as Stefan's fingers tensed against her palm. She knew it was nothing more than a spontaneous response to the cold of the snow, but for an instant it felt more like a plea. She risked a look at his face, but his eyes were closed. Yet she could not deny that his touch had moved her. He might not look like Michael or George, but in sleep he was no different than any patient she'd ever nursed. This was a human being in pain and relieving pain was her job.

She cleared her throat and assumed her professional tone. "That should do for now. I'll take first shift," she said, handing her mother a towel for drying her hands. "You should get some sleep."

As the night deepened and the storm clawed at the windows, there were times when Stefan thrashed about, calling out names and lapsing into mumbled ramblings in his native tongue. From time to time he would slip back into an exhausted sleep. But Maggie was wide awake. If anyone had told her this scenario was possible, she would have thought them mad. Yet here she was. More to the point, here *he* was. In spite of her determination to ignore the man but for the care her profession demanded, she was incapable of turning away. As she watched him toss and turn through the night, she could not help wondering why he cried out with such pure panic in his delirium, as if he had somewhere to be or something urgent to do.

She had resolved to view the man impassively as just another patient, yet her innate curiosity got the better of her. What if he was married and had left a wife — and even children — back in Düsseldorf? If so, was he likely to have defected, as she had heard her parents speculate earlier? She wondered if the wallet her father had found had contained any other clues about the man. Were there photographs? Some token of remembrance such as the cross she had given Michael the day he left for Europe? And even as the unanswered questions plagued her, she kept watch lest he take a turn for the worse.

Just after three Stefan's breathing changed from even to ragged and labored. Maggie had heard that sound before. It was the same sound her Grandmother Emma used to make in those last days before she slipped into sleep and never awoke. She was hardly surprised to find that she was concerned. This was her patient, after all. But her worry for his well-being, like her grief for Michael, took the form of anger — rage at the toll in human suffering this war was bringing and her lack of control to stop it.

"You will not die under our care," she murmured as she pressed a piece of fresh snow from the bucket her father had replenished against his chapped and dry lips. "I will not allow you to bring more sorrow to

these people that I love — do you understand me?" She shut her eyes tight against
the exhaustion and fury that threatened to
overwhelm her. "No more death," she
prayed. But having turned her back on God
the day she'd learned of Michael's death,
who did she think was listening?

Stefan was vaguely aware of the presence of
the two women through the night. The elder
one spoke to him always in soothing mater-
nal tones, while the younger one — a nurse,
by her dress, he guessed — gave commands
even when she whispered them. The burning fever had robbed him not only of physical strength but also of clarity of mind.
Events ran together, overlapped, came at
him out of sequence. He dreamed in English
but cried out in his native tongue.

Now he was aboard the U-boat, waiting
for the right moment. He had one chance.
The U-boat captain had been disappointed
with their position and vowed to exit the
Nantucket waters and head farther south.
He would surface once to give the crew time
on deck. This was Stefan's one opportunity,
and he had volunteered to take the watch,
giving him reason to don the diving suit.
The bitter cold and howling winds had
aided Stefan in his escape, for few crew

members had elected to go on deck. When the call came for all on deck to go below, it had been easy to conceal himself in the shadow of the conning tower.

Then he was in the two-man lifeboat he'd managed to slip into the water. In the icy sea he struggled to paddle as fast and far as possible before he would be pulled down into the vortex as the ship submerged. But the lifeboat had tipped, and in fighting his way to the surface, he'd lost his paddle. He'd climbed on top of the overturned boat and clung to it for what seemed like hours in the endless howling of the wind and pounding of the waves. Then miraculously the small craft had bumped up against an ice-covered rock, and when Stefan looked up, he saw the rhythmic, sweeping light from a lighthouse and knew that he had found the shore.

And now he was in this house surrounded by strangers speaking too rapidly for him to catch every word. His command of English for reading and writing was exceptional; understanding the spoken language was more difficult. But even as he hovered between consciousness and sleep, trying to decipher the jumble of words he'd heard that evening, he was aware of the nurse ministering to him. She covered him against the chills that racked his body, rubbed fresh snow over his toes and fingers, ordered him to take a sip of honeyed tea or beef broth and then took the cup away too soon. He clung to a single fact. She had confirmed that he'd reached his destination. He was on the island of Nantucket, and as soon as he could escape, he would head for the wharves, where he would meet his contact.

On the few occasions when he was lucid, he was aware that the storm had not abated, and he thanked God for that, knowing instinctively that the storm was somehow protecting him, buying time he desperately needed. The high winds of the storm had produced waves large and fierce enough to push him toward land. The interminable time in the water — minutes? Hours? And then the blessing of feeling himself caught and hauled upright when he had been certain that he would die before dawn. He hadn't even cared who his rescuers were or what they might do. He knew only that he could stop fighting — at least for the moment. He had murmured a prayer of thanks and then closed his eyes, content in the knowledge that he had at least made good on his escape. God willing, he would be as successful in the rest of his mission.

He remembered only snatches of what had

happened once his rescuers had discovered him. Semiconscious, he'd felt himself half dragged and half carried. For one moment he had found land legs enough to stumble along through the fog. His two pairs of thick socks had done little to soften the sharp edges of the rocks along the path, and yet his feet were numb and he was incapable of making them perform properly. When he'd collapsed, the men to either side of him had carried him toward the lighted windows of a large house. But try as he might, he could not stay conscious as the men hauled him the last few feet up the steps of the house and he heard a girl scream, "Papa!"

His own father, mother, sister were all gone now. He had tried to tell his rescuers that he was alone in this world, and it had been his last thought before succumbing to the blessed blackness of unconsciousness.

When he awoke, he found himself face-to-face with the most beautiful girl he'd ever seen. Hair that was thick and shiny and the color of a raven's wings. Eyes that were clear and direct and unexpectedly violet in color. Skin that was so unblemished by sun or wind that it reminded him of the pearly inside of a lightening whelk shell he'd found once. And a voice that showed no pity — only outrage.

Pure pride had made him reveal that he understood English. He was an officer, an educated man, and well knew that it was no accident he was on Nantucket, in Massachusetts, in the United States, for that had been the plan. However, revealing his knowledge had been a mistake because now they would question him.

Now, through eyes bleary and swollen nearly shut after the long battle to fight his fever, he studied the woman who pressed a lump of ice to his lips. He saw that in spite of her beauty she was not a girl, as he had first thought. In the glow of a single lamp he translated the shadows beneath her eyes first into sleepless nights, but then into something more familiar — that hollow-eyed mask of grief he'd seen all too often on the faces of his countrymen. Sorrow that was unadulterated in this moment when she thought no one was watching. He knew that depth of grieving. It lay at the very foundation of everything he was risking.

Then he recalled the way she had spoken to him in that high-handed manner that told him she thought herself superior to him. He had heard stories of these American women and dismissed the rumors as exaggerated. But if this woman was any measure of the level of impudence his shipmates had described, he had little hope for the ability of the American male.

Stefan tried to think about steps he would take if he survived his ordeal. What would this family do? Would they nurse him back to health only to turn him over to the local authorities? And what of the contacts he must make here on the island? When he didn't show up, would they take him for dead? What became of a man who defected to the enemy to help them defeat his own homeland? What kind of a man did such things?

You are a traitor, Stefan Witte.

Stefan felt hands on his shoulders and heard the urgent command of his nurse. "You will not die," she whispered fiercely.

May it be God's will that you are right, he thought and surrendered once again to the darkness that drowned out the pain.

CHAPTER THREE

At breakfast the following morning, Maggie's father once again stressed the importance of keeping the German's presence in their home a tightly held secret for the time being.

"Why are you protecting him?" Maggie was no longer able to hold her tongue. "He has survived the night. There's no more we can do for him."

Papa frowned at her, and Mama reached over and placed a silencing hand on Maggie's. Maggie knew better than to dispute Papa's decisions.

But Maggie kept her eyes locked on her father's. Finally he sighed and attempted to explain his reasoning. Throughout her childhood, she had constantly raised impossible questions, such as why she had to wear dresses when George and Michael could wear pants, especially if the three of them were off to dig for clams.

51

"Maggie, if Dr. Williams and I can determine what threat or harm this man intended in coming to our shores, we might well prevent some action that could take weeks or months to uncover if we turn him over to others. Besides, until he is strong enough to face the kind of interrogation he'll have to endure, common decency demands that we provide him with basic shelter and medical care. Your mother and I are quite agreed on this point. We are Christians as well as Americans, Margaret Rose."

Maggie swung around. "But, Mother —"

"That's quite enough, Maggie. Now finish your breakfast. Then I want you to go to your room and get some proper rest. You were supposed to wake me but instead took almost the entire night's watch."

"Isn't Dr. Williams coming back today?" Maggie asked as she picked at her eggs and sipped her milk.

"He said he would come by. I expect he's had an emergency to see to, but he'll be here," Papa replied. Then he frowned. "Even if there's no one around other than Sarah, Sean and us, it must appear that Tom has merely stopped for a social visit. For if anyone happens to pass him on the road coming or going — well, you know how fast news travels here on the island."

"They'll only think he has come to attend me," Mama said softly. "You know how others have fussed over me. No one will suspect —"

"I don't want people making assumptions about your health, darling," Gabe replied, and as usual, when her parents looked at each other across the length of the table, Maggie felt as if she had quite suddenly disappeared.

It struck her that she and Michael would never have the chance to know that level of devotion — the kind of love that comes only after years of togetherness facing life's challenges as well as its joys. The looks that she and Michael had exchanged had been more innocent, a little wondrous that a childhood friendship had blossomed almost without their awareness into the promise of marriage.

She cleared her throat, drained the last of her milk and stood up. "I'm wide awake. I'll go look in on the Ger—"

"Our guest," Mama corrected her.

"Our guest. Then I must get to the hospital."

"You can ride into town with Tom," Mama suggested. "Until then, go and lie down. You need your rest."

"I'm not the least bit tired," Maggie

53

insisted, although she could feel the heaviness in her limbs that accompanied a night without sleep. And yet her curiosity about the man in room three outweighed her weariness. The truth was that she wanted to see what she could find out about him. The question was why?

Her father studied her long enough that she felt color rise to her cheeks, and this time she could not meet her father's gaze. "Get some rest, Maggie, for we may all be facing a difficult time over the coming days. This young man is far from being out of danger."

Maggie could not dispute that. On every level, starting with his health, the German was in jeopardy. Although the fever had broken sometime around dawn and the man had finally fallen into an undisturbed sleep, he was weak and pale, and there was still the matter of the frostbitten toes and fingers. He would suffer significant pain over the coming days, but Maggie doubted it would lead to amputation. Of more interest to Maggie than the German's physical condition was his purpose in coming ashore in the first place. There was always the danger that someone had missed him and sent out others to find him and bring him back. Or more likely, at least in Maggie's mind, his

cohorts here in America would come looking for him, for surely he had contacts, if
not on Nantucket then on the mainland.

Maggie excused herself. In the lobby she
saw the German's wallet on her father's
open rolltop desk. She paused and listened
for the exchange of quiet conversation
between her parents. She heard her mother
refill her father's coffee cup and then pull a
chair close to his as the two of them talked.
She ran her fingers over the wallet's damp
leather as it lay flat, spread out, on the desk.
Her father had arranged the contents indi-
vidually on pieces of blotting paper to dry
them. She saw what looked like a photograph and carefully turned it over.

It was a picture of a young woman. She
looked boldly toward the camera and
smiled. She was holding a child of two or
three. The child stared directly at the
camera with one tiny fist raised in blurry
defiance. He had the German's piercing
eyes. The woman's eyes also were impossible to turn away from. They challenged
and demanded a certain respect. So he has
a wife and child, she thought and wondered
at the kinship she felt for the woman in the
photograph as well as the twinge of sympathy she felt for the man upstairs.

When she reached her room, she removed

55

her shoes and lay back on her bed. She was indeed very tired, and yet sleep would not come. Whenever she closed her eyes, she saw the faces in the photograph. Then she remembered the many expressions she'd seen on the German — fear, panic, weariness beyond exhaustion and surrender — when he finally understood that for better or worse he was at their mercy. And just before she fell asleep, she saw Michael's face, and wondered if he, like Stefan, had known similar moments of fear and ultimately resignation.

Stefan awoke to find the man whom he'd decided was head of the household sitting across the room. It was afternoon, judging by the angle of the sun, and the man was reading.

"Ah, *guten tag,*" the man said as he laid his book aside. "I must admit that's the extent of my knowledge of your language." His eyes narrowed slightly. "But you speak mine, do you not?"

"*Ein bisschen,*" Stefan replied, aware that he should take care before revealing the extent of his understanding. He tried signaling with his fingers, but they were bandaged into stumps. "A little," he translated.

"Very well, then we shall forge ahead."

The man stood and moved the rocking chair closer to the bed. "We need to discuss your future, young man."

"I am Stefan Witte," Stefan replied, prepared to chant the information he would give if captured.

"Yes. Yes. I am Gabriel Hunter, and this is my home — and my family's business. We run an inn here on Nantucket — profitable business up until recently." He sat in the rocker and leaned forward, resting his folded hands on the edge of the bed. "What is your business here?"

"*Ich heiße* Stefan Witte —"

Gabe leaned back in the chair and closed his eyes for a moment. Then he opened them and leaned forward again. "You are in grave danger, young man. I am trying to find a way to help you make the best of your situation."

Stefan searched the man's features for any sign of cunning and found nothing but weariness. "Why would you do that?"

"Quite honestly? I have no idea. It's just that it seems there has been so much loss and suffering and —"

"You have a son?"

"I have a daughter — Margaret Rose — Maggie. She's a nurse. She attended you during the night, along with my wife."

So the nurse has a name.

Stefan nodded. He was about to ask why she had not come near his room all day, but decided that might alarm the father. The man's wife had checked on him a few times, but he had been groggy with the drugs the doctor had ordered and unable to decipher anything she had said. Once, he had heard the nurse's voice outside his door, but she had not come to his room.

He waited for what the man might ask next. Instead Gabriel Hunter handed him a photograph.

"We found this with your papers."

Stefan felt his throat close and his eyes burn with unshed tears. "Uma," he whispered, fingering the photograph.

"Uma is your wife?"

"*Schwester* — sister," Stefan explained.

"Ah. And that is her little boy?"

Stefan nodded as he ran his thumb over the cherubic face of the child. "They are dead now. Also my parents." He swiped at a tear that had escaped. He made no effort to control the internal weeping that was breaking his heart.

Gabriel cleared his throat. "I am sorry for your loss."

"*Danke,*" Stefan whispered and turned the photograph facedown on the bed. "I can

58

tell you nothing," he said in a voice resolved to show his strength and determination.

"But why did you come and from where?"

"Nothing," Stefan repeated as he studied his captor, wondering if indeed he might be able to trust this man. "You also have suffered loss," he said after a moment.

"My wife and I have been blessed not to have suffered directly, but our daughter was to be married to the son of the doctor who treats you. He and a dear friend were killed in the war. So, yes, within these walls there is much grief and suffering."

Perhaps that explained the nurse and her hostility. Stefan understood that kind of inner rage — he felt it every time he thought about his parents, his sister and her son.

"Do you believe in God, Stefan?"

Stefan was taken aback at the man's sudden shift in topic. "Yes."

"I thought as much." He showed Stefan the gold chain with the small cross. "You were clutching this when we found you, and last night you called out to God."

Stefan fingered the cross his sister had given him the day he left to report for duty. "It was a gift," he murmured.

Gabriel stood and fastened the cross around Stefan's neck. "And perhaps it is God's gift that has brought you here to us.

Perhaps He has a plan for us to do something to help each other. Think on that, Stefan Witte. We will talk again."

Within two days the household quickly settled into a routine. Maggie attended to her duties at the hospital while her mother and Sarah divided their time between ministering to their guest and managing the normal household tasks of the inn. And although Stefan triggered painful memories of receiving the news about Michael and George and others, the women were diligent in administering the treatments and medications Dr. Williams had prescribed. He assured Lucie that no one thought anything of his coming so often.

"They assume I am meeting with Gabe on security matters," he said. "Of course, they are correct."

After three days Stefan began sleeping through the night and there was no longer a need to keep watch. Gabe decided that they would all retire to their rooms at night, but Maggie did not miss the fact that her father bolted the door to the German's room. Even so, Maggie's mother still insisted on sitting with the seaman after supper and reading him passages from the Bible until he slept.

For her part, having followed the doctor's

instructions for getting their patient stabilized, Maggie kept her distance. Every evening she sat by the fire, feverishly knitting socks to send to the Allied troops overseas before climbing the back stairs to her room in the tower, which faced her grandparents' cottage and the stillness of the frozen harbor beyond. And still she listened for any information about this intruder. When she heard that the woman in the photograph was his sister and not his wife, she was inexplicably relieved.

Why should she care if he was married? Did it lessen the tragedy if the child was his nephew and not his son? What was wrong with her?

"Maggie, wake up."

The urgency in her mother's voice brought Maggie awake instantly. Outside a light snow was falling, and Maggie shielded her eyes from the unusually light morning sky. A warming trend had allowed the harbor to reopen the day before, and Maggie could not help wondering how long before it would close again on their opportunity to rid themselves of Stefan Witte. One look at her mother told her that something was afoot. Perhaps this was the day — the day her father and the doctor would turn the German over to the coast guard.

Her emotions were in complete turmoil these days. Hadn't she campaigned for that very action? Then why should it be that the realization that the day would come sooner rather than later came with a vague sense of disappointment?

"What is it?"

"We need to move Stefan."

Maggie had noticed that the entire household had begun treating the man as if he were a member of the family or a special guest. "Why?"

"Dr. Williams and your father think the cottage would be best, at least for the moment. But we must hurry. There's no time to spare."

"But why now? It's snowing and —"

"Your Auntie Jeanne has just arrived on the morning steamer." Mama began laying out clothes for Maggie.

"In the middle of winter?"

"She called to say that she's come to look at some property. Apparently she's considering building a home on Nantucket and wants to see what it would be like to live here in all seasons." Mama gave a sigh of exasperation.

Jeanne Witherspoon Groton-Hames was a dear friend of the family and, from the time Maggie had been a toddler, she had insisted

Maggie refer to her as "Auntie" even though there was no blood connection at all. Jeanne was the daughter of Gabe's former business partner. She was a gifted artist, a delightfully flirtatious woman and the widow of a British duke, eighteen years her senior, who had left her with a sizable fortune. Maggie adored her.

As a child she had been delighted to learn that at one time Jeanne and Maggie's father — who liked to refer to her as "Duchess" — had considered a union, which everyone agreed would have been one of convenience rather than love. In fact, Maggie's parents and Mrs. Groton-Hames often laughed about those early days. These days Lucie and Jeanne were the best of friends, much to Maggie's father's consternation. He had only limited patience with Jeanne's chatter and spontaneity, which seemed always to assume that others would simply be delighted to follow her lead.

"But surely Auntie Jeanne can be trusted —" Maggie began.

"Your father is concerned." Lucie handed Maggie each item of clothing in order to speed her along with her actions. "She was deeply devoted to the duke and well, his family has ties to the Austrian royal family and —"

"Austria is on the same side as Germany," Maggie said, finishing the thought. "But still the duke was assassinated in Austria when he tried to stop the war."

"Even so, Jeanne's penchant for speaking whatever is on her mind at any given moment could spell disaster," Lucie reminded her.

Maggie couldn't argue with that. More than once Jeanne had blurted out some private detail of the days when she and "darling Gabe" had been courting, much to Mama's amusement and Papa's mortification.

"Besides," Maggie's mother continued, "she's bringing others with her — her maidservant and her traveling companion, Sir Frederick Groton, a nephew of the duke. Plus, I suspect that at least a portion of her motive in coming is to lighten the burden of your grief over Michael. She's fond of you."

Maggie certainly appreciated that it was far too risky to involve any more people in this matter until they could be certain what Stefan Witte's purpose truly was. Of course, there was a solution for that but she knew better than to suggest how simple it would be to load the German up and deposit him on the steamer that brought mail and passengers and supplies between New Bedford and Nantucket twice daily weather permitting.

In spite of occasional bursts of sympathy for a patient in pain, she continued to argue that turning the German over to the authorities and letting them sort it all out made a great deal more sense than keeping him at the inn. But all her protests had fallen on deaf ears — in fact, with each day the seaman was under their roof, everyone else in the household became more attached. The world had indeed gone mad.

"Just let me get dressed," she said with a long-suffering sigh.

Lucie nodded and turned to leave. "And bring your coat and scarf and mittens. There's a strong north wind and it's very damp and raw out."

Maggie did as she was told. Wrapping her wool scarf twice around her neck, she took the back stairs to the second floor and hurried down the hall to room three. Overnight, the German had taken an unexpected turn for the worse. And now he was lying flat in the bed, his eyes closed, his face as pale as the sheets. Every few minutes his entire body was racked with coughing and Sarah ran to attend him.

"Ah, Maggie," her father said. His voice was reassuring but his expression showed clearly the worry and concern he had for this new development. He was wearing his winter coat and gloves and scarf. He took Maggie's hands in his and drew her to one side of the room while Sarah wrapped Stefan in layers of blankets. "Here is the plan. We are moving Stefan to the cottage for the time being. Given his state of health, Tom thinks it best that you stay with him."

"I have my work at the hospital," Maggie protested.

"That's all arranged. Doc has told the staff that he plans to move all of his surgical patients out of the hospital to private homes and cottages to be cared for until the threat of influenza has passed. Everyone will simply assume we are caring for such a patient and Doc is making his usual rounds in the community instead of the hospital."

"But you can't possibly expect me to stay alone with him. Once he's stronger, Papa —"

"Sean will be just outside the back door in his workshop, repairing his nets. He and Sarah will take the nights. We're installing locks on the door, and we've nailed shut the window of the downstairs bedroom. You will be perfectly safe. The man is weak as a kitten —"

"But Auntie Jeanne will wonder why I'm

66

not here," Maggie protested, searching for any possible way she might avoid the assignment her father was giving her. She felt almost desperate to avoid such close contact with Stefan Witte. Something happened to her sense of propriety whenever she was near him, and the only sensible way to fight that was to maintain her distance.

Over the German's coughing, Maggie continued to protest, "I'm to be his nurse and warden?"

"We will all help you, Maggie," her mother assured her, coming to stand with Papa — a united front. "Besides, it's only until Auntie Jeanne and her party leave. How long can that be?"

Well, let me think now — two summers ago when she "visited" she stayed for three months. What if she decides she likes it here so much that she decides to stay permanently?

Maggie felt outnumbered, not to mention confused. What was it about this man that had her parents inventing whole strategies to keep him with them? Maggie glanced toward the bed and then back to the eager faces of her parents. "That man is not a son of Nantucket," she whispered.

"No," her father replied. "But what if he has been sent to us by God?"

67

"For what purpose?" Maggie asked.

"To give us the opportunity to save another mother's son — to give us the challenge of forgiving our enemies," her mother said gently, her eyes brimming with tears but her expression filled with hope. "Do this for your father and me, Maggie. Do it for Sarah and Sean. Do it for the memory of Michael and George."

She understood that they had discussed it already, and in the face of her parents' steadfast faith, Maggie could not refuse. "Very well," she said.

Moments later Sean pulled a wagon mounted on runners up to the back entrance of the inn. Upstairs Sarah opened a folding cot and placed it next to the bed. Using the skills she'd developed in training, Maggie orchestrated the transfer of the German from the bed to the cot. Immediately, Maggie's mother and Sarah began adjusting and adding covers until the man looked like some kind of mummy, his face barely visible. Through it all he floated in and out of consciousness.

"Ready?" Gabe said as he positioned himself at the front end of the cot while Sean took the back. Together the two men maneuvered their heavy burden down the back stairs. Once there, they loaded the cot onto the back of the wagon and slowly made the short journey over the frozen and snow-covered yard down the slight hill to the smaller cottage.

"You should go," Maggie's mother said when Maggie hesitated in the kitchen. "Jeanne will be here soon and everything needs to be in place."

"What if Auntie Jeanne insists on coming to the cottage?"

Lucie laughed. "She would never traverse the yard in this weather," she predicted. "She'd ruin her expensive shoes. No, she'll be disappointed to find you away but will wait to see you this evening. Now, go. I need to prepare her room."

Room three, Maggie thought as she wrapped her scarf once more around her face and started across the yard to where the others had disappeared into her grand-parents' former home. It was the house where her father had grown up and the place he had run away from when he was a few years younger than her own nineteen years. Her heart lightened. Perhaps the German would escape — run away. But she immediately felt contrite at the trouble such a thing could bring for the doctor, the Chadwicks and her parents. Before Michael died, she would have uttered a short prayer begging forgiveness for even thinking such a thing. But in this new world where the insanity of war ruled everything, Maggie had difficulty rationalizing a benevolent God.

By the time she reached the cottage and removed her coat, scarf and mittens, the German was settled in the first-floor bedroom her grandparents had used. It had also been the room Sarah and Sean had shared before George's death until Sarah had insisted they move down to the inn. When Maggie reached the room, Sarah was offering a groggy but conscious Stefan Witte a verbal tour. Maggie saw the effort for what it was. Sarah had come to see in Stefan the ghost of her son, George.

"We can leave the curtains open or closed as you prefer, and here I've put your sister's photograph in this frame so it will sit here where you can see it." She placed the frame on the bedside table and turned it so that Stefan only had to turn his head to see it. "Shall I get you something to eat? Or water. A pitcher of water." She started for the door.

"Sarah?" Gabe's voice was always gentle and quiet, especially when he spoke to Sarah. "Let Maggie take care of that. You'll be needed back at the inn."

Sarah glanced at Maggie. "Get those

blankets off him," she instructed as Maggie walked with her and Sean back to the front foyer. "I've brought a kettle of soup. It's on the stove. Sean can light it. And upstairs —" She faltered as she looked up to the closed door at the top of the stairs and Sean put his arm around her shoulder as he added, "In George's room, there are books and a chess set for when he's feeling better."

"I'll be all right, Sarah," Maggie said gently. "Everything we need is here."

Sarah kissed Maggie's cheek. "Darling girl," she murmured. "Take those dustcovers away in the parlor and dining room so you can be comfortable. I'll keep a plate warm for your supper."

Maggie's father kissed her cheek and handed her a large cowbell. "If you need anything ring this loud and long. Sean will be just outside that door."

Maggie wondered what sorts of emergencies her father had imagined as he searched for something she could use to sound an alarm. She took the bell and tried it. Satisfied that she had everything she needed, everyone left — Sarah to help Lucie ready the inn, Gabe to meet Jeanne at the wharf and Sean to get back to work.

Maggie placed the cowbell on the bedside

table and looked down at Stefan Witte. "Don't get any ideas," she muttered, but the man was quite unconscious.

Maggie had decided to think of him as simply "the German," for that impersonal tag would surely stem the tide of her curiosity about his past. He slept most of the morning. Maggie looked in on him several times as she uncovered the furniture, stirred the fire in the parlor, set the soup on simmer, then stood at the dining room window across the hall from the bedroom. There seemed little point in literally watching him sleep, and Sarah had already changed the man's bandages for the day.

Just before noon she saw Jeanne and her entourage arrive. The sounds of Mama's enthusiastic welcome and Jeanne's bell-like laughter carried across the yard on the cold air. Maggie saw a small older woman — obviously Jeanne's maid — scurry into the inn carrying the smaller two pieces of Jeanne's luggage. Behind her was a man about Jeanne's age who helped Gabe unload the rest of the luggage. She envied her mother and Sarah the opportunity to hear Jeanne's chatter about things in Europe and in New York, where she had been living ever since the duke's death.

Turning from the window, she prepared

herself a bowl of soup and a plate with cheese and two thick slices of the bread that Sarah made each morning. She settled in on the cushions that lined the window seat of the dining room's large window, where she would have a good view of any further activity at the inn as she ate. But aside from a lamp in room number three, obviously lit to offset the gray gloom of the day, there was little for her to see.

A crash from the bedroom startled Maggie, and she dropped her bowl of soup onto her grandmother's frayed Oriental rug. The silence that followed had her imagining everything from the German now waiting for her, armed with one of Sean's hunting rifles that he'd managed to slip from the locked case in the front hall, to the possibility that he had made good on an escape through the window. She crept across the hall and pushed the half-closed door open with a force that made it bang against the wall. The German had obviously tried to get up and in so doing had knocked over the bedside table. As soon as he saw her, he fell back onto the bed, which brought on a howl of pain followed by a bout of coughing that led to choking. With each cough he jangled the cowbell Maggie had inadvertently left on the bedside table — the cowbell he now held in one hand — with the table and its other contents strewn across the floor.

"Give me that," Maggie snapped as Sean came at a run and stopped just inside the doorway. Maggie pushed the German forward and pounded his back with the flat of her hand. "Breathe," she ordered, trying to temper her own irritation with a little of the gentleness her mother would use under similar circumstances.

Maggie signaled to Sean that everything was under control, and after he retreated, she turned her attention back to her patient. "Slowly. Deeply." She forced herself to modify her tone and draw out the words as she allowed him to relax his weight against her. In spite of the hollow sounds of his breathing, she could not help noticing that he was muscular and rock solid for all his frail health.

"Now out," she coached. "That's it. Again."

After a few minutes the man drew in a shuddering breath and let it out without coughing. He nodded and she allowed his weight to collapse onto the pillows. Maggie felt a chill as if the absence of his warmth had suddenly changed the temperature in the room.

"I'm going to get you some tea with honey to ease the rawness in your throat. Understand?"

He nodded.

"Stay where you are," she warned.

The German gave her a weak salute. Nonplussed by his obvious attempt at humor under such circumstances, Maggie fled the room. When she returned with the tea, he was once again asleep and she breathed a sigh of relief. She could handle him when he slept, but when he was awake, those piercing green eyes seemed to follow her with the same curiosity that she could not deny every time she was in his presence.

By the end of the day Maggie was so exhausted it was all she could do to make a grand show of delight at seeing Jeanne. Unsettled by being cooped up in the cottage with a man who was now awake and following her every move when she was within his range of vision, she had scrubbed the kitchen floor, wiped down the cabinets, washed all the dishes and put fresh linens on the upstairs beds.

"Look at you," Jeanne exclaimed while holding both of Maggie's hands as she looked her up and down. "I go away for a few short months and you've blossomed into a woman."

Maggie blushed with pleasure. "I am tired and hungry," she said, brushing aside the compliment.

"No, no, no," Jeanne instructed, wagging her forefinger like a schoolteacher. "The correct reply is, 'Why, how kind of you to say so.' Go on, we're all waiting."

Maggie dropped into a curtsy and murmured, "Why, how kind of you to say so, your Grace."

"Stop that," Jeanne scolded, but she was laughing with delight. "Now, come into the dining room and let me sit with you while you have your supper so you can tell me everything — and I do mean *everything.*"

Maggie made a face. "There's a war on — is there anything more I need say?" She blushed scarlet. "Oh, Auntie Jeanne, I am so sorry. I didn't mean to imply —" How could she have forgotten for even a moment that Jeanne's beloved also had perished in this war?

Jeanne waved off her apology. "Dodging the question never works with me, young lady. And I have not come all this way — at great expense and danger to myself, I might add — to have you avoid me. Do you realize that it took over two hours for the steamer to traverse a single mile over that ice-packed harbor?" She shivered, then

76

pointed her finger at Maggie. "I will not be brushed aside with oversimplification. Now sit down here and tell me how you are getting along. So, you've decided to become a nurse." Her raised eyebrows made it clear she was questioning the wisdom of this decision.

Maggie shrugged. She had begun her nurse's training right after Michael announced his plan to volunteer. She had never told anyone that it had been her plan to follow him to Europe and the war.

"I applaud your desire to get on with your life, Maggie. Still, I can't help but wonder if you are doing this as some sort of tribute, or perhaps retribution in memory of your young man?" Her voice softened. "Such dedication is admirable, but you mustn't abandon your life for a memory. It's been what — almost a year?"

"Just shy of six months," Maggie replied, her voice suddenly unsteady.

"Oh, sweet child," Jeanne exclaimed and pulled Maggie to her.

"Sometimes I can't seem to remember his face or the sound of his voice," Maggie confessed. "It's like losing him in pieces."

Jeanne nodded. "I know. I do." She cupped Maggie's face with her hands, stroking her cheeks with her thumbs. "And you are not going to believe what I am going to suggest," she said, "but you must remember that I too lost the love of my life."

"I know."

"It's been two long years, and I too have felt the last memories of his face, his voice — his touch — fading."

At last someone understood — really understood.

"How have you managed?" Maggie asked, feeling the tension ease through her shoulders and neck.

"It occurred to me that those lapses in memory were my signal, my message from the duke and from God that I must begin to move forward — even to love again."

Maggie was stunned. The love that had existed between Jeanne and her duke — in spite of the difference in their ages — had been the stuff of fairy tales, complete with her own castle. How could she even entertain the idea?

"I believe that it is time you considered that there will be another love for you, Maggie. You are far too young to close yourself away from such opportunities."

"Even if that were true — even if I had the slightest interest in such nonsense," Maggie protested, "well, the male population here is —"

"Come now, there must be other young men on this island, someone who has not yet heeded the call to battle? Or better yet, a hero just returned safely home?"

For an instant the image of Stefan Witte flashed unbidden across Maggie's mind. She could practically feel her eyes flashing with shock and her mouth curling in disgust.

Jeanne laughed as she studied Maggie's horrified expression. "Oh, don't look so stunned. God surely has no need for a lovely thing like you to go through life alone."

"I shall never —"

The tall, portly man she had seen arrive with Jeanne stepped into the room, his dark hair gleaming in the lamplight, his eyes settling on Jeanne first before he turned politely to Maggie. "Ah, so this is your niece," he said.

"Maggie, I would like you to meet the duke's nephew, Sir Frederick Groton. Freddie, this is Margaret Rose."

"Charmed," Frederick whispered as he took Maggie's fingertips and bowed low over them. For a moment Maggie thought he might actually click his heels together and then kiss her hand.

Maggie withdrew her hand from his and cast an incredulous glance at Jeanne.

Jeanne laughed. "Don't you just love the

Europeans? So courtly and utterly charming, every one of them."

I wouldn't be so sure, Maggie thought. These days she couldn't seem to help questioning the motives of every European — friend or foe.

CHAPTER FOUR

Stefan fought weakness and exhaustion to stay alert as he translated all that was happening beyond the closed door of the room where they had brought him. The fisherman and his wife had returned at dusk, and he had been on alert. In these moments when he was not in pain or fighting the delirium of high fever, it was important to learn as much as possible about these people. He well knew that they might be pleasant to his face but was certain that only the foul weather prevented his arrest and transfer to a prisoner-of-war camp at the earliest possible moment. So he listened, straining to hear the soft, weary voice of the young nurse for what information she might give the others.

"He's sedated," he had heard her tell the couple, who would watch him now. He took a moment's satisfaction in realizing she had not noticed him hiding the pills she'd brought him between his gum and cheek until he could remove them. Gritting his teeth against the pain that electrified his fingers and toes from time to time, he had ground them to powder with his thumbnail.

"He'll likely sleep through the night, then," the fisherman had replied.

He'll likely keep his wits about him and plan his escape, Stefan thought. He had to reach his contact. But every attempt he made to roll over or sit up brought excruciating pain and drained him further of what little strength he had.

"The man must eat something," the fisherman's wife protested. Stefan thought of what the nurse's father had told him of the couple's loss. He thought of how the woman had fussed over him during the transfer from the inn to this cottage. She would be useful. He could play on her sympathies, gain her trust — not like the nurse, whose demeanor was as stiff as her crisply starched apron and nurse's cap. She kept watch even when he pretended to be drugged, as if at any moment she might be called upon to shoot him.

"You can rouse him long enough for that, Sarah," he heard the nurse reply.

"Go on, then," the elder woman replied. "The duchess is anxious to see you."

The duchess? Since when did Americans take the titles of royalty? Surely he had not heard correctly.

And then for the first time he heard the nurse laugh. The sound was musical — lively, sweet notes that trilled in the cold, still air. Maggie they called her and hearing her laughter, he thought the name apt. He imagined her running lightly over the freshly fallen snow. He envisioned her bursting through the door of the inn and rushing into the welcoming arms of "the duchess" who was . . . What?

Stefan shook off such thoughts and concentrated on the moment at hand. How many days had passed since he'd jumped ship? Surely the contact he'd been told to find at the wharves as soon as possible would not wait forever. If he failed to keep that appointment, all would be lost; he would have defected for nothing. Either way his fate was sealed. He squeezed his eyes shut as pain shot through his toes and fingers. Could the end be any more painful than these sudden shocks that paralyzed his limbs without warning, leaving him helpless as a newborn? Would his interrogators torture him to gain information? Would his death be painful? Would it come from a firing squad or hanging? And would anyone ever know that he had died a patriot? He had died because he loved his country — his homeland?

The turning of the doorknob brought his attention back to the here and now. He rolled onto his side and forced his breathing to be deep and steady in spite of the pain. Through the dim light and one eye opened a mere slit, he saw the fisherman's wife ease into the room. She put the tray she was carrying on the bedside table and stood for a long moment looking down at him.

"Ah, Georgie," she whispered and her voice caught. "If only this man were you come back to us." Then she dropped to her knees next to the bed and began praying.

Stefan pretended restlessness and rolled away from her, giving her privacy. After a long moment he heard the rustle of her skirts as she stood. "Stefan Witte," she whispered, touching his shoulder gently. "You need to wake up and eat something. Build your strength."

She's right. I cannot expect to make my way to the wharf in the state I'm in. Stefan faked a moan and rolled onto his back. When the woman touched his shoulder again, he opened his eyes.

"There. That's much better. Can you sit up a bit, dearie?" While he pushed himself to a half-sitting position against the pillows, she bustled about lighting a lamp, then spreading a napkin under his chin and bringing him the hot broth. "Maggie — Nurse Hunter — suggested perhaps a mug might make things easier than trying to use a bowl and spoon. Can you manage?"

Stefan nodded and took the mug from her, cradling it with his palms. Instead of leaving him alone as he had hoped she might, the woman pulled a chair closer and watched him. "It's *gut* — good," Stefan said, nodding toward the broth.

"Thank you. So, you speak our language," she said, raising her voice and slowly enunciating each syllable.

Stefan continued to sip the broth as he considered his options. Surely the more he could remind this woman of her son, the more helpful she might be. "I try," he admitted with a shy smile.

"I'm not sure we've been properly introduced, you being out of your head with fever much of the time since you arrived. I'm Sarah Chadwick. My husband — the fisherman who found you — is Sean."

"The nurse?"

"Oh, surely Margaret Rose has introduced herself, although she prefers to be known as Maggie. These modern young women," she added, shaking her head with obvious disapproval. "Her parents own the inn. Sean and I work for them. You simply will not find a finer couple than Gabe and Lucie Hunter. You have little to worry about, Stefan," she assured him. "Between Mr. Hunter and Dr. Williams, you will be treated fairly — and humanely." She took the empty mug and placed it back on the tray. "Now then, the way you managed that, I don't see why you can't try something a bit more solid. Some bread or cheese perhaps?"

Stefan stifled a yawn. "Very tired."

"Of course. I'll come check on you later, then." She touched his cheek. "Why, you're burning up. Sean! His fever is back. Send for Maggie at once."

By the time Dr. Williams could arrive, it was late evening and the patient had a raging fever and was struggling for every breath.

"I was afraid of this," the doctor said, more to himself than to Maggie.

"But he seemed so much better earlier," Sarah protested, wringing her hands as she hovered near the bed.

"It's not unexpected in a case like this," Maggie assured her. "There's nothing you could have done to prevent this." She saw relief flood Sarah's eyes. But the truth was that she was wondering if indeed they had overestimated the extent of his ability to fight off the pneumonia that might well kill him before the firing squad got its chance.

No! Not as long as you are under my care.

For three days Maggie barely left the man's side. If he choked, she was there to pull him upright and administer the breathing treatments she had once helped dispense to her grandmother. If his fever worsened, she was there with cloths soaked in alcohol to cool him. When he shook with chills, she was ready with extra blankets, which she wrapped him in as tightly as she might swaddle a child. For three nights she stayed at the cottage, sleeping in spurts on the sofa in the Chadwicks' parlor while Sean attended Stefan, waking the moment she heard a cough or sensed a change in his condition.

And all the while she could not help but admire his determination — even in his state of semiconsciousness — to fight the fever, to refuse to surrender to the attacks of pain and infection that racked his body. Finally when she woke on the fourth morning, after spending the last three hours in the rocking chair by his bed, she found him sleeping peacefully. His breathing was regular and his fever had passed. Maggie felt triumph mingled with relief. She had stayed with him every minute, forcing him to take fluids, holding him when he choked and coughed, massaging his cramped muscles, sleeping only when he did.

When she was nursing him, she had stopped seeing him as the enemy. He was a human being in pain, in real danger of not making it through another night. She had fought alongside him as she would have fought for the recovery of any patient.

"He's come through it," Dr. Williams announced with some degree of disbelief mingled with admiration. "You've brought him through it, Maggie. Now I want you to go to the inn and get some proper rest or it will be you I'll be coming to treat."

"As soon as Sarah comes this evening," she promised.

Dr. Williams looked at her for a long moment. "Your devotion to your patients has often impressed me, my dear, but this man — this man is out of danger. You have done good work here. There's no need to exhaust yourself in further effort."

He was right, of course, and the truth was that Maggie was every bit as mystified as the doctor appeared to be regarding her reluctance to leave Stefan Witte's care to others.

"I'm up," she said with a smile and a shrug. "And as you say, there is little to do but watch him sleep until Sarah returns this evening. I'll be fine."

"Come to town with me tomorrow," Jeanne urged Maggie that evening as they sat in the parlor together. "We'll go shopping. That uniform is impressive in its symbolism, but as the latest fashion?" Jeanne arched one eyebrow in disapproval.

Shopping with Jeanne was indeed an adventure, and Maggie was tempted. "I have to attend my patient," she reminded Jeanne.

"Nonsense. By all reports your patient is improving. Are not Sarah and Sean seeing to him at night?"

"Yes, but . . ."

"Then Sarah can see to him for one afternoon. You go in the morning and make sure he has survived the night. Get him set for the day with his medicines and treatments and then off we go."

Maggie had always envied the way Jeanne seemed to assume that all things were possible simply because she wanted them to be. On the other hand she reminded herself that Jeanne had suffered a loss as great — perhaps greater — than hers. Was this sudden urge to shop really about Maggie's need for clothes, or did it go deeper? She studied Jeanne's beautiful face — the smile that always seemed only a hair away from exploding into girlish giggles. But closer examination revealed that in spite of her smile and teasing, Jeanne's eyes had been robbed of their usual guileless sparkle.

"The selection on Nantucket may not be quite up to your usual standards," Maggie warned. "No Parisian gowns here."

"Of course not. There's a war on, after all. We shall simply do our part to support the economy no matter what the selection. If I decide to move here, I'll have need of some items — a muff for every day, proper boots, a sweater or shawl for these insufferable winter nights. Perhaps I can entice my dressmaker to open a shop."

"Why would you come here to live when you can live practically anywhere in the world?" Maggie asked.

"Because I can't be in Europe right now and Nantucket — well, it's as close as I can come to Europe for the time being, at least geographically. Besides, I have this delightful young friend who needs cheering up." She tweaked Maggie's nose and laughed.

"Now tell me about your patient. Why all this devotion? He's no longer so very ill, is he?"

Maggie stumbled for words. "He is . . ."

But Jeanne thought she had confirmed the man's state of health and pursed her lips sympathetically. "Has he a family?"

"A sister and nephew." At least that much was true.

"They don't . . . live here."

"Then you must write them — have him dictate a letter for you to send them. They must be told that he is in the best of hands. The man is not — that is, he isn't going to —"

"He will not die," Maggie replied firmly.

"Oh, Maggie, are you so fierce about all your patients, or perhaps this man has attracted you in a different way?"

Maggie was shocked at the very notion that she and the German might find any attraction. Of course, Jeanne was completely unaware of the man's national ties. "He is . . . we could not . . ."

Jeanne burst into laughter. "If you could see your face, child. Perhaps the man is much older? Of course he is. For as you noted, who else is left on this island when it comes to the male population but the old and the very young?"

"I do not consider myself either old or very young," Gabe protested, brushing the snow from his camel-hair overcoat and sable bowler as he entered the room. He glanced at Maggie and nodded slightly, and she understood that he had been up to the cottage to check on the German. "And yet I reside on this island, Duchess."

"So you do, Gabriel, and thank heaven for that." She accepted his kiss on her cheek. "You could use a new scarf, Gabe. Something a bit more stylish for a man of your position, I should think. Maggie has agreed to come to town with me tomorrow for some shopping. Perhaps we will surprise you."

"My beautiful daughter made me this scarf when she was no more than ten — it is irreplaceable," he replied with a wink at Maggie.

Maggie blushed with pleasure, as she knew that the scarf was filled with dropped and added stitches and other mistakes and yet her father wore it with great pride.

"Your daughter is a woman now, and hopefully her knitting has improved. Perhaps she might consider knitting you something new? Haven't you a birthday coming soon?" Jeanne reminded them.

"And are we to have the pleasure of your

company for that occasion?" Gabe asked, his tone jovial, but Maggie saw that his eyes were searching Jeanne's for some clue of her plans. His birthday was still months away.

As usual the duchess batted her eyes flirtatiously and laughed. "We shall see how things transpire," she said. "I might have to leave sooner rather than later. I have some important business to attend to in New York."

Gabe couldn't help himself and laughed. "More shopping?"

Jeanne shrugged. "On the other hand, perhaps I could extend my stay if you and Lucie have the room available?"

"You know you are always welcome, Duchess," Gabe replied, but as he turned away to light his pipe, Maggie saw the frown that creased his forehead. Having Jeanne and her entourage on the premises would complicate things, no matter how they tried to keep her away from the cottage and the German they held prisoner there.

"You are much distracted today," Stefan said the following morning in a voice made raspy by sleep and near-constant coughing. Maggie rushed around preparing his medications and treatment supplies so Sarah could manage them for the day.

"And you are somewhat improved," she countered.

"And yet you bother with these details — these matters that Mrs. Chadwick has already seen to." It was not an accusation. His intent was only curiosity.

"I am simply trying to make sure you have the proper care," she replied, avoiding his eyes as she had all morning.

"Are you going away?"

She released an exasperated sigh. "I am going into town for some shopping with my — a guest of the inn."

"The duchess?"

Maggie whirled around to face him. "How do you know of the duchess?"

Stefan shrugged and locked his eyes on hers. "It is a small house. I hear things — and your cook, Mrs. Chadwick, talks to me."

"About what?"

"Her son mostly. Her husband — and you and your parents. You are much like family to her." Maggie turned back to her work, but he continued. "She told me of your father's good work in the city — how he made retribution for past wrongs in his business, although they were not his to make right. How he rescued her family from certain ruin."

"My father is a good and kind man. For several days now you have been the benefactor of that kindness."

His eyes widened. "How many days? How long have I been here?"

"Well, you came to us the night of the twelfth and today is —" he watched as she mentally calculated the date "— the twentieth." Stefan felt a rush of pure panic. He reached for the covers to throw them aside, and demanded, "I would wish to speak with your father."

"There is no need to call him here to thank him. You'll have ample time for that, I'm sure."

Still weak, in spite of feeling better than he had since being brought here, he sagged back onto the pillows.

"No — yes, I would thank him, but I need to speak with him about an urgent matter."

"This morning? Now?"

"That would be good."

"He's — about what?" Her eyes narrowed with suspicion.

"A business matter."

Maggie laughed.

"I amuse you?"

"You are hardly in a position to discuss anything, much less business, with my father," she said.

"Only your father can decide that. Shall I ring for him?" He gestured toward the cowbell that Sarah had left on his bedside table in case he needed her in the night. "Or should I make the trek through the snow?" He made an effort to sit on the side of the bed and place both feet on the floor. The pain that shot up his legs could not be disguised. He grimaced and bit his lip to keep from crying out.

Maggie was at his side instantly, grasping his arm and easing him back onto the pillows. "Get back in bed. What on earth are you thinking?"

"I must speak with your father," he hissed through teeth gritted to hold back the cries of pain. "It is most urgent."

Maggie hesitated. "Very well. I can call the inn and see if he is available."

"Danke."

When her father arrived a few minutes later, Maggie crossed her arms and remained at her post near the foot of the bed. "Please," Stefan said quietly, "may we speak in private?" He glanced over at Maggie and Gabe nodded.

"Maggie? Give us a moment, dear."

Stefan saw resistance tense every muscle

in her body. Surely she would not defy her father.

"Maggie?"

She glanced at her father and seemed about to say something, but then her gaze shifted to Stefan. And in her eyes Stefan saw the same boldness he had seen in a woman's face only once before. Uma had looked at him with that same defiance. He saw now that Maggie Hunter had stayed because she was protecting her father. It was ludicrous, of course, but she, like Uma, would do whatever it took to safeguard the people she loved. He had the passing thought that such loyalty must surely extend to her community — her country — as did his. Was it possible that this woman, so small and yet so outwardly strong, also possessed the inner courage that would be required in one who must stand against the masses?

She was watching him now, her eyes fiery as usual. She cast him a look of warning and left the room.

In the time her father spent with the German behind the closed door, Maggie made a fresh pot of tea and cut vegetables for the stew Sarah would serve at noon. Dr. Williams had prescribed a more substantial diet for the man — lamb stew with vegetables,

97

bread, cheese. "Now that he's apparently out of danger, he needs to rebuild his strength if we're to get him on his feet again," Doc had announced that morning. "Maggie, you should try getting him to stand next to the bed starting tomorrow and by the end of the week perhaps a few steps."

"Yes, Doctor," Maggie had replied.

She glanced toward the closed door. She had expected her father's stay to be a short one, but he'd been in there now for well over half an hour.

Finally the knob turned and her father emerged, his expression unreadable.

"Is everything all right?" she asked as she held his overcoat for him.

"What? Yes, fine." He bent and kissed her cheek. "I'll send Sarah down so you and the duchess can be on your way."

But before stepping off the porch, he turned. "Maggie, stop by my study before you leave. I have an errand for you to run as long as you're going to town, all right?"

Maggie searched his expression to see if there could possibly be any connection between this errand and whatever had transpired with the German. But her father was already headed back toward the inn. She stood for a moment in the open doorway, trying to find some clue in the set of his shoulders, the tilt of his head.

The slightest ring of the cowbell interrupted her thoughts.

"You rang?" she said with just enough sarcasm to let the man know she did not appreciate being summoned in this way.

But he was collapsed back onto the pillows, his face contorted with pain, his cheeks flushed as perspiration dotted his furrowed brow. Maggie's ingrained sense of compassion overcame every suspicion and doubt. At this moment this was her patient and he was in pain.

"Where is the pain?" she asked, keeping her voice calm.

"Legs," he managed. "Feet."

Maggie reached for the bell and rang it with all her strength. "Get me a bucket of snow," she said when Sean came at a run.

She arranged the covers to expose his calves and feet and eased a rubber sheet under both legs. "Sorry," she murmured when he stiffened and bit his lip against crying out.

Sean returned with the snow and Sarah. "What can I do?" Sarah asked, shrugging out of her coat, scarf and mittens. "He was doing so well."

"It's a good sign. The pain means he's regaining some feeling. Repeat the massages every fifteen minutes or so for the next hour — longer if the pain doesn't abate." Maggie scooped up snow and began massaging Stefan's feet and ankles. "Perhaps I should stay."

"No," Sarah assured her. "I can do this, and it wouldn't do to disappoint the duchess. She's talked of nothing else all morning."

Seeing that the massage was already bringing relief, Maggie found the tube of ointment the doctor had prescribed for his nearly healed fingers. She squeezed some into her palm and spread it over the back of his hand and then down between the fingers and over the palm, then repeated the same on the opposite hand. "Better?" she asked in her generic nurse's voice when she'd finished.

He closed his fingers around hers, his eyes locked on hers. In that instant she was aware of one thing only — the warmth and strength of his fingers on her skin. Maggie felt a wondrous sense of connection instead of the revulsion she might have imagined at the very idea that this man might touch her intentionally.

"Thank you," he whispered.

Flustered by the sudden assault on her senses, she pulled her hand free. "Not at all," she said. "Mrs. Chadwick is a natural nurse." She dunked a small towel into the bucket of melting snow, squeezed the excess moisture from it and placed it on his forehead with the professional efficiency that came with having performed the same task dozens of time. "I leave you in good hands here."

"Have a lovely afternoon," Sarah said. "Let the duchess spend her money on you. Goodness knows she has enough of it."

Maggie smiled the first genuine smile she'd given anyone all day. "Sarah!"

"Well, she does," Sarah replied defensively.

"Then I shall see if we might bring back something for everyone — even you," Maggie teased as she put on her coat and wrapped her shawl over her hair and shoulders.

"If it's a gift-giving mood you're in, don't forget our guest here." Maggie saw Sarah actually wink at Stefan and was rooted to the spot by the door when his face, so recently contorted in pain, was transformed by his brilliant smile.

In spite of his poor health, his smile radiated strength. If Maggie had passed him on the street, she would have thought him interesting, appealing, someone worth getting to know. She might have instantly identified him as a kindred spirit. She might have smiled back, even greeted him. There had been a time when she might even have flirted with him. His eyes moved from Sarah to her, and his smile wavered.

"Have you forgotten something?" Sarah asked, glancing back at her as she continued to massage Stefan's feet.

"No. I —" She could not seem to look away from Stefan — nor he from her. Shaking free of his gaze, she reminded herself that this man she had momentarily thought attractive was German. He was the enemy. "No," she said firmly as she turned away. "I'll return as soon as possible," she called.

"Not likely we'll see her 'til tomorrow," Maggie heard Sarah confide to Stefan. "The duchess does love to shop."

CHAPTER FIVE

Maggie barely heard Jeanne's chatter as Frederick drove the three of them in the carriage into town. Jeanne was going on about how much more comfortable it would be if they were riding in the automobile Frederick had left in New York.

"You would love it, Maggie," she gushed. "On the open road it can be a little like flying. Freddie has promised to teach me to drive this spring. Won't that be something?"

Maggie hadn't really been paying attention and hoped that nodding and smiling would suffice. She was still confused by her father's strange assignment.

"I want you to meet this afternoon's steamer," he had instructed as he finished scribbling a note and then sealed it securely in an envelope. "The person you're looking for will be wearing a blue scarf and carrying an umbrella. He will be part of the crowds but not necessarily a passenger. When you see him, pass by and say, 'Peace be with you.' If he replies with, 'And with you and all your countrymen,' give him this envelope."

"But who is this man and what's in the envelope and why all the mystery and —"

Papa stopped her with a look. "It is business, child."

In other words, do not question, Maggie thought as she turned the envelope over in her hands. It was slim and could not possibly contain more than a single slip of paper. It was sealed tight. "And after I hand over the envelope?"

"Go about your shopping."

"What am I supposed to tell Aunt Jeanne?"

Papa frowned. "Tell her you have an errand for me."

"She'll want to come along."

"Then say you want to get something for her — a surprise."

Maggie's eyes widened. Her parents had never asked her to lie; in fact, they had punished her more than once for doing just that in order to get out of school on a beautiful spring day or avoid chores when she'd rather be at the shore. "I am to — deceive Aunt Jeanne?"

Her father sighed heavily and reached into

his coat pocket for his wallet. He handed her several bills. "No, at least not entirely. Here, choose something for her on your way back from the meeting."

Maggie accepted the money. "Papa, is this — business — to do with the German?" She cut her eyes toward the window and the cottage beyond.

Her father smiled and came around his desk to enfold her in a hug. "Oh, my little one, always so curious." He squeezed her tight and then leaned back so he could see her face. "We are in a time of war, Maggie. Will you do as I ask?"

Maggie nodded but did not miss the fact that her father had avoided answering her question.

"I have an errand to run for Papa," she blurted now as Frederick turned the carriage onto Main Street. He guided the matched team of horses cautiously over the uneven cobblestones, set decades earlier to make it easier to roll the barrels for storing whale oil to and from the docks. "I won't be long. Shall I meet you both at the tearoom?"

Jeanne sighed. "Leave it to your father to see the opportunity to inject a bit of business into a pleasure excursion," she grumbled. "Very well, let's get it done."

"No!" Maggie protested so vigorously that both Jeanne and Frederick turned to her. "That is, well, it's true I need to run a quick errand for Papa once the steamer docks, but I had also thought to have a moment to choose a gift for you," she admitted, her face flaming with the half lie.

Jeanne squealed with delight and hugged her. "As usual you have solved a little problem of my own — namely, how to distract you so I could purchase *you* a special something to cheer you up a bit. Perhaps from that shop there?" She pointed in the direction of a ladies' boutique on the street a block from the steamer dock. She waited for Frederick to come round and help her down from the carriage. "Now hurry along and do your father's bidding. I want you to have plenty of time for choosing my gift," she teased as she fumbled under the frilly ruffles of the silk scarf that filled the neckline of her fur coat and highlighted her strawberry-blond curls. She consulted the gold watch she wore on a chain. "Shall we meet at the tearoom in an hour?"

Relieved that Jeanne had raised no further questions, Maggie stepped down from the carriage, waved goodbye and headed for the dock at a quick pace. The steamer was just coming into the dock.

So many blue scarves, she thought as gentleman after gentleman came off the steamer.
But not one of them with an umbrella. She
frowned. Her father had indicated the
person might not be a passenger. Maggie
glanced around. One man was wearing a
blue plaid scarf but carrying a walking stick,
so perhaps she'd gotten the instructions
wrong?

She eased toward him, fingering the envelope in her coat pocket as she did. She
waited until they were side by side and
murmured, "Peace be with you."

The man glanced down at her, scowled
and hurried on without a word. The last of
the passengers had disembarked and there
were fewer people around. What now? Maggie thought. She studied the passengers
waiting to board, but not one of them fit
the bill. She glanced at her watch — only
thirty-five minutes before she was due to
meet Jeanne and she still had to buy some
token.

As she hurried toward the shops, it began
to snow. She was surprised to see Frederick
raising an umbrella over himself and Jeanne.
They were strolling slowly along the wharf,
their heads bent low in conversation. Jeanne

was wearing a blue scarf. Frederick had an umbrella but a white scarf.

Now you're seeing blue scarves and umbrellas everywhere, Maggie reprimanded herself and ducked into a shop that specialized in nautical antiques. Hastily she selected an ivory scrimshawed comb with rose and hydrangea blossoms for Jeanne.

When she emerged from the shop, the steamer horn blasted the warning for all returning passengers to be on board. A man raced past her, waving an umbrella as if to get the steamer captain's attention.

"Peace be with you," she shouted after him.

He slowed and glanced over his shoulder, and her heart raced as she half pulled the envelope from her pocket. Then she saw that he wore no scarf at all. He waved and grinned at her but kept running as Maggie shoved the envelope back into her pocket and crossed the street to the tearoom.

By the time the threesome completed their shopping and returned to the inn, it was nearly time for dinner. When Maggie found the opportunity to return the still-sealed envelope to her father, he was strangely calm about her failure to complete the assignment. When she told him what had happened, he nodded solemnly and murmured, "As I thought." He seemed more resigned than disappointed as he ripped the envelope in half and fed it to the fire.

"I'm sorry, Papa," she said again.

"No, I am the one to apologize for cutting into your time for shopping with Jeanne. Did you and the duchess have fun?"

Maggie blushed. "Auntie Jeanne insisted on buying me so many beautiful things. I'll return them, of course, once she leaves. We'll donate the money to the war effort."

Her father studied her for a long moment. "Surely you can keep one or two items. You've hardly worn anything other than your uniform since —"

"I am a nurse," she reminded him, interrupting before he could form the words *Michael died.* "Besides, where would I wear embroidered leather evening gloves?"

Her father's dark eyebrows shot up, and then he smiled and shook his head in wonder. "That's our Duchess," he said. "Was there nothing more practical?"

Maggie pretended to consider, then grinned. "Yes. One item. She bought me a handknit cardigan of alpaca and silk. It seems she recalls that Grandma's cottage was always drafty, and she thought I should have this to wear when I am there."

"Alpaca and silk?"

"It cost a fortune when a serviceable wool sweater would have done as well, but she insisted." Maggie shrugged. "She bought presents for everyone — even you."

"Not a scarf, I hope."

And immediately Maggie was back to the question of why her failure to make contact with the person in the blue scarf was not more upsetting to her father. "Could this person in the blue scarf have gotten the date wrong?" she suggested. "Or perhaps he simply forgot the umbrella part?"

Her father glanced up at her over the top of his reading glasses. "No. The details were very clear," he said. "Very clear, indeed." He leaned back in his chair and stared out the window, where the glow of lights from the cottage spilled across the snow. And in that moment Maggie knew that she had been right. Whatever her errand, it had something to do with Stefan Witte.

Stefan was agitated and out of sorts the following morning when Maggie arrived, while she was still caught up in the pleasure of the shopping venture. It was always fun to spend time with Jeanne, and she'd been delighted to find that Frederick was just as witty and lighthearted as the duchess. After dinner the evening before, Jeanne had insisted that Maggie model each purchase for her parents, and the five of them had spent a lovely evening admiring the craftsmanship of the garments and speculating on occasions that Maggie might find to wear them.

For perhaps the first time since Michael's death, Maggie had hardly given the war a thought. Her failure to complete her father's assignment aside, she had been captivated by the adventure Jeanne and Frederick had created for her. For the first time in months she had slept soundly and awakened rested and eager to face the challenge of getting Stefan Witte on his feet and out of their lives.

"Dr. Williams says we are to begin standing and even walking today," she announced as she threw open the curtains and ignored his growl of protest at the sudden bright light that filled the room. "I have brought you this robe of my father's and some slippers. Can you manage the robe, or shall I call Sean to help you?"

"I want proper clothes."

She ignored his protest. "The robe will suffice during your convalescence. I hardly think you'll be going outside anytime soon. There's a foot of snow and ice on the ground now and more coming if the skies are any indication." She gave the robe a slight shake, and he took it from her. "Do not try and get up on your own," she instructed as he moved to sit on the side of the bed. "Even though your toes and fingers seem to be healing more quickly than we might have expected, this will take time."

"I must speak with your father," he announced.

"About using his robe? He won't mind. He has another."

"About . . ." He broke off and clamped his mouth shut. "I thought he would come this morning."

"He has a business to run and . . . other responsibilities. Perhaps later. For now the doctor wants you to try sitting up and then —"

"We will walk," he said in a voice that demanded rather than questioned.

"Yes, eventually, but I would think you might not be so eager to regain full strength and movement." She studied him curiously.

He glanced at her, his scowl momentarily replaced by a questioning frown.

"Once you are well enough to move around, no doubt we shall be turning you over to the authorities on the mainland." The look that passed over his haggard features was one of forbearance when she might have expected panic or even rebellion.

"We will walk," he repeated, thrusting one arm into the sleeve of the robe.

"As you wish," Maggie answered as she held the other sleeve for him. "But first we will stand." She was careful to keep him covered as she helped him to the edge of the bed. She had left the door open and could hear the rattle of Sean's newspaper as he sat in the kitchen just across the hall. "Sit for a minute," she instructed, taking the opportunity to assess her patient.

The effort of putting on the robe and moving to the position of sitting on the side of the bed had taken its toll. He was breathing heavily. She bent to work his feet into the slippers that were large enough to allow room for the protective bandages, giving him the time he needed to regain his strength. When she stood up, he was watching her, his eyes troubled.

"What is it? Your feet? Cramping?"

He shook his head impatiently. "Why do you wear that?"

Maggie thought for a moment he might be hallucinating. Then she saw that he was looking at her hair, at her starched nurse's cap. "It's part of the uniform," she answered. "As a military man, I should think you would realize that."

"But here, there is no need. This is not a hospital."

Maggie stood. "It's part of the uniform," she repeated, "and when I am on duty, it is what I wear. Now, shall we try standing?" She moved next to him. "Put your arm around my shoulders."

It was a mistake to think she could do this alone. It was not his weight or weakness that was the problem. Over her career she had performed a similar exercise with patients who far outweighed Stefan. It was being this close to the man. It was confusing the way her thoughts became tangled around the first sensation of nurturing and then that of aversion. It was the very fact that his arm stretched over her back and shoulders, the flat of one large palm pressed against her sleeve felt somehow as if he were supporting her rather than the other way round.

Shaking off such folly, she placed her arm around his waist. "Ready?"

He nodded and focused all of his attention on the floor, as if willing his feet and legs to do his bidding. Slowly she slid him forward until both feet rested flat on the floor, then wordlessly guided him to a standing position.

114

He gasped and then smiled. He looked down at her and grinned. "*We* are standing."

In spite of herself Maggie laughed. "Indeed we are." She loosened her grip on his waist and felt his body adjust to the change in support. He leaned toward her. "Steady," she coached while at the same time reminding herself to ignore the warmth of his side pressed against hers and the wintergreen scent of the soap Sean had used when helping him wash earlier that morning.

He tried to take a step and instead fell backward onto the bed, his hand slipping from her shoulder and tangling through her hair as he fell. Maggie shouted for Sean even as she braced him against the fall. Sean caught them both and eased Stefan back onto the bed. Maggie stood and straightened her apron and collar. "Are you all right?" she said, instinctively reaching to push pins back into the coil of hair she wore at the nape of her neck.

"Yes," he replied, then grinned as he held up her nurse's cap.

She snatched it from him and ignored the slight smile Sean tried to cover by turning away. "I do not appreciate your wasting my time, Stefan Witte." She turned to the mirror to replace the cap.

"I had a cramp," he protested.

Maggie glanced at him through the mirror and caught him exchanging a knowing look with Sean, who had clearly heard the earlier exchange about the cap and who now appeared to agree that it was an affectation for her to insist on wearing it here.

"Very well," she said. "That's enough for today, then." She wrapped the sheet over him and with Sean's help lifted his legs so that he was lying fully on the bed.

"No, wait. I will cooperate. We will stand again." His words hit the door she closed firmly behind her.

When he had stood for the first time, and she had laughed, Stefan had thought to charm her. After all, was she so different from the young women he'd known back in Germany? He had not lied about the cramp, nor had he deliberately taken her nurse's cap. And yet he had thought she would see the humor, the irony of it. Sean had.

Why? What did it matter if she liked him or even felt a bit more comfortable around him?

Because there was something about this woman — a connection between them. They were more alike than either of them was prepared to admit.

He had made progress with the others. Sean stopped by in the evenings, encouraging Stefan's childhood memories of fishing excursions with his father or sharing his own memories of teaching their son, George, to fish. Sarah continued to sit with him and knit or read passages from the Bible. Although Stefan had refused to say why the meeting was so vital, Maggie's father had given him the benefit of the doubt when Stefan had told him of the need to reach his contact. He had agreed to write a message explaining why Stefan could not keep the appointment and deliver it to the mysterious contact. Stefan knew that Gabe had agreed only because this was a way of testing Stefan's story. He could see in Gabe's eyes that he did not believe him. But it was just as evident that Maggie's father wanted very much to believe him.

Nevertheless, when Gabriel Hunter finally came to call on him later that afternoon, Stefan saw that doubt had won out. Gabe was stone-faced and unmoved by Stefan's protests as he reported that there had been no one in a blue scarf with an umbrella to receive his message. Gabe made it clear he now believed that Stefan's fantastic story of defection was pure fabrication, a ruse to buy time.

"I wanted to believe you," Gabe told him. "I so wanted to believe you that I did a terrible thing. I involved my daughter, my only child, in your deceit."

"I told the truth. You cannot blame me if you decided to send Mag— your daughter — instead of going yourself," Stefan protested.

"I blame myself," Gabe said in a low, tight voice that spoke louder than if he had shouted. "I trusted you, but we — Germans and Americans — are not to share trust, are we?" He did not wait for an answer but left the room, closing the door behind him, and Stefan could not hear what he was saying to the Chadwicks. He knew only that beginning that evening they did not come to sit with him to talk or read aloud.

In need of an ally, Stefan mentally ran through the remaining candidates. He had already decided against involving the Chadwicks, and that left only Maggie. She had suffered her own losses in this war. Surely if he could explain it all to her, she might even respect what he was trying to do. On the other hand, the little he'd been able to learn about her from the Chadwicks told him that the roots of her personal grief and anger ran deep. He well knew that she needed someone to blame for her loss — someone like him.

The Chadwick woman had told him how Maggie and Michael had seemed meant for each other and how Maggie had turned her back on God when she'd received news of Michael's death. Such powerful anger might be turned to his advantage if he could find a way to convince her that in helping him she was avenging the death of her sweetheart.

Now, as Stefan lay on the bed, his arms crossed behind his head, his eyes tracing the outline of the small water stain on the ceiling, he considered his next move. The contact had not been made. Now what? He had been through too much to give up now. If he could not convince Maggie to help him, then escape was the only other option, and unless he regained his strength, escape would be impossible.

He waited for Sarah to bring his night medicine, for Sean to look in and mumble his good-night before closing and locking the door. He heard the couple in the bedroom overhead, their voices seeping through the ceiling as they prepared for bed. He waited longer, his eyes riveted on the clock on the mantel. An hour passed. Above he could hear Sean's muffled snoring. Outside the snort of the horses. All else was silent.

He eased to the side of the bed and rolled onto his stomach. Panting, he lay there a moment gathering his strength. Then he twisted his lower body until his legs hung over the side, inching backward until his bare feet touched the planked floor. By that time his breath was coming in ragged gasps and his forehead was beaded with sweat.

Upstairs he heard a sound and froze. Someone coughed. Stefan waited for more but all was silent. He forced himself to relax and then placed both palms on the mattress and shoved himself upright. The pain that shot through his fingers and toes because of the pressure he placed on them was so excruciating that he bit down hard on the inside of his lip to keep from crying out. He collapsed back onto the bed, then tried it again, this time placing his weight on his palms and the balls of his feet to avoid the pain to his injured digits. Hunched over the bed, he relaxed his full weight onto his feet and legs and tried to stand — and fell forward. Again and again he worked until the light started to break over the snow and he heard Sean's heavy tread on the floorboards above him.

He had not stood alone, but he had gotten upright for several seconds, his fingers barely clutching the sheets for balance, and that was progress. Exhausted, he worked his way back into the bed and pulled up the covers. The last thing he heard before falling into a deep sleep was the click of the latch to his bedroom door — another problem to overcome, he thought, and accepted that now more than ever he needed the help of Maggie Hunter.

Maggie was confused and surprised by the report Sarah gave as they exchanged places for the day. "He's had a setback. No fever that I can tell, but I could hardly rouse him. And his bedclothes were damp as if he'd fought a fever through the night. All twisted up in the bedding he was. I had to get Sean to come in and help me get him straight. I brought fresh linens for us to change the bed. Those are a mess." She shook her head, mystified. "He's been improving steadily, although last night he did seem more agitated than usual."

And yesterday as well, Maggie thought. "Dr. Williams should be here soon," she assured Sarah. "And I can manage changing the linens. Mother needs you at the house. Don't worry, Sarah. A setback at this stage is not so unusual for one who has been so ill."

Sarah nodded. "I just hope it's not influenza. You don't think it's that?"

"Let's wait for the doctor," Maggie said. Of course the thought of influenza had crossed Maggie's mind. While the population of Nantucket had been fortunate to escape the numbers of cases that had plagued towns and cities up and down the East Coast, it wasn't beyond possibility that the man, in his weakened state, might have contracted the virus. And might it spread to others in the household in spite of everyone being inoculated? To Sarah and Sean or her beloved parents? Her mother, who'd already been infected once?

The very idea gave fresh fuel to the fire of her determination to get this man out of their lives once and for all. By the time she reached the door to Stefan's room, Maggie was fairly seething with the injustice of having to deal with this German at a time when she and her family had already faced so much. She entered the room briskly and opened the drapes. The lump in the bed did not stir.

She went about her morning duties — preparing his medication and fresh bandages to apply once she had drained the blisters that had finally formed, signaling further healing of the frostbite — just as she would have if she had been in the hospital.

She tapped the silver spoon against the ceramic bowl with extra vigor after mixing his medication. She washed her hands thoroughly, allowing the water to run even though the pipes clanked and groaned in protest. And all the while she watched the bed. She saw him pull the covers over his face to shut out the light.

"Well, good morning," she said in her professional voice. "Sarah tells me you had a restless night."

The bandaged fingers clutching the covers flinched slightly, and his body went too still for him to be sleeping. He was listening, waiting for what came next.

"Are you hungry?" she asked as she shook the thermometer, then pulled the covers free of his face and thrust the thermometer between his lips. "Under your tongue, please," she instructed as she took his wrist and measured his pulse.

Fast, she mentally noted. She checked the thermometer. Normal. She saw him watching her through the puffy slits of half-open eyes.

"*Lass mir lien,*" he muttered and reached for the covers.

"Later," she said and pulled the covers down just past his shoulders, lifting one hand and then the other as she unwrapped and examined his fingertips. "Sarah said you've had no breakfast."

He grunted.

She moved to the foot of the bed and raised the covers to expose his toes. "You're making excellent progress," she observed. "The color is almost normal, although there is a bit of swelling. Still, the return of color means better circulation and that's a good sign. Any cramping overnight?"

"Some," he confessed. She rested her fingers on his foot, taking the pulse there as well. When she looked up and straight into his eyes, she mentally recorded his pulse but seemed incapable of breaking the contact.

"Your hand is warm," he said softly.

She jerked it away from his ankle as if she'd just touched a hot stove. "The water — hot water when I wash," she said, wondering why she was explaining herself. Just then she heard the jingle of a harness and the soft whisper of runners on snow. "Doctor is here," she announced unnecessarily and hurried from the room.

"Good morning, Maggie. How's our patient?"

Maggie gave both Sarah's report and her own to Dr. Williams as she took his heavy coat and hung it on the hall tree.

"Hm-m-m" was all Dr. Williams said as he entered the bedroom and went immediately to Stefan's bedside. He repeated the same basic examination that Maggie had already done, confirming her findings. He took out his stethoscope and listened to Stefan's heart and lungs.

"You look a bit done in, my boy," he said. "Your recovery from the frostbite seems to be coming along nicely, and the lungs are sounding better." He glanced over his shoulder at Maggie. "Have you been working on the standing this morning?"

"I just got here," Maggie explained.

The doctor frowned. "Well, maybe we're rushing things. Maybe hold off for now. Make sure he eats and let him rest for the day."

"No," Stefan objected before Maggie could reply. "I — we will stand," he said, his eyes on Maggie.

Maggie felt the rush of color along the collar of her uniform and up her neck to her cheeks as she recalled the previous day's attempt. Unconsciously she reached up and straightened her nurse's cap. She felt her color deepen when she realized Dr. Williams had spoken and she hadn't heard. He was studying her, his eyes sympathetic.

"Maggie? I said that perhaps you should

train Sean to work with him at night. Mr. Witte here is a large man."

Maggie forced her thoughts to focus on her patient, for that was what Stefan Witte was. They might do things differently where he came from, but Americans were kind and caring to people in pain or need, even to their enemies. "I can do it."

"Nevertheless, let's have Sean assist you." The doctor seemed to be having second thoughts.

"Yes, Doctor," she said, addressing him as she would have in the hospital to reassure him. "I'll go heat up his breakfast while you finish your examination."

In the kitchen she stirred the oatmeal that Sarah had left on a low fire and set the tray with a napkin and utensils. She'd left the door open a crack so she could use her toe to open it all the way when she returned with the tray. But she paused outside the door when she heard Dr. William's low voice.

"Now see here, young man, Mr. Hunter has told me all about this business of meeting some imaginary contact at the docks. Don't you think that after everything the folks here have done for you already, you owe them a bit of respect, not to mention honesty?"

"It is the truth," Stefan insisted, his voice a low, bass hiss.

"You were to make contact with someone at the docks by the twenty-fifth of this month and then what?"

There was a long pause and then with a tired sigh Stefan admitted, "I don't know. I was to be given further instructions. Surely you understand that in times like these such matters demand secrecy even among those involved."

"Yet the fact remains —"

"Perhaps the person could not come. There are still three days until the twenty-fifth, are there not? We could try again."

The bed creaked and Maggie knew that Dr. Williams had gotten up. She could hear him replacing instruments in his bag. "Here's the thing, young man. No one blames you for coming up with some story that might save your hide, but mysterious messengers in blue scarves carrying umbrellas is a little melodramatic, even for times like these."

Maggie's hand shook slightly, rattling the china. She pushed the door open and carried the tray to the bedside table. "Here we are," she announced as she removed the warming covers and set them aside, releasing steam and the inviting scent of oatmeal with apples and cinnamon in the bargain. She handed Stefan a napkin and then the oatmeal, all without once meeting his eyes.

"Looks good and smells better," the doctor said as he snapped his bag shut and headed for the hall.

Maggie followed him, her mind brimming over with questions, questions she would have thought her father might have answered before sending her off on that wild-goose chase. She watched Dr. Williams climb onto his sleigh and knew this was neither the time nor place to question him.

"I'll stop by this evening," he said. "If he's truly up to it, then by all means try to get him standing, Maggie. And keep in mind that he has every reason *not* to want to stand given the fate that likely awaits him. If you need to, use Sean to force him." He pulled on his gloves and let himself out.

Maggie watched Dr. Williams snap the reins. The horse tossed his head and started forth. Alone with their prisoner, she marched back down the hall and into his room, closing the door behind her with a bang that made his head jerk up and the spoon clatter back into the bowl. "Now then," she announced, "since you claim to be so anxious to get back on your feet, suppose we strike a bargain."

His eyes narrowed with suspicion and caution.

"I will help you walk *after* you tell me what's going on and why you are involving my father and me in your schemes."

CHAPTER SIX

If Stefan had thought he might have the upper hand in the battle of wits with Maggie because he was a man, even one with compromised health, he was wrong. She stood there, hands planted on her slim hips, her eyes locked on his, defying him to contradict her. He considered his options.

"I have the whole day," she reminded him with a little shrug as she turned to leave. "We can do this my way or not at all."

"What will you tell the doctor?" he asked when she was out the door and ready to close it. "Has he not ordered you to work with me — to make me stand and then walk?"

He had barely said the word *ordered* before she had covered the distance from the door to his bedside and was pointing her forefinger at his nose. "Be very clear about this, Stefan Witte," she said. "No one 'orders' me. Do not for one moment think that because I am a woman and you are a man, you have any special power or rights over me."

"But the doctor is —"

"— in charge of your treatment. However, if *you* fail in following his orders for your care, he understands that I cannot force you. Keep in mind that he and my father are already suspicious of your will to recover, given the fate that awaits you."

Stefan scowled at her but she did not blink, only lowered the accusing finger. "Now, if there is nothing else," she said and turned once again to leave.

"Please sit," he said wearily. "We will talk and then we will stand, yes?"

He saw her study him, searching for some sign that this was a trick. "You'll tell me about the ruse to meet a contact at the docks?"

"It was no ruse," he protested. "You must — I need for you to believe that."

"Why should I?" She pulled the rocker closer and sat down. She rocked forward, her elbows resting on her knees. "Why should any of us believe a word you say?"

"Because we are on the same side," he replied and was pleased to see that this statement had finally garnered a reaction other than suspicion and anger. Her eyes flashed with interest and surprise.

"You confuse me, Stefan Witte," she admitted as she rocked back and folded her arms as if to create a barrier between them.

Stefan smiled. "Then we are — how do you say it? In the same boat?"

"How can you make light of this? You are in serious trouble and I am trying to understand you."

"Why?"

Her eyes widened as if the question had not yet occurred to her. "I have no idea," she said softly. "It just seems that perhaps it might be important."

"It is more important than you could possibly imagine, Maggie."

"That you were supposed to meet someone wearing a blue scarf and carrying an umbrella?"

He waved her question away impatiently. "That is but a small kernel of the whole." He sighed, slumped back onto the pillows and glanced toward the window. Outside the snow had started again and the wind had picked up. "Perhaps God has changed His plan," he muttered, more to himself than to her as he fingered the small gold cross at his throat.

Maggie abandoned the rocking chair and began pacing along the foot of the bed, her hands clasped behind her back. "You can't honestly believe that you are on some sort of mission here."

"We are all on God's mission," he replied, giving her his full attention once again. "Even you, Maggie Hunter."

She paused in her pacing, but the look she gave him was filled with cynicism.

He seized the moment to press his advantage. "Mrs. Chadwick has mentioned that you think you no longer believe in God."

"We are not discussing my faith, or lack thereof, here. We are not discussing faith at all. Your so-called mission is political. Please don't put any other face on it."

"But you have doubts? You ask why God could allow such a thing as this war?"

"Of course I do," she snapped.

"Then you have faith," he replied. "Because the only solution to doubt is faith."

"That's a ridiculous logic."

Stefan smiled at her with something he knew Maggie read as pity. "In life we never know what a new day will bring and yet we go on. We believe that the sun will rise, that the fog will lift, that the flowers will conquer the snow. We believe that the storm will abate and calm waters will eventually carry us to port." He shrugged. "Faith."

Maggie frowned, then turned briskly to

her duties. "So, besides being a spy, traitor and deserter, you are also a minister?"

"I am no traitor and no spy." He ground out the words as if each were a bitter pill.

Maggie kept her back to him, but he knew that he had touched a nerve.

"If you think of doubt as questioning your faith, then perhaps you will see that I am correct," he continued in the pleasant voice of a teacher. "And if events that challenge your beliefs have made you doubt — made you question what God could be thinking in allowing such things — then you have faith."

"You are speaking in riddles." But she turned to face him and moved a few steps closer to the bed. "I will grant you that I have wondered about . . . things that have happened recently."

"The death of your intended," Stefan said.

"That and other things," she admitted.

"And you wonder why God allowed this good man to be taken from you at the very moment in both your lives when you were just beginning to find your way in this world?"

She raised her head and met his empathetic stare with a stony glare. "I see what you are trying here, Stefan Witte. Well, it won't work — not with me. You may have hood-winked others with your gold cross and your pretense at being a friend, but . . ."

Stefan sat forward, every muscle tensed as if at any moment he might literally leap from the bed and take her by the shoulders to shake some sense into her. "I have left my homeland and risked my life to come here," he pointed out. "Few people would make such sacrifices for mere political gain. What do you take me for?"

She met his challenge with her own. "I take you for the spy that I believe you to be. I take you for someone who has come to this island in order to find some way to the mainland where you and those who probably came with you that night —"

"For the last time, no one came with me," he said, his voice hoarse with frustration. "It is complicated," he admitted after a minute. "How to make you understand that I believe you and I share the same goals when it comes to this war."

"I doubt it." Maggie flung the words at him.

"Then I am wrong that if you had the power, you would end this tomorrow?" The question hung there between them, Stefan stubbornly waiting for an answer and Maggie just as stubbornly refusing to give one. "I am not a traitor to my country or a spy for yours, Maggie."

She narrowed her eyes. "Your English is exceptional. Of course, as a translator you would be proficient."

He could see that she was working through the questions that would naturally spring to mind. "I am German," he assured her. "I am a translator for the German government. All of this is true."

Now she was frowning. "How can we possibly be on the same side?"

"I do not mean that I am in favor of what your country and its allies are doing any more than I believe my government is right to pursue this quest for domination — not at the cost of its own citizens. Not at any cost."

"America is there to try to end this," she argued.

"As am I on the side of ending this war. From what I have learned and seen in my short time with you, I believe that you and your family also are in favor of such a thing. So you see, we are not so different after all."

Maggie rocked back in the chair and folded her arms. She seemed about to say something but simply pursed her lips and waited for him to continue.

"I do not like what is happening to my country, my homeland," he said quietly. "In the name of war, many innocents are suffering, dying."

Maggie glanced toward the photograph of his sister and nephew on the bedside table. "Your family?"

Stefan closed his eyes against memories he did not want to relive. And yet those memories might be the very thing to finally get through to her before it was too late. "When the British succeeded in blockading the North Sea, a blockade that prevented food and other essentials from reaching the innocent citizens of my homeland, I blamed them. It was then that I volunteered for service. I could not stand by while the very old and very young were denied the basic things necessary for survival."

"Go on."

He opened his eyes and looked at her, trying to decide if it was worth continuing. "My sister, Uma, married young. Her husband was a soldier and he was killed in the beginning days of the war, leaving her and my young nephew, Klaus."

Maggie picked up the photograph and studied it closely. "Your sister is very beautiful."

"Yes, she was — once. That picture was taken in happier times."

"What happened to her?"

"She died," he replied, his throat closing over the words. "And Klaus, as well."

"How?" Maggie whispered as she continued to study the photograph.

"They starved," Stefan replied and watched her carefully as the words sank in.

"Starved? I mean how could that be? They were — they look so . . ."

As was always the case when he forced himself to recall the process that had led to his sister's tragic end, Stefan had to fight against his rage at the unfairness of her death. "She did not have enough to eat," he snapped. "How else does one starve to death? And what she had for herself she fed to her son — to no avail, for he died, too."

Maggie's features contorted and for an instant Stefan thought she might burst into tears. "That's barbaric," she whispered, running her thumb over the laughing faces of Uma and Klaus.

"Yes."

"You must have been so very angry," she said, her eyes meeting his.

"Yes."

"At the Allies — your enemy." She was watching him carefully now. "Certainly the British for the blockade."

"At first," he admitted. "But then two things happened that changed everything for me. Our parents had died before the war, so there was only Uma and me. When I went to bury my sister and nephew, I made a startling discovery. My sister was working with the underground, people in Germany and Austria who believed the war was wrong and were working to sabotage the effort."

"Traitors?"

Stefan shrugged. "Or heroes — only history can truly say. Either way, I was doubly angry now, for I wondered if she had been denied food rations because the authorities suspected her." He stared at Maggie for a long moment. "In many ways she was a little as you are, outspoken, even defiant."

"But how did you know she was working against her own government?"

"At the cemetery, a man came to pay his condolences. He pulled me into his embrace and whispered some startling words to me. 'Your sister was a patriot, and now you must take up her cause.' Later that evening as I was emptying my pockets, I found a postal envelope with a key inside."

"No message?"

"None. I recognized the key as the kind that fits a postal box. So I went to the postal station nearest my sister's apartment and opened the box that matched the number on the key."

"And found?"

"A single sheet of paper, an advertisement for a pain medication."

Maggie actually looked disappointed.

"I tossed the paper in the trash as I left. Then a woman came running after me waving the paper. 'Sir, you dropped this,' she called to me." Stefan's attempt at a falsetto imitation of the woman's voice sent him into a fit of coughing.

Maggie was immediately at his side, lifting him so that he could lean forward, then holding a basin with one hand while she supported him with the other. He gagged and coughed until he was able to force out the phlegm and breathe again.

"Deep, slow breaths," she coached as she set the basin aside and lightly rubbed his back and shoulders. "That's good." She eased him back onto the pillows and went to attend to the basin. When she returned to his bedside, she looked uncertain.

"Perhaps this is too much," she said, more to herself than to him. "You need your rest," she announced in her nurse's voice.

"No. I will finish this part for there is much to tell and as you have reminded me, time is not on my side."

Maggie sat on the edge of the rocker. "Only this part — the woman in the post

140

office — then you must rest."

Stefan nodded and cleared his throat. "When she was close enough for me to explain that I had deliberately discarded the advertisement, she pressed the paper into my hand and said softly, 'Read this carefully — for Uma.' Then she was gone."

"I don't understand," Maggie said.

"Neither did I, but I had to report back to my unit. We left that very night for the front in Belgium."

"But the paper?"

"On the train north, I read it more carefully."

"And?"

Stefan shook his head. "The only odd part was that the source for purchasing the concoction was from a chemist shop in a small town in Belgium, the town where my unit was being sent." Stefan fought against a grimace as pain shot up his fingers and toes.

Maggie checked the small watch she wore on a thin gold chain around her neck. "It is past time for your medication — I apologize." She turned to the dresser where she had set up his medications.

"Do you believe what I have told you?" he asked as she held out the pills and a glass half-filled with water.

"I haven't heard the entire story," she hedged. "What happened once you reached Belgium? And you said there were two events that changed your mind, your loyalty."

"Never my loyalty," he announced, nearly choking on the pills. "I love my country."

"Yes, as do I love mine," she said firmly. He saw that the interruption had given her the moment she needed to remind herself who he was.

"Let me tell you the rest," he pleaded, sensing that he was losing her. "Then perhaps you will understand."

"Later. For now please swallow those pills and rest." He took the pills in his mouth and held out his hand for the water glass. To his surprise Maggie pressed two fingers gently to his throat. "Swallow," she said as she watched his throat convulse with the action. "Now open." Using her fingers she stretched his lips apart and checked the inside of his mouth. "Good," she said. "If you want me to consider believing you, a good first step is to stop hiding your pills and discarding them once I leave the room."

She offered him one more drink of the water, which he refused. "It occurs to me that under different circumstances you and I would have shared much in common. We could have become friends, Maggie," he said, watching her as she refilled the water glass.

"Do not think anything has changed between us," she replied evenly, but he did not miss the way her hand trembled as she set the glass on the bedside table within his reach.

In the hallway Maggie rested her head back against the closed door and drew in several deep breaths. The truth was she had gotten completely caught up in his story. His lightly accented but nearly perfect English had made her forget for a time that he was German. The story of his sister had been mesmerizing and never more so than the moment when he related that she had been working against her own government.

Of course, she reminded herself, gaining her sympathy had been his intent. And how better to do that than to use the photograph of the laughing young mother — a woman about Maggie's age — holding her cherubic child on her knee, their heads bent close? She'd gotten so caught up in the image of Uma and Klaus slowly wasting away that she'd failed to notice that none of this had in any way answered the question of tricking her father into sending her off on that wild-goose chase at the docks. She would not be so easily taken in again, she vowed as she set about dusting and sweeping the parlor and dining room and washing the breakfast dishes.

On the other hand, there was something about Stefan Witte. Something familiar about his eyes and their depths of sadness and bewilderment at what his world had become that she recognized. Clearly she had never met the man before he showed up half-frozen at her family's inn. And yet she felt as if they understood each other on a level beyond the understanding she received from her parents or friends. What if her mother and Sarah were right? What if God had sent this man to them?

You no longer believe in God, Maggie reminded herself.

"Enough," she whispered aloud. "Think on something else," she ordered herself and forced her thoughts to the inn. She wondered what Jeanne was doing. She had mentioned something about going into town again. Then Frederick had reminded her of the need to attend to some correspondence that was long overdue and Jeanne had made a face. Frederick had promised that if she worked on that project with him, he would entertain the family that evening by playing piano for a sing-along.

"Lovely," Jeanne had exclaimed. "Frederick is a gifted pianist," she had assured everyone at the breakfast table. "And Gabe, I seem to recall that you have a passable baritone?"

"Gabriel sings in the church choir," Lucie said before Gabe could reply. "Last Christmas, he had a solo," she added with obvious pride.

"Perhaps Frederick might perform a concerto for the church one Sunday while we're here," Jeanne had suggested. "Wouldn't you love hearing a Bach on that fine old organ, Maggie?"

"Or perhaps we might invite neighbors and friends here while the inn is quiet to enjoy a musical evening and one of Mother's wonderful buffets," she suggested instead.

It was obvious that her mother had confided in Jeanne that Maggie had abandoned the church after Michael's death. It was the one thing that had caused Mama the greatest worry. Now Jeanne had evidently decided to find some way to draw Maggie back into the fold. On the one hand, Maggie saw this as yet another sign of the deep friendship that her mother and Jeanne shared. On the other, Maggie was no hypocrite; her ties with God and all matters religious had been irrevocably broken the day she'd gotten the news of Michael's death.

Now, as she had from the day she'd gotten the news of Michael's death, she waited for the tears, but she felt only the now-familiar emptiness. And marching alongside that emptiness were the loss and feelings of abandonment she fought against every day. Mama promised that life would go on, that she would find new meaning, new purpose, but when?

Catching sight of her reflection in the glass of the kitchen window, she drew in her breath and leaned closer until only her eyes stared back at her. There was the same heartache and sorrow she had found so hauntingly familiar in the eyes of her patient. Stefan Witte had suffered and not just physically. He was emotionally ravaged, and in that she could not deny that they shared a common ground, a kind of temporary truce.

A movement outside brought her attention back to the present. Her mother was coming down the path, wending her way carefully over the rutted snow and ice, a basket over one arm. At the same time the pot with the onions and potatoes she had set on the stove for her patient's lunch began to boil over. Maggie whirled round to the stove and wrapped the hem of her apron around the heavy iron pot handle as she dragged it off the hot surface.

"Hello?" her mother called, letting herself in and stamping the snow from her feet in the hall. "Maggie?"

"In here," Maggie called, adding as soon as Lucie came round the doorway, "You shouldn't be out in this weather, Mama."

"I'm perfectly fine," her mother protested, setting the basket on the table and unwrapping the tea towels that covered its contents. "Sarah baked bread."

Maggie slowed her stirring. "Yes. She left two loaves here. There was no need . . ."

"How is our patient?" Mama whispered.

"Somewhat improved." Maggie knew full well that Dr. Williams and her father discussed the German's progress daily as they debated their next step. "Mama, has something happened?"

Mama touched Maggie's cheek. "I just wanted to see how you were doing."

"But Aunt Jeanne . . ."

"Has gone into town with Frederick. She was quite at loose ends all morning. In fact, ever since the three of you returned from your shopping excursion she's not been herself. Perhaps I should be asking you if something happened there?"

Maggie well knew that her father had not told her mother about Maggie's assignment in town. "Let's not worry your mother with this" had been his parting words as she left his study after returning the undelivered envelope. But Lucie Hunter was an observant and perceptive woman. There was not much that went on in her family that she was not aware of.

"I cannot imagine what might be upsetting the duchess," Maggie replied. "We had a lovely day in town. Perhaps she is regretting her decision to come here at this time of year. The weather has been worse than usual, and she does hate being shut in with nothing to do."

Mama set the bread on the sideboard along with a hunk of hard cheese and a jar of jam. "Perhaps. You've been out of sorts yourself lately."

"Not at all. I was tired. Shopping with Auntie Jeanne can be exhausting."

"I was thinking of the way you reacted to Jeanne's suggestion that Frederick play at the church," Mama said as she cut slices of cheese and arranged them on a small plate. "Was it the idea of Frederick playing or the thought of returning to the church?"

148

"Mother." Maggie's tone sounded a warning.

"It has been months now," Mama continued as if Maggie had not spoken. "Even for Christmas Eve you found an excuse."

"I was attending you," Maggie protested. "You were very ill."

"Eleanor Pritchard told me she offered to stay with me while you went with your father to services but you refused."

Maggie stirred the pot and eased it back onto the heat. She added the cod and spices and set the lid in place. "I wasn't — it was too soon."

"And now?"

"Oh, Mama, please don't fret over me. I will be fine but it will take time."

"It would be easier if you would share the burden of your grief in prayer," she replied. "I'm going to look in on Mr. Witte, a man of deep faith according to Sarah."

"He's sleeping," Maggie reported, but Mama took the plate of cheese and crossed the hall anyway. Do not be fooled, Maggie wanted to warn her mother, but she knew such warning would be useless.

Lucie Hunter's devout belief that God solved all problems was unshakable. Normally she was not given to the kind of missionary zeal practiced by some, but when

149

she saw someone in the throes of deep distress, she firmly believed that that person needed God's help. Further, she was convinced that such help was readily at hand if only the person would turn to God through prayer rather than away from it. "The answers are there," she had assured Maggie after Michael and George had died on the battlefield. "You must only listen and hear God's answers for your grief and pain."

Maggie found herself dwelling on thoughts of Michael as she ladled chowder into a bowl and added three thick slices of Sarah's rye bread. More specifically, she found herself comparing Michael with Stefan, not physically, but in the way she felt whenever she was with the German. With Michael she had always felt as if nothing bad could ever possibly happen to either of them. Their childhoods had been idyllic and their courtship the stuff of fairy tales. But whenever she was with Stefan, her mind was filled with far more serious matters, the hard challenges of life that she and Michael had never had to face, living as they did on an island far removed from the everyday stresses and troubles of the rest of the world.

With Michael she had never known a care, but the very presence of Stefan raised all sorts of weighty questions, matters that previously Maggie had been willing to leave to her parents or Michael. And the way Stefan looked at her, the way he seemed to assume his own suffering and loss connected somehow to hers, made her want to rise to the unspoken challenge she felt emanating from him.

Outside the bedroom door, she hesitated because rather than the low murmur of her mother's prayer or Bible reading, she heard laughter — her mother's and Stefan's. And when she pushed open the door, she saw that her mother was shaving off Stefan's beard and keeping him entertained with stories of her coming to America. Stories Maggie had heard as a child.

Stefan was more at ease than she'd ever seen him. Gone was the wariness that always clouded his gaze when he looked at her. As he conversed with Mama, his facial features were rested and relaxed with none of the tenseness and caution that she'd become accustomed to seeing. Without the heavy beard and mustache he looked younger, more vulnerable somehow. He laughed and she saw the fullness of his lips and the whiteness of his teeth. Was this an act put on for Mama's benefit to gain sympathy?

Stop it, she ordered herself. Stop questioning his every word or glance.

"Feeling better, are we?" Maggie said and hated the shrewish tone of her voice. She placed a napkin under Stefan's chin while Mama took the shaving brush, razor and basin to the sink to rinse them out.

Mama turned and addressed Stefan. "Now, Stefan, you mustn't overdo it. Dr. Williams tells us that you are still at risk for pneumonia, so you must be sure to get your proper rest and nutrition." She dried her hands and returned to his bedside as he took the first spoon of chowder. "How are your fingers and toes coming along?"

"Better, thank you," Stefan replied. "Later, Maggie — Nurse Hunter — will help me to stand and perhaps in a few days to walk."

"Well, won't it be lovely to get out of this room for a bit?" Mama said. "You can sit in the parlor for part of the day or perhaps go outside to the porch for some fresh air. Sean can lend you a coat."

"That would be very nice."

Maggie bustled about adjusting the draperies to allow in more light, straightening the precise order of medicines on the dresser, folding hand towels and hanging them in a perfectly aligned row on the washstand. The very idea that he could go outside, where anyone might see him, was ludicrous. What was Mama thinking?

"Well, Stefan," she heard her mother say as she stood with a rustle of her wool serge skirt, "I am pleased to see that you are making progress. You did give us all a terrible fright that first night, but clearly God has work for you to complete here on this earth before He calls you home." She brushed back a lock of golden hair that had fallen over Stefan's forehead.

"Thank you for your kindness, ma'am," Stefan replied.

Mama smiled and headed for the door. "I'll see you at home, Maggie," she said.

Stefan watched the tall, stately woman go and marveled at the gift she had brought with her. Not the cheese or bread but the sense of normalcy. Of all the Americans he had encountered, only she had treated him as something other than either the enemy or a reminder of those they had lost. Others had been kind in their acceptance of him, but Lucie Hunter had come immediately to his bedside and set about straightening his pillows and inquiring about his comfort. All the while she had talked about the weather, the goat cheese she had brought and the fact that the room he occupied had once belonged to her husband's parents. She had

153

not asked a single question or tried to pry information from him by referring to the war or his unusual appearance in their midst.

In her presence he had felt the tension that had become his constant companion slip away. And when she'd offered to shave him, it had felt like a gift. A kind of emancipation.

But the mood had changed the moment Maggie entered the room, for her very presence reminded him of who and what he was to these people. Although he had grown somewhat accustomed to her shifting moods, sometimes he found her aloof attitude irritating and confusing.

"So, now we will stand," he announced as soon as Mrs. Hunter was gone. He pushed aside the covers and moved toward the edge of the bed.

Instead of rushing to his side as he had expected, Maggie remained at the dresser. "We had a bargain," she reminded him.

"It's apparent that you have decided not to believe the story I told you of my sister, so why should I tell you more? The doctor wants me to stand, so I will stand — with or without your help." He pushed himself upright and sat on the side of the bed, his feet dangling inches from the floor. He glanced around. "Please bring that chair closer."

"You cannot support your weight on that chair. It rocks and you could fall."

"Then give me something else," he demanded, casting his eyes over the furnishings of the room.

"Oh, very well," she huffed and came forward. "Stretch out your arms."

He did so and she wrapped her fingers around his forearms. It seemed natural for him to do the same, although she had rolled back her sleeves, exposing bare, freckled skin that was warm to his touch.

"Hold on and ease forward," she instructed, pulling him slightly toward her. "That's it. Feet flat on the floor and rest." He saw her study his features and take note of the beads of sweat on his brow. "Perhaps that is enough for now."

"We will stand," he said and tightened his grip on her as he raised himself to his feet. They teetered for a moment as if engaged in some sort of childish dance, and then he found his balance.

Her breathing had escalated along with his, and they were both gasping as if they'd just run a race. "We are again standing," he whispered and grinned down at her. She stared at his freshly shaved cheek, and for an instant she seemed about to raise her hand to stroke his face. Instead she cleared her throat and concentrated on his feet.

"Not standing yet," she replied, and he felt her loosen her grasp on his arms, her fingers resting only lightly on his skin. He followed her lead, adjusting his weight to accommodate the change in support. She let go, her hands still hovering in front of his chest and ready to push him back onto the bed should he pitch forward. She looked up at him and she was smiling. "*Now,* you are standing," she said.

Their eyes met in the mutual triumph of the achievement and lingered. "You are very beautiful. Like your mother," he said.

Her smile faltered and she glanced down, then back at him. Once again her expression was that of the nurse. "That's enough for now. We will try again later." Once again she wrapped her fingers around his forearms. "Just sit down," she instructed as she gently pushed him back onto the bed. He could not help but notice that from this position she was able to keep her distance. There would be no repeat of yesterday's collapse.

"Very good." She waited for him to reposition himself in the bed, then tucked the covers tightly and precisely under his armpits.

He reached for her hand and held it, forcing her eyes to meet his. "Let me tell you the rest," he said, and although she could easily have broken the contact, she took far more time than was necessary to pull her hand away.

Maggie rubbed the back of her hand, not because his touch had been harsh but rather because it had been so gentle. Wasn't it bad enough that her duty to him as his nurse required contact? And yet the touch of Stefan Witte was somehow consoling. She reminded herself that it was only natural to feel such an emotional connection. After all, he had lost dear ones to the war as well. But until now she had never thought of those people America was fighting as much more than "the enemy" — a faceless, inhuman force standing against everything she held dear.

Stefan was changing that with his story. He had shown her Uma and the child, reminding her that they had suffered greatly just as people she knew had. She felt her certainty that all Germans and their allies were her enemy waver. In Stefan's presence, she found herself questioning everything.

Doubt, she thought.

"Very well," she replied. "Tell me the rest."

Chapter Seven

"Where were we?" she said, forcing a pleasant but bland smile. She sat in the rocker but left it where it was instead of pulling it closer. "Ah, yes, you and your unit were on the train for Belgium."

He nodded and launched once more into his odyssey. "It was common knowledge that our army had suffered heavy losses. It was also rumored that either we must defeat the Allies within the year or we would lose the war."

"So you were then a foot soldier, and now you are with the German Navy?"

"As a translator I go where I am told. That particular assignment was based on my command of the French language."

"You speak French as well as English?"

"And a little Italian," he admitted.

"Impressive. Go on."

"We finally settled just south of a town called Terhand. At night the English would make quick raids from their trenches, trying to break through our line so they could reach France. We suffered heavy losses from this unseen enemy. In the towns there was much destruction — houses burned and ransacked or taken over as headquarters for our officers. The locals often ran away, leaving everything behind. Meanwhile the line of stretcher bearers was unimaginable. . . . So much misery and for what purpose?"

Maggie saw that his eyes were closed and he was lost in his own memories of the horrors he had witnessed on the battlefield. "But you were safe?"

"We were camped on a farm near Vieux Chien. The Supreme Army Command ordered us to confiscate food and supplies from the locals. My job was to listen for and interpret local response to these raids. Command was always alert for the possibility of retaliation."

The sun had moved around to the far side of the cottage, leaving the room in shadow. The change in light seemed to fit the story he told. Maggie rocked without being conscious of her movement as she tried to digest the horrors he related.

"Every day the fighting became more fierce. The blood — it was like a river at times." His voice caught and choked but he pressed on. "More than half our men died there, boys they were. Death all around, not just human death but horses and other farm animals slaughtered and beyond that the skeletons of burned-out homes and farm buildings, and personal effects scattered across the earth like so many autumn leaves — clothing and books and photographs. The noise was horrific, shell after shell, hour after hour."

"That's barbaric," she said. "How did it all end?"

His eyes opened wide, and she could feel him staring at her despite his face being in shadow. "End? It doesn't end, Maggie. You know that. I am telling you of one battle, and you must multiply that by hundreds, perhaps thousands, as well as by weeks, months and years. And for what?"

She had never heard him speak with such passion. As always the effort cost him, since his throat closed and he was consumed by a choking cough. "Enough," she murmured as she went to him and helped him sit upright until the coughing passed and he could sip water. "That's enough for today."

"No. The paper, the advertisement. I want you to know."

"All right. Tell me that — only that." She eased him back onto the pillows and waited by the side of the bed.

"One night — unable to sleep for the shelling and artillery fire — I pulled the paper out and studied it closely. The chemist shop was in the same little town where we had set up headquarters. I could not help but think that God had brought me there."

"It could have been a coincidence," Maggie said. But she knew her mother would also see this as evidence of God's divine intervention, that God had brought Stefan to the very place his sister had wanted him to be.

"I thought that, as well," he said. "A few days later I was able to get away into the village. Everything was a mess, and the chemist's shop appeared to be as shuttered and abandoned as everything else."

"Seemed to be?"

"As I was checking around the back, a side door opened a crack, and I saw the nozzle of a pistol. 'Don't shoot,' I said in French and raised my hands. Two men came out of nowhere and surrounded me, taking me inside the shop, where I faced a third man, the one with the pistol."

"You must have been so frightened," Maggie said and then realized that he deserved to be frightened. She shook off her inclination to empathize with his feelings.

"At first I assumed I had walked into a trap — everything from the man at the cemetery to the woman at the postal station had been leading me to this. But when I told them how I had come there — when I said Uma's name — an incredible thing happened. The man lowered his weapon, and the three of them began speaking in French."

"Which you understood. What did they say?"

Stefan shrugged. "They were arguing about whether or not to trust me, whether my being Uma's brother was enough and if so, how they might make use of me." Again he seemed to drift off into his own memories of that day.

"And what happened?" Maggie asked impatiently. "Clearly you weren't shot."

"They let me go. I asked them if they weren't afraid I would turn them in, but they said that was the test. I needed to choose sides, as Uma had done." He paused for a beat, his eyes on hers. "As you may well have to do one day."

Maggie brushed aside his comment. "I have chosen sides — I am American."

"Sometimes it is a far more complex choice than one of simple citizenship."

"So, you did not report them," Maggie guessed.

"No, but neither was I ready to stand with them. The following day I received orders to go to Munich. And shortly after that I was scheduled to join the crew of a U-boat headed for the North Sea. Their purpose was to interrupt the shipping of supplies and food to England."

"As they had done to Germany with the blockade," Maggie said, shaking her head. "Sometimes war seems more like a game of tit for tat where the losers are innocents who never wanted to play in the first place."

He leaned toward her. "That is exactly how I have felt," he said. "I did not want to take part in the very tactics that had ultimately ended the lives of my sister and her child. There had to be another way. I made contact with the chemist, and he agreed to help." Stefan drew in a deep breath and stretched out his hand to her. "You understand why it was important for me to come here? To survive? To reach the proper authorities with the information I know? You believe me now?"

Yes, her heart responded at once. She shook off such foolishness and focused on the logic of his questions. "What does it matter whether or not I believe you? How can that possibly make any difference at all?"

"What if it's God's will that we work together to shorten the conflict between our nations? If we could do that by even one day, Maggie, it will matter. It will matter to those dozens — perhaps hundreds — of people who might have lost their lives on that single day." His passion for his cause flamed in his eyes. "I believe that this is God's purpose for my life now that I have lost everyone, but I cannot do it alone. I am pleading with you to help me, Maggie. Your father does not believe me, but there is still time. The contact will be there, I am certain of it. If you spoke to your father, told him my story —"

Maggie stepped away from the bed and backed toward the door. "I cannot. Don't you realize what you are asking of me?" She did not wait for his answer. "I must go. I'll send Sean to stay with you until Sarah comes."

Outside she forced her breathing to calm as she tried to digest what Stefan Witte had told her. What if?

The moment she reached the inn, she glanced at the calendar on the wall by the kitchen door and saw that it was the twenty-fourth. Had the contact come today? Would he come tomorrow? And then would he give up? She glanced at the clock. It was too late to meet the steamer today. But tomorrow . . .

Later that night Stefan saw the light go on in the tower window of the inn. Was that her room? Was she there now, or perhaps a house servant had entered the room to turn back the bed for the night? But Sarah had told him there was no extra staff over the winter. In spring they would hire help to thoroughly clean and prepare the inn for the influx of summer visitors.

He had asked the Chadwicks if he might sit in the rocker for his supper and for a little while after. In light of warnings from Gabe to be on their guard, the couple's demeanor had shifted to a polite and almost formal distance, and yet their curiosity about someone who had once lived where their son had died kept them coming around on some pretense or another. That very evening Sarah had suggested Stefan might want to sit up in the chair for a bit. But when he'd asked for the chair to be placed near the window, Sarah had protested that there was nothing to see with it being so dark. "Why not closer to the fire here?"

"I am used to being outdoors," Stefan

explained with a gentle smile. "It will comfort me to be near the window."

"We can do both," Sean said. "I believe the wheelchair that Mr. Hunter's mother used is still in the attic." He disappeared, with Sarah's protest that the chair would need a good cleaning trailing after him.

Stefan was elated. A wheelchair would give him some freedom. "It would be very kind," he said to Sarah, who sighed and went to gather the necessary cleaning supplies.

Once the chair had been cleaned to Sarah's satisfaction, Sean made short work of making the transfer. He was a large man with powerful forearms from his years of hauling in nets filled with cod, herring or other fish in season. As soon as Stefan was settled in the chair, Sean escorted Sarah to the door.

"We'll be down the hall," he said, and Stefan heard it for the warning it was. Sarah pressed her fist to her lips and glanced at her husband. Sean placed his arm around his wife's shoulders and gently guided her toward the door. "Come along, Sarah." When Sean left the door open a crack, Stefan knew that it was because while the man liked him, he did not fully trust him.

Now he wheeled the chair closer to the

window and used his hands as blinders to shield his eyes from the lamplight as he peered into the darkness at the light in the tower. He saw a silhouette at the window. Maggie. Have I translated the sadness, the rage in those eyes correctly? Are you as troubled by the course of this war as I am? Together we might do something that could help it end.

But his thoughts turned from the strategy of his mission to the woman herself — her smile, her incredible eyes, her fierce determination when she would have something. In another time and place, Maggie Hunter, you and I might have become more than friends.

He shook off such fantasies when the clock in the parlor chimed the hour, reminding Stefan of the passing of time. Every minute meant a minute less of his chance to make a difference, perhaps even change the course of things. Tomorrow was the deadline. If he did not show up at the docks tomorrow, then what? Surely the contact would come on the final day. Someone had to be there.

Maggie, I need you to persuade your father to give this one more try.

Stefan dropped his head into his hands. What was the use? If the contact was made, what then? If he got to Washington, D.C., with his information, what then? He'd already been unable to convince an obviously sympathetic but sharp businessman that he had come in peace. How could he possibly hope to reach officials within the American government?

"But I am but one small person," his minister had preached at the service for Uma. "What can I do to make a difference?" The man had covered the underlying message to Uma's comrades that she had done a great deal by playing up her love of family, her kindness to the poor and suffering, her willingness to share whatever she had with those less fortunate. Her love of country.

He rolled the chair toward the door, feeling the ache in his muscles with just this bit of exertion. "Mrs. Chadwick?"

"Yes?" She appeared at the parlor door at once, her face lined with worry. "Has something happened? Are you in pain?"

"No, ma'am. I was wondering if I might have pen and paper."

She hesitated, glancing over her shoulder at her husband.

"I thought perhaps writing would help exercise my fingers," Stefan added.

"Oh. Well, I can't see why not," she

decided. "There's some stationery in the desk. I'll bring it to you."

"Thank you."

Settled in the wheelchair with pen, ink and paper, Stefan wrote furiously for an hour, heedless of the cramping in his fingers. He had to get it down. He had to give her the whole of it. Any day her father and the doctor might have him transferred. And he little doubted that once he was in the hands of the military authorities on the mainland of America, no one would believe him. He would have failed, and it would all be for nothing — unless Maggie believed him.

Maggie Hunter was his last hope. In spite of everything she did to cling to her belief that he and his countrymen were evil, he had seen something in her eyes when he'd told her about Uma. He had seen sympathy, yes, but something more. He had seen that same outrage he had felt when he'd found his sister and her child starved to death. What he had seen and heard in her questions went far deeper than simple understanding. Maggie had the courage to take action, and if she believed deeply in something, she would take that step. He was sure of it.

He recalled that what the minister had left unsaid that day in the cemetery was that the actions of one person could inspire another and another until the few became many and the tide of events was transformed. He had to find a way to convey that idea to Maggie Hunter.

He wrote until Sean came to get him back into bed for the night. Then, when the house was quiet, he eased himself to the floor, crawled to the table, took down the pen, ink and papers and continued to write until he heard the first stirrings in the bedroom above him.

"Another restless night?" Maggie asked as she took his temperature and pulse the following morning.

Sarah had given her report as she and Maggie exchanged places for the day. "You must have the doctor look at his fingers. He wanted to write something — I thought perhaps letters to loved ones should he . . . well, once he's given over to the military. I was sure there was no harm in it, but now his left hand — it's just awful."

"You did no harm," Maggie assured the woman. But the minute she entered his room, she came straight to his bedside and lifted his left hand. She saw that his fingers were stained with ink but also purple from the swelling and overuse. "What was so urgent that you had to risk setting yourself back by days — or was that the intent?"

"No," he protested wearily. "I am not deliberately trying to worsen my condition in spite of what you may think."

"Then why?"

"To ask you to open your mind to the possibility I am telling the truth. I didn't know how much time I might have or if you would listen."

"I have listened," she protested.

"Then please read this and keep the sealed envelope safe." He reached under one of his pillows and handed her several folded pages and a sealed envelope. "Please?"

She considered the papers covered on both sides with his small, shaky script and then read the inscription on the envelope: *To be opened in the event of my imprisonment, deportation or death.*

She saw a glimmer of hope in the way he watched her, so she folded the sheets around the envelope and placed both in the pocket of her apron. "The doctor will be here soon," she said and left the room.

Dr. Williams left instructions for reducing the swelling in his hand and observed Maggie as she assisted Stefan to stand. "Once he is steady enough, take a few steps with him. Have Sean help you. We must keep moving forward. This weather is improving steadily." He did not need to add that it was only the unusually cold and bitter winter that was keeping people from making the usual neighborly visits.

"Yes, Doctor," Maggie said as she saw him to the door.

"The wheelchair is a good idea, Maggie." The doctor lowered his voice. "Perhaps sitting up in that for an hour or so in the afternoon, but take care that he does not move beyond that room. You must always remember that he has one goal and that is to avoid becoming a real prisoner of war. He knows the fate that awaits him, and you must understand that he will do anything to avoid that fate." He studied her for a long moment. "In fact, I believe I will speak to your father. The stronger our guest becomes, the less prudent it is for you to be alone with him, even with Sean nearby."

Maggie placed a protective hand over the papers in her pocket. "I have an errand in town. If it would be all right, I'll have Mr. Chadwick stay with our patient for a few hours at lunch."

The doctor was already climbing onto his sleigh. "You're going out?"

"It's something that can't be postponed," she replied.

"Very well, but take care. The road into town is foggy," he called and snapped the reins.

Maggie waved and returned to the house. Uneasily she glanced at the partially closed door. Had she lost her senses? The doctor was right. It was madness to go off on what was surely another wild-goose chase, and yet she had to know. She had to be sure that Stefan Witte was lying to them. Only then did she feel she would regain her bearings, know right from wrong, black from white.

"Dr. Williams says you may sit in the wheelchair for a few hours this afternoon," she announced. "I've asked Sean to come and help with your standing and walking."

"That would be good," he replied, watching her with a curious expression. He sat forward and she took a step back. "You read my pages?" he asked.

"Not yet."

She kept her distance through the whole of the morning's routine. She even devised a method for placing his medicines on a tray and passing that to him when before she would simply have handed him the pill or potion and the water glass and stood guard to make sure that he swallowed. Following her instructions, Sean helped him stand and balance and then walk the short distance

173

from the bed to the dresser and back again. She kept the wheelchair between herself and him every step of that journey, telling both men that if Stefan felt pain or weakness, he could simply sit in the chair.

Once Sean had settled him into the wheelchair and gone to the attic to find the tray that attached to the chair's arms, Maggie straightened his bed linens.

"That was quite good work," she said. "Before you know it, you'll be back to full strength. Now that you can sit in the wheelchair for a time each day, you can have your meals there. Perhaps you'd prefer to be closer to the window? It's going to be a nice day as soon as the fog lifts — cold, to be sure, but sunny and clear."

She was well aware that she was chattering on. Rarely did she squander words for describing the weather or handing out compliments, and here she was doing both without ceasing.

"Why are you suddenly afraid of me? I thought that yesterday we made progress together."

She gave him an impersonal smile. "Of course. You stood on your own."

"I am not speaking of my health," he snapped, then saw that she rested one hand on the pocket where she'd put his letter. "I need you to read what I have written. In those words I have asked that you go to your father and persuade him to go to the docks. It's the last day," he pleaded.

"I don't need to read your pages, because I have decided I will go myself," she said without looking at him. "As for your letter, I will read it later."

"You cannot go. I won't allow it."

Her eyes flitted about the room as if seeking another bed to be made, another patient's needs to occupy her. "I cannot convince my father if you refuse to tell me everything you know. Besides, wasn't the intent of telling me Uma's story to win my sympathies, to show me how similar your sister and I are?"

"My intent was to ask you to speak with your father."

"And tell him what? That I believe you in spite of the fact I know nothing new? My going to the dock is not something you get to decide, Stefan."

"Your father will be angry and . . ."

"Ah, Sean has found the tray," she said, her voice rising with relief. "Here, Sean, let me give that a proper wash."

By the time Sean had installed the tray, Maggie had brought his food. She passed the dishes from the tray to Sean to Stefan.

She could see that Sean was as mystified by this as Stefan was, but he was accustomed to doing what others asked of him, so he made no protest.

"If there's nothing else, Maggie," he said softly once the food delivery was completed and Stefan had started to eat.

"Would you mind staying with our patient for an hour or so after lunch? I have something I need to do in town."

"Very well." Sean obviously answered with surprise. Maggie could see his mouth working as if he wanted to say more, but all he said was, "Would you like me to hitch up the cutter for you?"

"I'd appreciate that."

Sean nodded to Stefan and left.

Maggie started to follow, but Stefan stopped her with a single request: "Tell me about your fiancé."

Instantly she felt her features shift to stone. "No."

"Why not?"

She sucked in a long breath and let it out slowly, leveling him with a look of cold fury. "You are only trying to prevent me from going."

"Tell me."

"He died. I do not wish to say more than that." Once again she turned to go.

"I do not wish to hear of his death, Maggie. I wish to know of his life, the kind of man he was. I know of his father and I know of his friend, the fisherman's son. And I know a little of you. This man must have been very special, for he was most fortunate in those who cared about him."

She chewed her bottom lip and hesitated. In all the long months since Michael had died, no one had thought to talk about his life. She leaned against the frame of the door in need of its support. She felt as if all the restless energy she'd displayed earlier had been squeezed out of her. She rested the side of her head against the door.

"Why would you possibly care?"

"Because yesterday when I told you about my sister, you cared. You cared very much. I saw it in your eyes, heard it in the way you questioned, felt it in the very air between us. Now I would like to know of your Michael."

"It won't stop me from going to the docks."

"Perhaps not, but it will give us a better understanding of one another and is that not the first small step toward a peaceful coexistence? To find the things we share in common rather than dwelling on the differences?"

"Someone on your side killed Michael. Someone on our side set things in motion that ended in the deaths of your sister and nephew. Our countries are at war," she reminded him.

"But I did not kill Michael, and you did not starve Uma or Klaus. You and I are not at war, Maggie," he replied.

She looked at him with the cynicism that had become almost second nature to her this last year. When had she lost her wonder? Her trust of others? Her belief that things happened for a reason? And why did the most minute interaction with this German make her feel that perhaps one day there could come an end to it, the pain and grief that they had both suffered?

She made a lunch for herself as well as Stefan and returned to sit with him.

"He was to be a doctor like his father," she said, taking a seat in the rocker on the far side of the room. "He volunteered, he and George, the day that America entered the war. Michael volunteered as a medic. He was so certain that it would all end quickly even though it had already gone on for years."

"Is that when you became a nurse?"

"I was determined to follow him, as far as possible."

178

"Why would you place yourself in such danger?"

"If he would not listen to reason and stay here where it was safe, then I would go with him. We had always done that since we were children. If one did something the other followed."

"He would allow such a thing?" Stefan saw the look she gave him and amended the question. "That is, he was in agreement with this plan?"

"He knew nothing of it — nor did my parents." Then she looked away. "Not that any of that matters now."

"You loved him very much."

"I loved him," she replied, but her voice was oddly uncertain. She blushed at the realization that sometimes she doubted that love and had nearly admitted as much aloud.

I am questioning my love for Michael. I have doubted the reality of a loving God. Could this man be right that such questions can only be born of faith?

She stood up and took her tray. "So, now you know about Michael. We have both suffered terrible losses, but we are still of different minds when it comes to this war."

"Are we?"

"I see what you are doing, and it will not

work with me, Stefan Witte. I am sorry for your loss, and I believe that you are truly sorry for mine, but there it ends." She balanced her tray and then picked up his with her free hand.

"And what if I could convince you otherwise?"

"Please don't do this," she said, her tone weary, almost defeated.

"Do what, Maggie?"

"Make me question what I cannot change."

"We only live this single moment in time, Maggie. How we spend it is up to us."

"I know that," she replied irritably.

"But?"

She let out an exasperated sigh. "But one woman on Nantucket cannot possibly change the outcome of a war between nations around the world. One so-called translator, regardless of how compelling his message may be, cannot hope to do that, either."

"Why not?"

She looked at him as if he had just sprouted a second head. Her lips moved but no words came out.

"What if you had the potential to make a difference — no matter how small? Wouldn't you want to at least try?"

She sighed heavily and turned to him. "We are simple people, Stefan, people who have already risked a great deal on your behalf. I will go to the docks and, assuming this contact of yours is there, I will deliver your message. But if, as I suspect, there is no contact to be made, then you owe us the courtesy of accepting your fate whatever it may be without further involving — or endangering — my family."

The steamer was delayed for over an hour because of the fog that had crept over the harbor like a thick, impenetrable shadow, and the waiting room was more crowded than usual. Maggie pulled up the collar of her coat and kept the brim of her felt hat at a low angle as she burrowed her gloved hands in her sleeves and waited for the steamship to arrive. In the meantime, she watched carefully for the infamous contact in blue scarf with umbrella. No such person appeared.

She found herself thinking of Michael and realized that the relationship they had shared since childhood seemed a little unreal, like something one might read in a novel. Had she loved him? Of course. He had been her best friend, her closest ally. Everyone had assumed they would marry.

Had she assumed it, as well? And what of the fact that it was shortly before they were to celebrate their engagement that Michael had declared his intent to volunteer? What was it he had said that day she'd seen him off?

"I just have to do this, Maggie. We'll have the rest of our lives together, but understand that I need to do this."

That day she had been so overcome with tears that she had nodded and accepted his quick kiss before he ran up the gangplank and onto the ship that would take him away from her. But now as she sat staring out into the gray emptiness of the Sound, she recalled something more. Michael had not looked back. He had stood at the railing of the ship and looked out to sea, and he had been smiling, leaning forward like a figurehead, as if he couldn't wait to begin this new adventure.

"Freedom," she murmured, understanding for the first time that what he had been trying to tell her was that before he settled into the routine of the life as doctor, husband and father that his father and grandfather before him had lived, he wanted this one grand adventure. Of course. As children they had both fantasized about the day when they would be old enough to be out on their own. As children they had shared their dreams of grand adventures. She had talked of following in Jeanne's footsteps. She would find her true calling in New York or perhaps Paris. Michael had dreamed of the West and the ranch he would have, the horses he would raise.

But then they had become teenagers. Maggie had taken on more responsibility at the inn, while Michael had assisted his father at the hospital and applied to medical school in Boston. They had attended every church or community event together, inseparable as they had always been. And gradually they had begun to believe what the adults around them believed, that they were destined to be together.

Had she loved him? Had he loved her? Of course. His death had been like losing half of herself. Who was she without Michael? With him her destiny had seemed so clearly mapped out until Michael had volunteered. She realized now that all those hours she had spent in the cupola above the inn had not been about grieving. They had been about seething over the unfairness of it all. They had played by all the rules, she and Michael. They had done what was expected of them without rebellion. So why?

A flash of blue silk caught her eye, and

she shook off her ruminations and turned quickly. Jeanne and Frederick had just entered the waiting room. Frederick closed the umbrella he always used to protect Jeanne from the elements and shook it out as Jeanne looked around the crowded room.

I can't have them see me, Maggie thought as she pulled her scarf up to cover her hair and half her face and turned away. From the corner of her eye she saw Jeanne say something to Frederick. Maggie took advantage of the moment to make her escape out the side door and practically collided with Eleanor Pritchard.

"Why, Maggie Hunter! Whatever are you doing in town, and here at the dock at that?" Mrs. Pritchard prided herself on knowing everything that went on with the population of Nantucket. She considered herself the island's matriarch, coming as she did from one of its oldest and most respected families.

"Good afternoon, Mrs. Pritchard," Maggie said, ignoring the question. "It's so lovely to see you. How are you?"

The thing about Eleanor Pritchard was that if you asked after her health, she assumed you truly wanted a report. "Oh, my dear, this damp weather has just played havoc with my rheumatism. Well, you're a nurse. You of all people understand such things. I have asked Tom Williams any number of times if there isn't some new medicine or treatment we could try, but he just pooh-poohs the whole matter."

"Now, Mrs. Pritchard, I'm sure that Dr. Williams is sympathetic. It's just that for these last weeks we've been so busy at the hospital. The influenza epidemic on the mainland has everyone here on the island suspecting the tiniest symptom of a common cold to be the dread disease."

Mrs. Pritchard eyed her more closely. "Yes, I had heard that Tom moved some of his noninfected patients into private homes. You have such a patient at the inn, I believe?"

"Yes ma'am." Maggie did not like the way the conversation was going and searched her brain for a topic that might distract the woman. "Have you had word from Benny?"

Mrs. Pritchard's eyes filled with tears, and she pulled a lace-edged handkerchief from her fur muff to dab at them. "He writes me daily from his post in Washington. He's quite involved in the War Department, you know. Why, the president himself has commended him for his work."

"And it's well deserved, I'm sure," Maggie said, placing her hand on Mrs. Pritchard's arm in a gesture of sympathy before turning to go. "Well, it was so nice running into you. . . ."

"I should call on your patient," Mrs. Pritchard announced. "Yes, I'll bring by some of my Russian tea and a tin of my homemade ginger cookies. Benny has so often reminded me of how important it is to do everything possible to raise the spirits of those in pain, be they soldiers or not. Perhaps I should visit with our prayer circle. Yes, I'll call Reverend McAllister today." She turned to go, then turned back. "I mean your patient is not contagious or anything?"

"We aren't really sure how his recovery will progress," Maggie said. "I'll be sure to tell him of your kind offer."

Mrs. Pritchard frowned as if something unpleasant had just struck her. "Are you alone with this man, Maggie?"

"I am his nurse."

"Nursing in the hospital is one thing, but as I understand it . . . Oh my, is that the duchess?" In an instant the woman was off. "Yoo-hoo! Your Grace," she called in a voice that caused passers-by to turn and smile.

Glad for the unwitting rescue yet not really wanting to explain her presence in town to Jeanne, Maggie didn't know whether to remain where she was or walk away. But apparently Jeanne was no more anxious to encounter Mrs. Pritchard than Maggie was to have Jeanne and Frederick spot her. Ignoring Mrs. Pritchard's cries, Jeanne took Frederick's arm, and the two of them boarded the tram taking steamer passengers to one of the local hotels.

Stefan checked the clock on the mantel numerous times throughout the afternoon. Was it a good sign that she was taking so long? His heart soared with the hope that the contact had been made and even now Maggie was bringing news that would allow him to deliver his information to the proper authorities in Washington. He was so filled with thoughts of what might happen next that he failed to realize she had returned until he heard her voice in the hall outside his door.

"Yes, thank you, Sean. I'll stay with him until Sarah comes."

It seemed an eternity between the thud of the outside door and the click of the knob to his room. Then the minute he saw her, he knew.

"No one came."

"I can't be absolutely sure," she said as she pulled the rocking chair close to his wheelchair so she could speak in low tones in case Sean came back. "The ship was late and before it docked, our guests, the duchess and her companion, came to the docks unexpectedly. I couldn't let them see me there. It would have raised so many questions. Then I ran into a woman from the church, Mrs. Pritchard. She's very much the busybody and has a knack for smelling something amiss. I had to leave."

"Thank you for going," Stefan said as he tried to deal with the full impact of her news.

"I went to the next wharf and stayed until the arriving passengers disembarked," she said. "No one was wearing a blue scarf that I could see." When Stefan remained silent, she added softly, "I'm truly sorry."

"I don't understand. The contact was to come every day because there was no certainty to when I might reach the island. Surely on this final day . . ."

"Perhaps you misunderstood the instructions," she suggested sympathetically.

Stefan looked up at her and smiled. "Does this mean you have had a change of heart, Nurse Hunter? That you believe me?" He cupped her cheek with one hand.

"I . . . there are parts of your story that have touched my heart," she admitted as she savored the warmth of his touch. Then she came to her senses and pulled back. "But I would remind you that your government has sent its army to occupy lands that had no quarrel with them."

"Governments and their armies are not countries, Maggie." He reached out to her again, his fingers finding a strand of hair that had escaped when she removed her hat. "You are very brave, Maggie. And very kind," he added, his voice husky as he concentrated on twisting the curl around his finger.

He leaned closer as if he would share a secret and kissed her lightly on the cheek. "In spite of your doubt, you have done as much as anyone could have asked — and more. Thank you." It was the voice of a condemned man.

Maggie pressed her fingertips to the place where his lips had touched her cheek so lightly that she might have thought she had imagined it were he not right there, a breath away. "Sarah will be here soon to give you your supper."

When she stood up, he brushed her hand with the backs of his fingers and she felt an enormous desire to surrender to that touch. Not in a sensual way; it was more that she had so wanted to believe in something again. Over the long months since Michael's death, her anger and depression had found no real target. Somehow Stefan Witte seemed to know not only whom he was fighting but why. She envied him that.

They both heard Sean's step in the hall — the stamping of his boots followed by the slamming of the outer door intruded on the moment. Maggie focused on Stefan's hands, strong and nearly whole again now. She thought of the times when she had laid impersonal fingers on his throat to be sure the pill went down. Only now she recalled the touch in detail — skin roughened by the elements and the stubble of his golden whiskers but so alive with the strength and fervor of a man bent on completing his mission. And always the glint of that small gold cross, this beacon in the darkness he must surely face.

Even as they heard Sean call to her, she did not move away. Rather she lifted Stefan's hand in hers and stroked his palm with her thumb. Then, as Sean stepped through the door, she found Stefan's racing pulse and counted its rhythm to her own while focusing blindly on the small watch she wore around her neck.

CHAPTER EIGHT

That evening it seemed forever before Maggie was able to escape to her room and retrieve the folded sheets of paper Stefan had given her. Through the long ordeal of dinner, she had thought of little other than those pages and the sealed envelope she'd left in her room. But Jeanne had insisted on giving them all the information she and Frederick had gathered that day about possible houses for sale on the island. She described each one they had visited in minute detail, laying out the features that she found attractive, while Frederick gave a more realistic picture of each house's problems.

"That one will need constant upkeep," he declared after Jeanne had gone on for several minutes about the charm and quaintness of a three-story Greek Revival mansion just off Main Street. "The gardens alone will cost a small fortune to maintain."

"Well, Freddie, I happen to have a not-so-small fortune," Jeanne had replied snappishly. "One, I might add, that at the moment is doing little good for anyone."

Frederick had reached over and taken her hand. "One must be realistic," he said quietly, and everyone was relieved when Jeanne's normal good spirits were immediately restored.

"Yes, one must," she agreed with a smile and a light touch of his cheek. "Which is the very reason I treasure having you with me to decide these matters."

From there the discussion had gone back and forth, the women rhapsodizing over the charms of each house, while the men continued to try to interject a note of common sense into the discussion. At last Jeanne had stood. "Well, no decision need be made tonight," she said, taking them all under the sunshine of her smile. "And frankly, house hunting can be quite tiring, so I will bid you all a good-night."

Frederick and Gabe remained standing until she had kissed every cheek and left the room. Maggie was relieved that Frederick soon followed Jeanne's lead, opening the way for Maggie herself to protest that she had to be up early.

"How did things go today — with his

standing?" her father asked in a low voice after checking to be sure both Jeanne and Frederick were out of earshot.

"He did well," Maggie replied. "He's not yet to the point of running a race, but —"

"You went into town today?" her father asked.

"I had an errand." Maggie met her father's questioning gaze but said only, "Good night, Papa, Mama."

In her room Maggie changed into her nightgown. She wrapped herself in her robe and the blue-and-white log cabin–patterned quilt Grandma Emma had made for her sixteenth birthday. As anxious as she had been to read the pages, she now felt a reluctance to do so. Whatever they contained was likely to create more questions, questions she had not permitted herself to consider since Michael's death. Questions that haunted her anew after she'd heard the story of Uma's tragic end. Questions that her mother would surely consider blasphemy. Questions about God.

She settled herself against the painted iron headboard and unfolded the pages. As expected, the letter began with a plea for her to talk to her father, but there was so much more.

I will tell you a story — a true story and one I lived. In the early days of the war, I was in the infantry and we were stationed along the front in trenches dug facing the enemy. One December afternoon a few of us left our trenches with hands raised to show we were unarmed and walked out into the neutral no-man's-land between the fighting armies. The British were wary but held their fire and watched as we began retrieving our dead and wounded from the most recent round of battle. Soon the Brits climbed out of their trenches to do the same for their lost brothers. Together we dug the graves heedless of whether a certain grave would be occupied by one of ours or one of theirs.

When the work was done, we stood for a time in that neutral space. We exchanged a few words and cigarettes, then returned to our respective trenches. We might have been neighbors who had gathered at a cemetery and then gone back home. That evening we continued to fraternize, calling back and forth to each other over the few kilometers that separated us. Many of those on our side had worked in England before the war and spoke the language. I had worked at the embassy in London and learned the language skills that would soon get me out of the trenches and living with officers behind the front lines. Others had worked in the restaurants and hotels of London because of hard times at home.

Although the Supreme Army Command expressly forbade such fraternization, most of the soldiers on both sides were farmers and local tradesmen who had joined the war in a burst of patriotism but now found themselves fighting for simple survival and the day they could go home. The fighting resumed the following day, but as Christmas Eve approached, soldiers on both sides received small gifts from their respective governments. I once saw a silver box embossed with the image of a woman and was told that this was given to the Brits filled with candies, tobacco and cigarettes. The woman is the daughter of their king.

"Princess Mary," Maggie murmured and continued reading, caught up now in the incredible story of soldiers at war so close to each other's front line that they could actually speak to their enemy.

On Christmas Eve, some of our soldiers got hold of small Tannenbaum — Christmas trees lit with candles — and placed them along the rims of the trenches up and down the German line. On the Allied side there was only silence, but then someone played carols on a mouth organ, and somewhere a soldier joined in on a concertina. Then as midnight approached, men on both sides began crawling out of their trenches and standing on the neutral ground where a few days earlier we had buried our dead. There we talked, laughed, shared photos of family members and exchanged the gifts our governments had sent. Even the officers looked the other way. In those hours before the dawning of Christmas Day we found common ground, if only briefly.

Maggie, I vow to you on Uma's grave that I indeed have information that could change the course of things, but it is complex and cannot be given to just anyone. It must reach those with the power to take action. The contact was to arrange that. But now I must ask myself what is to happen if I cannot reach that contact. Is my escape in vain? Will this information remain silenced because it cannot be heard by those who might change the course of things?

I understand what I am asking of you. I

am asking you to come out of the trench of your anger and grief and meet me on the common ground of our shared love of family and country. In the sealed envelope I have given you to hold are the details of my mission, the full explanation of the information I have brought with me. I cannot stop you from opening that envelope, from handing it over to others who might disregard its contents and cast it aside in their zeal to pursue me as their enemy. And yet you hold in that envelope everything that might keep me from a life in prison or worse. My fate is quite literally in your hands.

Maggie, I now believe with all my heart that it was no accident I was brought here and that you were the one to nurse me back to health. Surely you can see God's hand in all of this. You might deny that truth with your closed mind, but not with your heart if you will but open it to the possibilities. This is more than a plea to save a German's life, Maggie. This is a plea to help save many lives — on both sides of this war. Together we can make a real difference for so many others. I am pleading with you to believe me — to believe in me — and to help me.

Maggie let the last page fall to the floor next to her bed. She pulled the quilt high around her shoulders and covered her ears. Anything to turn off the images in her head. Michael, with his face uplifted to the horizon, his hands braced on the railing and everything about him saying, "I am free." Uma and her son staring at the camera, smiling and confident. Stefan challenging her with questions she had refused to raise, questions about faith that she had suppressed for these long months.

She gathered the pages of his letter and stacked them impatiently. How could this German for one minute have dared to think that she would lift a finger to help him? And yet she had. She had gone to the docks in spite of the fact that she knew her parents would not approve. She had studied every waiting and arriving passenger, and although there had been no contact there, she could not deny that she had believed him. That she still believed him.

She closed her eyes and saw his face, clean-shaven now, the green eyes bright with the truth of his beliefs and alive with the confidence that God had brought them together. To what end? What possible good could come of it? He is a condemned man.

But what if he could make a difference,

however small, in the outcome of this tragic war? What if she could be a part of that? Might that not give her life some meaning and purpose? Might that not be the first step on the road to rediscovering herself?

Stefan sat on the side of the bed and pounded his fists on his useless legs. Impatiently he had waited for the Chadwicks to retire for the night and then worked his way out of the bed to practice standing. He had even managed a few steps toward the window, where he'd seen the tower lamp glowing like a lighthouse across the snowy yard. Was she reading his letter?

To pass the time he repeatedly made his way around three sides of the bed and back again, managing only one or two steps while standing free of the bed. At this rate he would not be able to walk properly for weeks. He didn't have weeks — he might not even have days. On his fifth trip back around the bed and back to the window, he saw that the lamp had gone out. All was dark except for the long moonlit shadows of the trees and outbuildings stretched out across the snow.

He slumped against the side of the bed, his breathing shallow from the exertion of his exercise and from the emotional toll of accepting the reality that after everything he had been through, all might be lost.

Maggie, I need you to believe in me if I am to face what I must clearly endure.

The one thing he was certain of was that he had not misread her anger, her rage at the injustice of this war. When she had confessed her original plan to gain her nurse's training in order to follow Michael to the front, he had seen it in her eyes. Maggie would not go to fight for some political cause, but she would do whatever she could to protect anyone she truly cared about. And did she care about him?

When he had kissed her cheek, he had intended a chaste gesture of gratitude. But the smoothness of her skin, the whisper of her hair feathering against his finger, had changed all of that. In another time, another place, they might have come to mean so much more to each other than patient and nurse. If they had met before the war, when they were both free of the political restraints created by their governments, they might have had the freedom to truly come to care for each other. If she had not been with Michael — if he had not lived an ocean away . . .

She had been determined to follow Michael to the battlefields of Europe. He hoped that this man had realized how fortunate he was to have found such a woman. A woman who would consider leaving her family to follow her beloved to another continent — a continent at war. Such a woman had the will and the spirit to want that loved one's death not to have been in vain. Stefan felt a twinge of hope.

He smiled as he imagined her arriving the following morning, the silly nurse's cap propped on top of her raven curls, her eyes considering him for a long moment before she spoke. "Good morning," she would say as she had every morning, an impersonal greeting of nurse to patient.

And then?

Stefan closed his eyes and fell back onto the bed. Then she would say, "I read your pages."

And?

"Tell me how I can help."

"Do you believe in me?" he would ask.

"Yes."

"Then that is all I need."

Yes, it would be like that.

Energized by his fantasy, Stefan pushed himself to his feet and worked his way back to the window. He scanned the darkness, memorizing his surroundings. A barn several yards from the cottage and beyond that a pond, frozen now. No forest that he could see, only snow-covered fields of shrubs and grasses. This was disappointing. He swiveled his vision in the other direction. On a bluff sat the inn. Of course, it would have the better view for guests. It would overlook both the ocean and the harbor on the opposite side.

He considered each route for escape. The barn would stable the horses. The fields beyond the pond might lead to a road that would eventually take him down to the harbor. That would be the best route, the most likely place to find a boat. The weather indeed had warmed, as indicated by the patches of bare ground in the snow. At night he could hear the steady drip of icicles as he lay awake in the silent cottage. But if his way to the harbor was blocked, there was always the sea.

The obstacle between him and the ocean was, of course, the inn. More precisely the people inside the inn. The danger of being seen and apprehended was far greater. And he was quite certain that Maggie's father would not be sympathetic.

He turned his gaze back to the darkened window. Maggie. Stefan closed his eyes as the sensation of her small warm hands gripping his washed over him. He thought of the way the lamplight caught the blue-black richness of her hair on gloomy winter afternoons. He thought of her eyes, the way she watched him, first with suspicion and aversion but more recently with curiosity and interest. The same way he watched her. And he thought of the kiss and how much he had wanted to shift his lips that small distance until they met hers.

He shook off such impossible thoughts and turned his attention back to the pond and the fields beyond, rejecting the barn and the horses as too much of a risk. The best course would be through the fields to the harbor. Once he was strong enough. He edged forward and took hold of the levers for raising the window. He tugged and grimaced at the pain that stunned his still partially numb fingers.

"The window is nailed shut," Sean said.

Stefan had heard no stirring from the room above, no footfalls on the stairway. "I thought perhaps some fresh air. The room is very close," he explained and saw that Sean was not fooled. Scowling, the elder man approached him.

"Back to bed with you," the fisherman ordered as he took hold of Stefan's upper arm and steered him away from the window. Once he had almost bodily lifted Stefan onto the bed, he waited until he had covered himself, then handed him a glass of water. "This will cool you."

"Thank you," Stefan said, drinking and then handing back the water glass.

Sean stood where he was, his mouth working as if trying to form the proper words. "Do not dishonor these good people," he warned. "They have already put themselves at great risk to help you survive. They may yet pay a terrible price for their kindness."

Such an idea had never occurred to Stefan. He understood they might have problems but nothing they couldn't handle. After all, from what he had gathered, the doctor and Maggie's father were in charge of things here on this island. "What are you saying?"

"I am saying that should the news ever get out that we have been aiding a German officer, the Hunters — if they aren't arrested and jailed for treason — may as well close up the inn for good and move as far away as possible. For they will surely never do business or find forgiveness on this island after that."

"I did not ask them to take me in," Stefan protested.

Sean's smile was wry and devoid of humor. "Did you not now? Are you saying that when you lay there freezing to death you didn't once pray to God to send someone to help you?"

"I prayed," Stefan admitted.

"Best keep at it," Sean said, setting the glass on the side table and turning to the door. "You'll be needing God's mercy in the days to come."

In the darkness Stefan twisted himself around until he could just see the corner of the inn through the window. Maggie's window remained dark.

If Maggie had hoped that a night's rest would clear her head and bring her to her senses, she was mistaken. Surely she had given Stefan Witte every possible consideration. She had nursed him, listened to the story of his sister and nephew, read his scrawled diary of life on the battlefield and even kept that final appointment at the docks. And yet each step seemed only to move her closer to a precipice she could not fathom.

As she dressed for the day, she firmly reminded herself it was a given that he would attempt to play upon her sympathies. He had not turned to her originally because he had viewed her father as the more sympathetic. But now, having failed to gain her father's trust, or the doctor's, he had set his sights on her.

She studied the envelope, still sealed and lying on her dressing table. She picked it up, touched her thumbnail to the sealed flap, but stopped. What if this was truly information that could save lives? What if she could be a part of something that might shorten this horrible war by even one hour? What if . . .

She touched her cheek as she had many times while she read his plea for her to help him, then firmly withdrew her hand and put the kiss out of her mind. She was no one's fool — and certainly not Stefan Witte's fool. She dropped the sealed envelope back onto her dressing table, then took special care with anchoring her nurse's cap into place. She smoothed her apron, checked the turn of the three-quarter cuffs of the shirtwaist, turned sideways to examine the precision of the bow at her waist.

Very well, I will help him get his information delivered, and if it is a ruse, then he will pay the price and my conscience will be clear. I have saved your life, Stefan Witte, and now if you are to be believed, I can help save the lives of others. And if he was lying? Then may God have mercy on you.

Maggie shoved the sealed envelope into the pocket of her apron and headed downstairs to join her family for breakfast.

"Good morning," she said cheerfully as she took her place at the table.

"Well, this is an improvement," Jeanne said. "I take it you had a good night?"

"I slept well," Maggie said. "And you?"

"Quite well. Frederick and I are accompanying your parents to church this morning. You really must join us."

"I have a patient to attend," Maggie replied with an apologetic smile.

Her father cleared his throat. "I believe you could take today off, Maggie. Sean and Sarah will see to your patient."

"But . . ."

"You had the time to go into town yesterday. You can certainly come to church with us today." It was not an invitation.

"But . . . Yes, Papa, all right." She heard her mother's soft sigh of relief. "I'll just go and change."

"This afternoon perhaps we could go skating on the pond," Jeanne called. "Won't that be fun?"

Maggie changed into her best wool navy suit, with its three-quarter-length jacket belted at the waist and ankle-length full skirt. It had been months since she'd worn the outfit, and as she stared at her reflection in the mirror, she saw a woman who had

experienced the best and worst of life —
love and death — since the last time she
had worn the suit. So much had changed
and yet the suit fit her the same as it had
before. Only inside, in her heart and mind,
nothing seemed to fit at all.

When she returned to the lobby, the others were busy donning capes, cloaks and
gloves for the sleigh ride to the church. "I'll
be along, my dear," Gabe said as he kissed
Lucie's cheek. "As soon as Dr. Williams has
come and gone."

Maggie saw a look pass between her
parents. Something had shifted overnight.
The atmosphere surrounding the normal
routine of the house felt unsettled. In spite
of every effort to maintain normalcy for the
sake of Jeanne and Frederick, Maggie could
see that something had happened. It had to
be Stefan. Her heart pounded. Was he
worse? Had he fallen? Her earlier resolve
was forgotten in the face of her concern.

"I could come later with Papa," she said
suddenly. "If Dr. Williams has new instructions, I should hear them."

"Dr. Williams will speak with Sean," her
father said quietly. "Sean will be caring for
our patient until he can be transferred."

"What has happened?" Maggie asked,
heedless of the warning look her mother

sent her way.

Her father laughed, a false guffaw she'd heard him use in situations that made him uncomfortable or angry. "I am simply taking your Aunt Jeanne's words to heed, Maggie. You've been working too hard. It seems that Jeanne will not be here forever, as we might have hoped, so you should have the opportunity to enjoy the pleasure of her company for a few days."

A half truth at best, but Maggie knew better than to force the issue. She accepted the felt hat, with its wide satin band, that her mother had held for her while she had pulled on leather gloves.

"Now go along," her father urged, kissing her cheek and ushering them all to the door. "It won't do to be late."

The church was nearly filled and Maggie did not miss the fact that several of the regulars took note of her presence, whispering to one another behind gloved fingers or casting knowing looks at a neighbor across the aisle. Her mother led the way to the third pew on the right, where the family normally sat. Maggie, head held high, followed. If she caught the glance of any of the other parishioners she was greeted either by a smile that said the person was glad she had come to her senses or a scowl from a person who thought her absence had been an act of defiance. Eleanor Pritchard seemed especially taken with her unexpected appearance at services.

Ignoring them all, Maggie took her place next to Jeanne and rose with everyone else as the organist played the opening to the first hymn. By the final verse of the responsive reading that followed the hymn, her father had slipped quietly into his place on the aisle.

Maggie glanced over at him, but he did not meet her gaze. Instead he took her mother's hand, then focused all his attention on the service.

Maggie's mind was so filled with questions that she heard little of the message that day. Something about forgiving one's enemies and while that was beyond her ability to fully obey, surely she had done her best. At least where Stefan was concerned.

But the morning's events had raised new doubts and troubling questions. Her mind raced with thoughts of Stefan. The very idea that he might have taken worse or done something in his desperation to break free had sent her heart into spasms of panic and fear. It stunned her to realize that her fear was not for herself or even for her family.

She feared for Stefan. The hour flew by as she tried to untangle the mess of contradictory thoughts that pounded in her head. Before she knew it, they were standing for the final hymn and benediction.

Outside the little church she waited with her parents while Jeanne and Frederick chatted with several locals that Jeanne had met through her years of visiting the island. Given Jeanne's natural penchant for social conversation, this could take some time, and Maggie saw her opportunity. "Please tell me what has happened," she asked and saw by her father's look that he had no doubt what she was asking.

"Your mother and I simply believe that it is asking too much of you to spend all your time with him," Gabe replied.

"No. It's something more than that," Maggie insisted.

"Lower your voice," her mother warned.

"What is it?" Maggie demanded in a low hiss. "I deserve to know."

"He may be planning an escape," Mama said, turning away from a group of passing parishioners.

Maggie released a choked laugh. "How? He most assuredly cannot manage an escape. The man can barely stand and even then needs assistance."

"Sean found him trying to open the bedroom window last evening."

Maggie's look flew from her mother to her father. "How is that possible?"

"It isn't. The window is nailed shut. Still, it shows the way of his thinking." Papa sounded tired and worried. "Sean and Sarah had retired for the night after he asked to be left alone for the evening. Sounds from the room below them woke Sarah, and she sent Sean to check. When Sean came into the room, he was walking around unaided and attempting to open the window."

"I'll speak with him," Maggie said and realized she had almost said *warn him*. About what? And why?

"You will do no such thing," her father growled. "For now Sean will attend him — day and night. As soon as Jeanne and Frederick leave, we will turn him over to the coast guard for transfer to New Bedford. Now here they come. Not another word."

Maggie knew better than to debate the matter further, but that did not mean she was content to let it drop. She thought of the Christmas truce, and indeed had they not had a kind of similar truce here on Nantucket? By taking him in and caring for his injuries and poor health, had they not crossed the no-man's-land he had described

212

and looked at the other side? Or was she a fool? Had he made up the tale to gain her sympathy and, having second thoughts, had he decided to repay her family's kindness by trying to escape?

Her mother had always taught her that trust was a two-way road. Perhaps in the night Stefan had regretted giving her the envelope that could decide his fate one way or the other depending on whose hands it reached. If only she could see him, speak with him face-to-face about the letter, then she would know if he was lying to her.

CHAPTER NINE

The young minister and his wife joined them at the inn for Sunday dinner, and Jeanne kept everyone entertained with stories of life on the Continent before the war. Jeanne's personal maid had taken over the duty of serving the dinner while Sarah and Sean remained at the cottage with Stefan. Maggie had hoped to catch Sarah alone in the kitchen. She wondered what Stefan had been told or if he had simply accepted that he'd been caught in the act and this was the result. Had he asked for her? Was he at all distressed at this turn of events, or would he simply now turn the focus of his desperation on Sarah and Sean?

Well, so be it. Upon awakening that very morning, hadn't she already been thinking it would be best to return to their former status of patient and nurse? It was a relief to have her father decide she should no longer attend the man, wasn't it? Isn't this what she had wanted from the beginning? And yet Stefan's eyes and the touch of his lips on her cheek haunted her every waking moment.

She forced her attention back to the gathering at the dining table. The minister's wife was showing Jeanne a small framed photograph of her sister's child. Jeanne passed the photo to Maggie. The woman holding the child looked at the photographer with no expression, and the child appeared sullen and unhappy. Nothing like the photograph of Stefan's sister and nephew, both of them so happy and filled with the joy of life.

Once again doubt, her constant companion these days, raised troubling questions. What if he had fabricated the story of Uma? Was the woman in the photograph really his sister? She was a woman about Maggie's age with the same golden hair as Stefan, and the boy she held on her lap had Stefan's smile. In fact, pictures of Stefan at that age would surely be interchangeable with this child's image.

Uma Witte. Maggie's counterpart on the other side of the world but perhaps on the same side of this war. For if she was to believe Stefan, Uma had abhorred this war as much as Maggie did. But unlike Maggie she had not turned her back on it even after she had begun to feel its effects. For the war had not only taken her husband, it had then come to her very doorstep, her bare cupboard, her starving child. With official channels closed to her, she had fought back in the only way available to her. She had gone underground and joined the resistance. Maggie actually envied Uma her courage. Maggie had done little but isolate herself from the events and people around her. Oh, she had nursed the sick and been praised for doing so in the wake of her personal tragedy, but she felt something of a fraud. The nursing had been her refuge, her place to hide from the possibility of truly caring — loving — again.

"Not everyone has the luxury of simply going on with life," Jeanne was saying to the minister, and her tone, so serious, caught Maggie's full attention.

"Of course," the minister was saying, "those who live in Europe, who must face this war every day." His tone was patronizing, dismissive.

Maggie saw Frederick briefly place his hand over Jeanne's, an unspoken signal that Jeanne chose not to heed. "Forgive me, Reverend McAllister," she said quietly, "but the war has not yet truly come to your shores. Until the citizens of Nantucket find themselves living with the reality of a foreign occupation or imminent attack, it is impossible to understand what life is like for so very many innocent souls all over Europe now. Even in Germany and my late husband's beloved ancestral home of Austria-Hungary."

There was a stunned silence around the circle of the table. It was Frederick who broke the grip of that sudden quiet. "But enough of war and politics. The duchess and I were planning to go ice-skating this afternoon, Reverend. Perhaps you and your wife will join us?"

The minister's wife tittered with uneasiness as she glanced quickly at her husband, who was scowling at Jeanne. "It is the Lord's Day," he reminded them all.

"And what better way to praise God than to enjoy the beauty of His creation in this peaceful setting that offers God's own respite from a world in chaos?" Jeanne replied, meeting the minister's gaze until he dropped his eyes.

"Thank you for the dinner, Mrs. Hunter, but I'm afraid Mrs. McAllister and I must be going. We have some calls to make to the sick and infirm this afternoon. This too is the Lord's work," he added as he stood and pulled out his wife's chair. "In fact, Mrs.

Pritchard mentioned that you are caring for a patient at the cottage. Perhaps we should begin our visits there."

Maggie glanced at her father, but he remained perfectly composed. "Sadly, this patient's maladies are still under question, and until the doctor can determine their source, he doesn't want to risk having the man infect others." He smiled. "I'll be sure our patient knows of your concern."

"And our prayers," Mrs. McAllister added.

While Lucie and Gabe escorted the McAllisters to the door, Jeanne turned to Maggie. "Your minister is so very young, a child in the matter of real-life experiences. Was I too forward with him?"

"Yes," Frederick answered before Maggie could open her mouth. "You know very well that you were. You cannot simply go about telling people what you think, Duchess — not in times like this."

"And why not?" Jeanne replied. "Someone needs to speak up — August would have." She turned back to Maggie. "My dear husband was horrified by what was happening, and he certainly saw no reason to stay quiet."

"And when he went back to Austria to try to broker a truce, he was assassinated," Frederick reminded her gently. "Just be careful, please." His gaze was so filled with tenderness that Maggie realized Frederick was in love with Jeanne. This was the way her parents looked at each other.

Frederick noticed Maggie staring at him. He laughed then, and patted Jeanne's hand in an affectionate manner. "Now if you are quite finished with trying to solve the problems of the world, could we go skating? After such a feast as this, I need the exercise."

Jeanne caressed his cheek, and her entire expression softened as she looked at him for a long moment, oblivious to Maggie's presence. "We shall go skating," she said, "if that will make you happy."

Maggie was stunned, for Jeanne's tone and gesture spoke volumes. Not only was Frederick in love with her, but also Jeanne returned those feelings. How could that not be disloyal — even a betrayal — of the love she had lost?

"Coming, love?" Jeanne asked, and Maggie looked up, shocked that Jeanne would direct such an open endearment to Frederick.

But Jeanne was looking at her, as was Frederick.

"Yes," she stammered. "I'll just go and change."

■ ■ ■ ■

Stefan heard the laughter before he saw them, his ears alert to any sound that might signal Maggie's arrival. Sarah Chadwick had been polite but vague in answer to his question about Maggie's whereabouts.

"I believe the family has gone to church," she replied after delivering his breakfast tray. Her manner was that of someone performing an unpleasant task, and she did not look directly at him. In fact, she practically fled the room.

But now it was well past the church hour — well past the noon dinner hour — and still she had not come. Stefan had asked Sean to help him into the wheelchair after lunch, and the man had done so without a word. But his action when he went to the window and tried it to be sure it was still secure spoke louder than any words.

Stefan was dozing in the wheelchair when he heard her laughter. He awoke with a start and glanced around the room, searching for the source of the sound, listening for her step outside his door, but the house was silent. Then again came voices, high-pitched with excitement outside the window.

He wheeled himself forward and looked

out. The first to pass was a tall woman with reddish-blond hair, walking arm in arm with an equally tall man. Behind them came Maggie, hurrying to catch up to the longer strides of her companions over the packed snow. Each of them carried ice skates over their shoulders, the laces tied together, the blades sparkling in the bright winter sun.

He saw Maggie glance once at the cottage as she passed and then look just as quickly away, running now to catch up with the others. Her voice echoed on the cold, still air. "Wait for me," she shouted, and the handsome couple paused.

"Come along, little one," the man called with the clipped, precise accent of the British.

Then the woman added, "It's so cold, Freddie. You should have warned me." But her voice was full of gaiety and happiness, not reproach. The man tenderly pulled the woman's fur collar closer around her throat, his gloved fingers lingering to brush her cheek as Maggie reached them, breathless but laughing.

Fascinated at seeing this girlish side of the woman who for days had barely dared favor him with a smile, Stefan pressed closer to the window. He could feel the rush of cold air seeping in wherever the window frame was not properly sealed, and for a long moment he closed his eyes and gave himself over to the sensation of fresh, pure air — of freedom.

A shout from the pond brought him back to the present. The man had led the woman to the very center of the ice and was twirling her around. Despite her protests she cut a graceful figure, reminding Stefan of a music box Uma had once cherished upon which a ballerina pirouetted to the music when the key was wound.

When Maggie took to the ice, he saw that she was an even more accomplished skater than her companions, but unlike the tall woman, Maggie took no time for pirouettes or cutting precise, ladylike figures in the ice. Instead she struck out to circle the perimeter of the large pond, her feet driving the blades of the skates firmly into the ice as she gathered momentum. Even after working up to a fierce speed, she did not allow herself to coast. Rather she pushed herself as if this were some race she needed to win, making each turn by hunching low, her mittened fingers sometimes skimming the ice as she rode the curve of the circle. Over and over she followed the oval shore of the pond until her companions paused to watch.

"Maggie!" the woman shouted. "Stop

that. You look ridiculous. Besides, you'll fall and hurt yourself."

Maggie slowed her pace and stood upright, her hands clasped behind her as she made it another half lap around the pond before she glided to the center, showering shards of ice in all directions like the sparks of a fire as she came to a stop. She was breathing hard and laughing even as the woman continued to reprimand her.

"But, Auntie Jeanne," Stefan heard Maggie protest, "it's glorious — a little like flying I think." And then she twirled round and round on her skates, her head flung back and her arms outstretched.

Stefan's breath caught. In that moment she became the very image of everything that life had been before the war — free, self-reliant, beautiful. He could not deny that his feelings for her had progressed well beyond admiration and gratitude, and he knew without a doubt that this vision of Maggie Hunter laughing, spinning, lifting her arms to the heavens in an act of unadulterated peace and liberty would sustain him. Even if he went to prison, he would keep repeating his story until someone else believed him, someone with the authority to take action. And although Maggie might never realize it, he would be doing it for her family as much as to honor Uma's memory. Most of all he would be doing it because he was falling in love with her and it might be the only way he could ever honor that love.

Maggie did not return to the cottage that week. Instead she left with her father every morning for town, where she went to work at the hospital while he attended to the business of managing the many properties he owned in addition to the inn. In the late afternoon the family had dinner at home, then gathered in the parlor, where Frederick and Gabe played chess while Lucie worked on her needlework and Jeanne sat sketching the various members of the family. By week's end Maggie had begun to feel as confined as Stefan Witte was.

"I'm going for a walk," she announced one evening. She saw her mother cast a look at her father, who continued the chess game. Maggie knew that he had few concerns about her trying to visit Stefan, for she had already tried, twice, and been turned away, first by Sean and then by Sarah.

"I'll come with you," Jeanne announced.

Maggie had noticed that Jeanne was nearly as restless as she was these days. The duchess often seemed distracted, even irritated. The only time she showed any real enthusiasm was on the daily trips she insisted that she and Frederick make into town. But she always returned from those excursions even more out of sorts than before.

On most any other occasion Maggie would have welcomed Jeanne's company. In fact, more than once she had considered telling her all about Stefan, even about the kiss. But then her father would comment on the world situation and that brought her back to the realization that this was a time of war, a time of secrets too dangerous to share.

"It's so very damp and cold," Maggie said now even though a warming trend had melted a good deal of the snow and left the ice on the pond too thin for skating. She hoped she looked appropriately disappointed that Jeanne might not come with her.

"But not too cold for you?" Jeanne arched one eyebrow and smiled. "My dear Margaret Rose, if I did not know you better, I would think you had planned a tryst with some young suitor."

Maggie felt color stain her cheeks, and Jeanne laughed, her good spirits momentarily restored. "Aha! It is as I thought. I always hoped you would return to your routine at the hospital, where at least you had some chance of meeting others."

Maggie's father turned his full attention to Maggie, as did her mother. She read a mixture of hope that perhaps she had weathered the storm of her grief and at the same time concern that she might be seeing someone behind their backs. Apparently Jeanne read the same message in their surprised but curious glances, for she shook her forefinger at them and admonished them. "Now, the two of you, stop being so old-fashioned. This is the twentieth century, and she is certainly of an age that she could see anyone she pleases with or without your approval."

"I didn't say a word," Gabe protested, but his eyes remained on Maggie.

Jeanne took Maggie by the arm, leading her into the lobby. "Go now, child, before they start asking questions," she advised as she covered Maggie's head and shoulders with her cashmere shawl.

"I won't be long," Maggie promised.

Once outside she closed her eyes and gulped in the clear night air, then opened them, head thrown back to the star-filled sky. In the midst of such serenity how could the world be in such disarray, she wondered. She walked the length of the porch, following its path as it wrapped around the side of the house. Through the lighted windows she could see her parents and Jeanne and Frederick. They had returned to their occupations but were clearly engaged in a far more animated conversation than they had enjoyed earlier. No doubt they were speculating about Maggie.

She stepped off the side porch and struck out on the path that led to the cottage. In the days since she'd last seen Stefan, he had haunted her every waking moment and inhabited her dreams. She had read his letter again and again. *No-man's-land . . . truce.* The words spun in her brain like a constant whirlpool, and the sealed envelope called to her. The truth was she could no longer deny that she had feelings for him that went beyond her duty as his nurse. Sorting out those feelings was exactly what had driven her out into the cool night air.

Maggie knew there was little use in trying a third time to carry off a proper visit, so instead of going to the front door of the cottage, she walked around to the side. The piles of evergreen branches Sean had stacked around the foundation of the cottage as insulation muffled her steps. Her intention was only to assure herself that he was all right.

She saw a lamp in the window of Stefan's

sickroom, and then she saw him, hunched forward in her grandmother's wheelchair, reading a book. She watched him for a moment and then moved closer, scanning the room for any sign of Sarah or Sean. Seeing no one but Stefan, she pulled off her glove and tapped lightly on the glass.

His head shot up and he moved the chair closer to the window. His eyes widened with surprise and then wariness. He glanced toward the door and back again.

"How are you?" she mouthed.

He shrugged. "I am better," he mouthed back. He raised his fingers to show her that the bandages were off and the blisters had healed nicely. He pressed his palm to the glass, and she matched it with her own. Her heart quickened when he smiled, and she realized she was no longer looking with the eyes of an enemy. She was looking at a man for whom she cared deeply. Then suddenly he turned toward the door and rapidly wheeled the chair away from the window.

Maggie saw Sean enter the room, and she ducked beneath the sill. She waited a moment, listening to the muffled voices of the two men. After the lamp went out and she heard the door snap shut, she stepped back to the window. But now the wheelchair sat empty in a corner. Stefan was in bed. She turned to go, but a movement inside the room, which was lit only by moonlight now, caught her eye. She turned back and watched in amazement as Stefan eased himself to the edge of the bed, found his footing and walked steadily to the window. He grinned at her triumphantly; then as if realizing what he had revealed, his features crumpled with distress.

He leaned on the sill and she moved closer, raising herself on tiptoe as she clung to the outer sill, their faces close enough for sharing a kiss, one separated only by glass. Her heart pounded furiously as he placed his mouth close to the edge of the window frame and she heard the low rumble of his accented voice. "Will you tell them?"

She hesitated, wrestling with the "shoulds" and "musts" of her upbringing. Then she shook her head. "Not yet. But you must tell me what to do, how I can help you."

"I don't know," he said, his anguish clear in his tortured expression. "The contact was to arrange everything, and now . . ."

"We will find a way," she assured him.

His relief was clear. "I am glad you came," he enunciated each word on a whisper. "I have missed you."

And I you, Maggie thought. "I must go," she mouthed.

He nodded and leaned all his weight on his forearms. She stared in fascination at the rippled muscles exposed there, the long fingers almost whole again.

"Did you read it?"

Maggie nodded. Once, twice, a dozen times she had read the pages until now she knew them almost by heart. "Truce."

Stefan bowed his head for a moment, and when he looked up, his eyes had filled with tears. And yet he was smiling. "I'll be fine, then. You should go."

He was giving her the exit that just days earlier she'd been determined to take, and yet instead of accepting his reprieve gratefully, she bristled. He was giving up? Surrendering? Did he think she was not up to the challenge? Did he assume that because she was a woman she would not be able to do anything?

"You can't do anything from prison," she argued. "We must find another way." Without giving him the option of a response, she turned and walked away.

"No." His protest carried on the night wind as she retraced her steps to the front of the cottage. As she rounded the corner, she heard the sound of an upstairs window being raised. The Chadwicks rose before dawn and were in bed hours before Maggie or her parents retired for the night. Maggie froze for an instant while Sean leaned out. A moment later he turned out the lamp in the bedroom he shared with Sarah just above Stefan. The action seemed especially poignant given Stefan's nailed-shut window on the floor below.

We take so much for granted, she thought as she stared up at the dark house. We can open a window, go to town if we want, go ice-skating on a perfect winter's day. What if it were taken away regardless of our innocence? Such as in Stefan's case.

She realized that she needed to prove his innocence, even as the others assumed his guilt. This realization came with such clarity and certainty that she might have spoken the words aloud — shouted them. And on the heels of that came a single question: Why? Followed by a realization as clear as the cold night air. Because I believe him.

In spite of his concern for what Maggie might do, Stefan slept that night as he had not slept in all the time he had been at the cottage. His joy in the fact that she had come to him — defied her parents to come to him — and believed him brought with it such peace and comfort. Feelings he had not known in years.

His thoughts were filled with her, her smile, her laughter, the vision of her spinning on the ice. The fervor of those words — *We must find another way* — had echoed in his dreams. He awoke and immediately gave thanks for God's gift in bringing him to this place, to this woman, this incredible woman.

But as soon as Dr. Williams came to call, his spirits plummeted.

"Well, now, young man, we have a bit of a conundrum, don't we?"

"Sir?"

"You see, your frostbite has healed nicely, far better than I might have anticipated in such a short time. On the other hand, Mr. Chadwick reports that you have made some progress with your exercises and walking, but less than we might expect. Very odd, don't you think?"

"How so?" Stefan was well schooled in the way of using questions to answer questions in order to learn just how much information the enemy had gathered.

Dr. Williams chuckled but his eyes remained steely. "Come now. You are a man of some physical strength and ability given your build and age. The question is why you seem unable to build on that strength, compromised though it may be."

"My breath — breathing," Stefan said apologetically.

"Hm-m-m. And yet your lungs are clear." He pulled a chair closer and lowered his heavy frame into it. "Now see here, my friend, you and I both know the end to this tale. We have no alternative but to have you transferred to the mainland. The longer you stay here, the more you endanger the reputations of these fine people. They have done enough — more than enough. I would think you would be pleased to show your gratitude."

"I need only a few more days," Stefan said softly, knowing the doctor was right yet clinging to every moment he might have with Maggie.

"And then you'll be strong enough for the transfer to the mainland?"

Stefan nodded and lowered his eyes so the doctor would not see that his thoughts were already racing through possible alternatives to being handed over to the authorities.

The doctor pushed himself to his feet. "Well, it's your good fortune that the Hunters' houseguests will not leave until Monday. That gives you three days. But mind you, be prepared to go on Tuesday at first light."

"Yes, sir. Thank you, sir."

"Don't thank me," the doctor said as he packed up his equipment and snapped his valise shut. "Thank these people who have risked everything for you."

In the hall outside his door, Stefan heard the doctor giving Sean his instructions. "Regular walks every hour, and Sean, take special care — the man is stronger than he lets on. Don't leave Sarah alone with him."

Stefan heard Sean's mumbled agreement to these instructions as he accompanied the doctor out to his carriage. A minute after Stefan heard the retreating clops of the doctor's horse, Sean entered the room. He went straight to the window and tried it. Stefan held his breath.

He had spent most of every night using a small manicure file he'd found in the back of one of the bureau drawers to loosen the putty that held the glass in place. Would Sean see the scrapings? Would he be suspicious?

"The doctor wants you walking," Sean said, turning from the window. "Now," he added firmly.

"I heard the instructions. I should probably practice dressing myself, as well," he added, and when Sean seemed confused, he explained, "I doubt the prison wardens will be dressing me and undressing me and tucking me in at night."

The ghost of a smile passed over Sean's lips. "Aye. You've a point there."

To Stefan's surprise, the fisherman left the room and returned a few minutes later with a shirt and sweater that Stefan did not recognize.

"Sarah said I should give you these."

"I'll be sure to thank her at supper," Stefan promised as he reached for his underwear.

Sean folded his arms across his chest and grunted. "Maybe you could start taking your meals with us instead of my missus carrying trays in and out. Makes more work for her."

"Of course," Stefan agreed, hastily pulling on the new clothing. The shirt and bulky handknit sweater were loose on Stefan but too small for the heavier fisherman.

"These clothes belonged to your son?" he asked.

Sean nodded. "Might as well do someone some good," he muttered.

That evening he surprised Sarah by walking with a cane to the supper table. She made her usual fuss over him, ignoring her husband's warning looks.

"How are the Hunters?" Stefan asked as he shared their supper of cod, potatoes and lentils. He pretended not to see the look that passed between them.

"They are well," Sarah replied.

"And Miss Hunter? Has she returned to her work at the hospital?"

"Why do you ask?" Sarah eyed him with both curiosity and suspicion.

Stefan shrugged. "Mr. Chadwick and I have made many walks today, and I thought she would be pleased to know of my progress. She was the first to have me stand."

"Aye," Sean murmured. "Well, we'll let her know you've progressed." His tone declared that this topic of conversation was at an end, and they passed the rest of the meal in silence.

But later that evening Sarah came into his room to deliver the last of his medicines for the day and handed him paper and pen.

"You may not have a chance to thank the Hunters in person — they can't be part of your being transferred."

Stefan could not disguise his surprise.

"Sean says there will be no contact. It's for the best." She ran her hand over the wool of the sweater Stefan had folded over the back of the rocking chair. "You're such a nice young man," she said softly. "Why, in other times you might have been friends with my George."

"I believe we would have had much in common," Stefan assured her and gave her a moment to compose herself before adding, "Will you take my note?"

Sarah nodded. As soon as she left, Sean appeared.

"I'm thinking you can get yourself into bed going forward?"

"Yes, sir," Stefan replied.

Sean grunted and went to check the window again. "Finish your letter writing then and Sarah will take it to the Hunters in the morning," he said as he left and locked the door behind him.

"But, Papa," Maggie protested in a low, hushed voice as she sat on her parents' bed with Mama watching Papa tie his shoes, "if you hand him over to these men, they might — he has information that must reach a higher authority."

"So he keeps saying. Were he inclined to offer information, he would have spoken up before now. He's desperate, Maggie. He knows that his time here is at an end. He's likely to do or say anything to try to get you to help him stay."

Maggie felt her mother's eyes on her and turned to her for help. "Mama."

"Tell me why this change of heart, Maggie? We had to practically beg you to nurse the man. I would think you'd be relieved to know he will finally be gone."

"It's not him," Maggie said, knowing deep in her heart that indeed it was him. "It's his sister and her child who have touched me."

"And what if he made up that tale?" Papa said.

"No, the story is real," Mama said. "Why, the newspapers report horrible conditions and the duchess confirms them. It's one of the reasons she left Europe."

"Still," Papa said, and Maggie saw the opportunity to seize the moment.

"Let me return to the cottage today," she begged. "I will know if he is lying, for he believes he has won my trust and his guard will be down. You've always said I was a good judge of people, Papa."

"It can do no harm," Mama said, "and I could use Sarah here. There is so much to be done to ready the inn for the season."

Papa frowned. "Very well, but take care. He is stronger than he lets on, and while I don't think he would harm you, neither can we forget that his future is —"

Maggie hurried to his side and kissed her father's cheek. "Thank you, Papa. I promise I'll be careful."

In her wildest dreams she had never dared to hope her father would give his permission. Mama, however, was always the softer touch, and Maggie congratulated herself on making sure that both parents were present when she pleaded her case. And then as she passed their bedroom after gathering her coat and gloves, she heard the real reason her mother had taken her side.

"I think that God has touched her heart at last," Mama was saying. "Oh, Gabe, can't you see? Somehow God has sent us this man to give us back our Maggie."

Maggie froze.

"You truly believe that?" Papa asked.

"He's a Christian, Gabe. Whatever he may believe his true purpose to be, it seems to me that God's hand is in all of this."

Maggie stood at the top of the stairs and allowed her mother's words to sink in. Lucie Hunter was a romantic as well as a devout Christian woman. Of course, she would see God's hand in this as she saw His hand in everything that happened. Hadn't it been Mama who had assured Maggie that Michael's death would not be in vain, that God had taken him from her for some greater purpose?

"Maggie?"

Maggie glanced around and saw Jeanne

coming out of her room.

"How are you this beautiful morning?" she asked as she greeted Maggie with a kiss to each cheek. "More to the point, you were gone for some time last night and raced off to your room with barely a good-night. So, how is that young man of yours?" She held Maggie by the shoulders for a long moment. "Perhaps the real question is *who* is your young man?"

Maggie felt herself blush a deep scarlet, and Jeanne laughed. "Come," she said, pulling Maggie into her room — the room where they had first brought Stefan, the room Maggie would never again be able to look at in the same way. "It's high time you and I had a little talk."

Jeanne reclined on the chaise and patted the space at its foot. "Sit," she invited. "Tell me all about him."

Maggie perched on the edge of the chaise and folded her hands primly in her lap. How she longed to confide in this worldly woman!

"Let me guess," Jeanne said, "you are feeling guilty. You think that any attraction to another man is a betrayal of Michael."

"How did you know?" It was a relief to have her feelings recognized and expressed openly.

Jeanne sat up and took Maggie's hand in hers. "I know because I have felt exactly what you are feeling, my darling. I am sure you have noticed that my feelings for Frederick run quite deep — and that those feelings are returned?"

Maggie smiled.

"Would it surprise you to know that I have wasted so much precious time denying those feelings?"

"You were in mourning," Maggie protested.

Jeanne shrugged. "Ask yourself one question, Maggie. Ask yourself if Michael would want you to deny yourself a life of love and family. He died." She leaned forward and placed her forefinger under Maggie's chin. "But you didn't die, Maggie."

"But . . ."

"You must live, Maggie, as I must. Frederick wants us to marry, and I truly believe that the duke would approve that at last I am moving forward with my life."

"Still, this man . . ."

"If God has seen fit to bring this man into your life, do not turn your back on that. You believe that your faith died the day Michael did. Perhaps you might reconsider that decision, for if there's one thing I have learned, my darling girl, it is that faith and love go hand in hand."

Faith, hope and love, Maggie thought, but the greatest of these is love.

Stefan had just finished dressing and positioned himself in the wheelchair when he heard the unmistakable sound of Maggie's laughter. She greeted the Chadwicks with more enthusiasm than he ever recalled hearing from her. And when she burst through the door to his room, her cheeks were rosy with the cold and tendrils of her hair had been pulled free by the wind. She was not wearing her nurse's cap and her beauty was all the more evident.

CHAPTER TEN

"I am glad you are here," Stefan began, but Maggie cut him off.

"Your walking has improved a great deal," she said, speaking in a voice that was a little too loud. "Sean tells us that you have made remarkable progress."

"Yes," Stefan replied, watching her steadily, her arms folded now across her chest as she studied him in return.

"If you wanted to do so, you could surely escape today. After all, I have things to attend to, in the kitchen, perhaps even upstairs."

Stefan frowned. What game was this? Had she been sent by her father and the doctor to test him?

"There's a heavy coat and boots of Sean's by the back door," she continued. "They would serve you well."

Her attitude confused him. Hadn't she promised to help him? *We must find another way.* Was this her idea of helping? To have him make a run for it? "You are testing me," he said irritably.

She lowered her voice. "Not at all. I am simply trying to warn you of the obvious choices that could trap you."

"What choice is there in taking your hints and acting on them only to find the fisherman waiting to shoot me as I run?"

"Ah, you can not only walk but also you can now run?" She grinned at him. "That is indeed amazing progress."

"I don't understand you," he grumbled and turned the chair away from her.

She crossed the room in half a dozen steps and leaned her weight on the arms of the wheelchair. "Here is all you must understand, Stefan Witte," she whispered. "If we are to do this, then I must know everything."

"I have told you that I was to make contact with someone on this side."

"Yes, you have this information that could turn the tide of this war."

"Do not mock me," he growled. "It's all there. You have but to open the envelope and read it for yourself. The language is technical, but you are very intelligent and in time could translate its meaning."

Silence reigned as she turned to stare out the window. Outside Sean moved back and forth, laying out his nets over the thawed yard as he checked them for needed repairs.

"We are alone so just tell me," she begged without looking at him. "I want to help, but how can I if I can't understand?"

It was a moment of truth and one that required an act of pure faith. Stefan took a deep breath. "All right. There was a meeting in Munich," he said softly. "I was called there because a document had fallen into the hands of the high command — a communication between the French and British generals. I was there to translate the document."

Several more beats of silence passed until Maggie said quietly, "Go on."

"In the communication the French were asking the British to assume control over a section of the trenches near the North Sea."

"The British already control that part of Europe," Maggie said and, when she saw Stefan's surprise at her knowledge of this, added, "The newspaper publishes the lines of battle each week."

"Yes, but the French wanted the British to also take on responsibility for another twenty-five kilometers to the south."

"All right, suppose they did, how is it important whether that little part of the line is controlled by French or British soldiers?"

Stefan reached out and took her hand and she turned to him. "It's important because the British are already overextended. Their men are exhausted and shorthanded."

"So, why agree? The French —"

"Are also shorthanded and exhausted. The two sides have not worked well together, and there is the risk that the French will simply abandon that part of the line."

"But the Americans —"

"Are not yet up to the job," he explained. "By the time they get enough troops trained and in place, it could be too late."

"Very well, but the British have such a powerful fighting force," she argued.

Stefan shrugged. "In places, yes, but the general in charge of this area is known to be dull and uninspiring. He's already suffered many defeats."

"Then surely he will be replaced," Maggie protested.

Stefan smiled. "No doubt but perhaps not before it's too late."

"What are you saying?" Her eyes flashed with fear.

"Quartermaster General Erich Ludendorff has been given the task of building a series of spring offensives to sever the line held by the Allies before you Americans can provide the necessary fresh troops and artillery. He had been considering where to launch this offensive when this document fell into his hands. It was a gift."

"How so?"

"It recommends the best point for launching the attack — this twenty-five-kilometer link between British- and French-controlled territory. The line will be weakest there."

"Then it is already too late," Maggie said, her voice low with dread.

"No. The attack was delayed until this spring because Ludendorff needed time to amass his forces and artillery. Some 800,000 men are to be brought, along with tanks, ammunition supplies and the like. All of this takes time, and there is the weather to consider."

"Then what?"

"The master plan is to defeat the British, the theory being that the French will then surrender and you Americans will have no cause to fight. The war will be over, and Germany will control all of Europe."

The clock in the parlor chimed the quarter hour as Maggie digested all she had heard. "Perhaps you would like that," she said as the clock fell silent, her eyes locked on his even as she pulled her hand free of his. "Your country would be the victor."

"Maggie, how can you think that? I have

risked everything to bring word of this to the Americans. Only your government can possibly change the course of this matter."

"So why not tell my father or Dr. Williams your story from the start? Why waste all this time? I don't understand you at all."

"They would not have believed me. I wanted to tell them but decided to follow the plan. My hopes were high when your father agreed to meet the contact at the docks, but when no contact was made, I saw that he had never believed me, had meant only to humor me. The information I have is far too important to hand over to people like your father who already have doubts."

"My father is an honorable man," Maggie protested. "If you . . ."

"Ludendorff is planning a massacre. Thousands will be slaughtered and irrevocably maimed. I am telling you that there is no thought of the human toll, only victory."

"But this would end with victory for Germany, your homeland."

"At what cost? Are we forever to be known as barbarians? For those men in that room the enemy was nothing more than an enormous, faceless beast to be utterly destroyed. They thought nothing of the lost lives, the lost youth, the lost sons and husbands and fathers. Every soldier wearing the opposing uniform was nothing more than a lifeless dummy to them."

"And for you? Who is the enemy?"

"The enemy is power and politics — not people. I see your face, Uma's, Klaus's. I see the faces of the men, boys really, that I served with on the U-boat. I see the faces of the Belgian chemist and the fellow seaman coming here who was my contact. I ask myself, why are we working toward this senseless destruction?"

Maggie's violet eyes burned with her desire to believe him, believe in him. "It's all so far-fetched," she said. "Coincidences that took you to Munich and then, instead of to the North Sea, here to Nantucket."

Stefan ran his hand through his hair. "Yes, I can see that this is how it appears. But you must believe me that the resistance is very well organized, very well connected. They arranged everything."

"You expect me to believe that a Belgian chemist had such connections when he was himself hiding out?"

"I can offer you only the truth, Maggie," Stefan said wearily. "Believe what you will. I have not lied to you."

Maggie watched Sean working on his nets.

She saw the weaving and thought of the web of underground connections Stefan wanted her to accept. "I don't know what to believe," she whispered.

Stefan pushed himself out of the wheelchair and stood behind her, his hands resting on her shoulders. "I can only tell you what I believe, Maggie," he said, his voice almost a whisper.

She waited.

"I believe that you are the reason I was brought here. Whatever I must face, God has given me this time with you, Maggie Hunter, and my life is far richer for it."

Maggie reached up and crossed her hands over her chest, holding onto his. She closed her eyes. "Stefan," she murmured and allowed her head to rest against his shoulder.

A sound from the yard brought them both back to reality.

"Someone's coming," Maggie said softly, then added with more alarm, "It's Reverend McAllister."

"To your father's inn?"

"No, here."

They both heard the sound of carriage wheels stopping outside the cottage, then Sean's quiet voice. "Reverend."

"I have come to call on the patient," they heard the minister announce in a voice that defied Sean to debate his purpose.

"He is sleeping," Sean replied.

"Then I will sit with him and pray for him to recover."

Maggie and Stefan heard the minister's heavy step on the front porch.

"Get back into bed," Maggie ordered. "Hurry."

Stefan did as she instructed, pausing only long enough to discard the slippers.

Maggie pulled the covers high over his shoulders and around his neck. "Close your eyes and whatever happens, do not speak."

Stefan turned on his side and forced his breathing to a steady beat, while Maggie sat across from him in the rocker, a book open on her lap. Seconds later there was a light tap on the bedroom door, and without waiting to be invited, the minister entered the room.

"Reverend McAllister," Maggie said in a hushed tone that nevertheless expressed surprise at his visit.

Without a word the minister crossed the room to Stefan's bedside. He frowned. "The day is quite mild, Miss Hunter. Does your patient have chills? A fever?"

"On the contrary, he is doing much better," Maggie assured him.

"So many covers," he replied as he folded

his hands and bowed his head.

Maggie watched as he prayed silently, his lips moving without sound, his eyes open and studying Stefan. She held her breath.

"In the name of the Father . . ." Reverend McAllister said aloud, and Maggie quickly bowed her head as he pronounced the benediction.

"It was kind of you to call," she said, speaking in the hushed tones of the sickroom. "Will you stop at the inn? I'm sure that Mother would want you to stay for tea before . . ."

He sat down in the rocker Maggie had vacated at his entrance. "I will stay until he has awakened," he announced. "His name again?"

You have not been told his name, Maggie thought. "Steven," she said softly and, at the raised and disapproving look the preacher cast her way, added quickly, "Steven Wit."

"Wit? I don't believe I've heard of that name here on the island."

Do not force me to lie to you, Maggie begged silently. Just then Stefan moaned and turned to his other side, away from the minister and facing Maggie. His eyes were open and under the dual questioning gaze of both the minister and Stefan, she faltered for words.

"He's not from Nantucket," she whispered. "Begging your pardon, Reverend, but my patient needs his rest. Could we talk in the parlor?"

The minister pulled a Bible from his coat pocket and opened it. "Please go about your duties, Miss Hunter. I will sit with Mr. Wit — is it?"

Stefan cast her a pleading look but what could she do?

"May I get you a cup of tea, Reverend?"

"Very kind of you. Two sugars, please."

She left the door ajar and stepped into the hallway where Sean hovered near the door. He jerked his head in the direction of the inn. "Shall I go for Gabe?" he mouthed and Maggie nodded.

In the kitchen she put the kettle on and tried to think what to do. At some point Stefan would have to "awake" and the minister would expect conversation. She drummed her fingers on the table, willing the kettle to boil more quickly. She cast her eyes over the kitchen shelves, seeking inspiration. And then she spotted the canister of dry mustard next to a basket filled with garlic bulbs.

"A poultice," she murmured. "If Stefan cannot speak . . ."

She hurried to gather mustard, garlic and some of the bacon grease Sarah kept in a closed jar near the stove. Using a mortar and pestle to grind the ingredients into a foul-smelling paste, she then spread the mixture on a towel she had soaked in strong vinegar and folded lengthwise.

All her life Mama had taught her that in hard times there was always a choice — to act or not, and choosing to do nothing was in itself a choice. Well, she was now choosing to act. It was true. Faced with the danger that could accompany the minister's visit, she had made her choice. She pounded more of the poultice ingredients into a smooth paste and added the second batch on top of the first. The kettle whistled shrilly as she rolled the towel and placed it on the tray next to the cup and sugar bowl she had prepared for the minister. She poured water over the tea leaves and smiled.

"What is that — odor?" Reverend McAllister's nose puckered in disgust.

"Oh, so sorry. It's a poultice for the patient's throat." She set the tray down on the small table near the rocker. "Shall I pour?"

As she had hoped, Reverend McAllister stood. "Perhaps I should take my tea in the parlor while you treat your patient." He tucked his Bible under one arm.

"As you wish," Maggie said, handing him the tray and trying not to let him see her relief. "But this will only take a moment." She took the tea towel from the tray and unrolled it, sending the fumes from the poultice wafting under the minister's nose.

Without a word he turned on his heel and fled the room.

"He's gone," Maggie whispered as she moved to the bedside.

Stefan burrowed deeper under the covers.

"Stop that," Maggie ordered. "Either you endure this or pretend to sleep until he leaves. We are wasting valuable time here," she reminded him.

Stefan peered at her over the edge of the quilt. "You enjoy this?"

With the efficiency of her training she wrapped the towel around his throat. "I'm perhaps a bit more used to unpleasant odors and procedures because of my nurse's training. It's a matter of weighing the options — sometimes the cure seems worse than the condition."

"You *are* enjoying this," he said with certainty.

"I'll tell the minister he can return to your bedside," she said with a smile.

In the parlor Reverend McAllister's tea

sat untouched as he fingered the pair of Stefan's socks that Sarah had been darning and left with her basket near the fireplace. "Unusually heavy," he commented. "I have never seen such wool, so fine and yet the stitch is quite dense."

"Yes, Sarah is well known for her fine work," Maggie said, taking the socks from him and rolling them. "Does Mrs. McAllister knit, Reverend?"

"Yes, a little." He continued to stare at the socks as Maggie replaced them in Sarah's basket under two pairs of Sean's socks waiting for repair.

"Ah, Reverend McAllister," Gabriel Hunter said as he crossed the room and took the minister's hand between both of his. "What an unexpected pleasure."

"I am not here on pleasure, Mr. Hunter. I have come to minister to Mr. —" He paused and waited for Gabe to provide Stefan's name.

"Steven Wit," Maggie said, her voice rising in a tone that betrayed her desperation. "Reverend McAllister was kind enough to sit with him, although the patient was sleeping."

"I prayed for him," the minister amended. "It would be my hope that I might pray *with* him." He turned his full attention to Gabe, stepping between Maggie and her father as he asked, "Is the patient still so ill? It has been some time since his confinement, has it not?"

"He's improving," Gabe replied calmly but cautiously. He gave the minister a gracious smile but said no more.

"Well, I shall look in on him once again if you don't mind," the minister said.

"Certainly, Reverend," Maggie readily agreed and led the way from the parlor, ignoring her father's look of astonishment. "I've applied the poultice and he's resting comfortably," she added.

McAllister hesitated. "Ah yes, the poultice." He made a show of looking at his pocketwatch. "Well, if he is resting, perhaps I will come another day. I have other calls to make."

Sean waited by the door with the minister's coat and hat, and Maggie's father walked with him out to his carriage.

"Dr. Williams has arranged for our patient to be transferred to the mainland on Tuesday," Maggie heard him say. "But we will certainly let him know of your concern and your prayers. He's a devout man and will appreciate your intercession on his behalf."

"Your daughter," Maggie heard the minister reply. "I have concerns, sir."

"How so?"

"Her absence from regular church attendance has caused talk, and Mrs. Pritchard tells me that she is spending an inordinate amount of time alone with Mr. Wit."

"She is a nurse by profession," Papa replied evenly.

"Still, the patient appears quite young, only a little older than your daughter, by my guess. I had thought him to be elderly."

"What are you implying?"

There was a pause and Maggie strained to hear the minister's response. "I am implying nothing. Your daughter is a single woman. Surely you and Mrs. Hunter can understand that —"

"What we understand, Reverend, is that our daughter has suffered a terrible loss, and in spite of that she has chosen to dedicate herself to the healing of others. She does not discriminate among her patients, for all are in need of her care. Please give our regards to Mrs. McAllister."

Maggie smiled, imagining that Reverend McAllister had been rendered speechless by her father's response. But her smile faded when Papa came back inside. "Sean, would you give me a moment alone with my daughter?"

Sean nodded and headed for his work-shop.

"The minister has gone," Maggie re-minded her father when she saw his frown.

"Yes, but for how long? He has questions, Maggie, and he is unlikely to keep his concerns to himself. No doubt there will soon be a parade of concerned church women calling on your mother and me."

"Well, let them. As you said, I am simply doing my job. If they have nothing better to do than to make something of that, then —"

Her father peered down at her. "But the question, Margaret Rose, is whether or not they have some cause for concern. After all, you were relieved of your duty to this particular patient and yet you pleaded to come back. Why?"

Maggie lowered her gaze. "It's — I am only trying to —"

"Mr. Hunter?"

Both Maggie and her father turned at the sound of Stefan's voice. He was standing in the doorway, the foul-smelling poultice removed. Maggie saw her father take in the fact that Stefan was fully dressed except for shoes. "Well, now," he said slowly. "What is this?"

"Please, may we sit together?" Stefan

asked, indicating the doorway further along the hall that led to the parlor. "I have something to tell you."

"I'll make a fresh pot of tea," Maggie said, but her father stopped her before she could escape to the kitchen.

"No tea is required, Margaret Rose. Come along."

Stefan led the way, walking upright and normally except for a slight limp. Maggie watched her father following him and saw that he was surprised at the agility with which Stefan moved.

"You've made great strides, I see," he said with a hint of sarcasm.

"I have and forgive me for keeping my recovery disguised before now. I needed the time to think through a strategy that might benefit us all."

Papa's response was a skeptical smile.

"You see, sir, I have not lied to you or the doctor. I jumped ship in order to make contact with someone here on Nantucket. Someone unknown to me. This person was to take me to certain officials with the power to act on this information."

"What information?"

"It's the Germans, Papa," Maggie interrupted. "They are planning an enormous attack on the Allied forces."

Both Stefan and Papa looked at her. Stefan sighed. If he had wanted to use caution in revealing what he knew, there was little point now. Papa laughed.

"I would remind you, Margaret Rose, that the bearer of this astonishing news is German. I would further remind you that you warned us repeatedly to use caution in what we believed about this man. Again I must ask you, what has changed your mind?"

"I believe him," she said with a shrug. "Why would he lie?"

Clearly Papa could think of multiple answers to that question, but instead he turned his attention back to Stefan. "I'm listening."

Stefan repeated the story he had told Maggie earlier that morning. "After the meeting in Munich I made contact with the resistance and gave them the news I had learned. They were able to get my orders changed. Suddenly the Supreme Army Command felt that I could be helpful in decoding communications to get past the American patrols."

"And you did that very well, apparently."

"As I have told you, not well enough to satisfy the captain. He decided Nantucket was too far from the mainland and planned to move farther south," Stefan replied.

"And this contact that never material-
ized?"

"It was on the voyage over that a fellow
seaman passed me word of meeting that
person. I can tell you nothing more about
that than you already know."

Papa shook his head. "Surely you can see
that you have no proof of any of this."

To Maggie's astonishment Stefan nodded.
"Yes, sir, I can. And yet once when you
barely knew me, you were willing to give
me a chance. Surely you can see that even a
man facing my fate would not be able to
concoct such a tale."

"He's telling the truth, Papa. I know he
is."

Papa maintained his focus on Stefan. "Do
you know the precise timing of this alleged
offensive?"

"I know what was decided at that meeting
— timing may have changed. Still, that is
the one piece of information I cannot reveal
for once I give up that I am just another
prisoner of war, am I not?"

"I see your point."

The two men fell silent, and Maggie
thought if one or the other didn't say
something, she was going to scream. The
tension in the room felt tangible. Finally
Papa stood and began to pace the room, a

good sign, Maggie thought, for she knew it meant that he was working through a plan.

Stefan glanced at Maggie but neither of them spoke.

"Tomorrow is Sunday," Papa said. "It would be best to maintain the appearance of normalcy. The family should attend services. The Chadwicks as well. Meanwhile you and I, Stefan Witte, will take the morning steamer to New Bedford. I know the authorities there well. You will not be mistreated, and perhaps we can persuade them to allow you to get a message to someone in the War Department in Washington."

"But . . ." Maggie began, but her father silenced her with a look.

"It's the best I can offer, Stefan. Anything more would raise questions of my loyalty and patriotism, endanger my family and probably destroy our livelihood."

Stefan stood and faced Gabe. "Thank you, sir."

The two men shook hands, and to Maggie they looked like two diplomats affirming a treaty. Her eyes welled and she was stunned to feel a single tear working its way down her cheek. "Surely there is something more to be done," she protested.

"No," Stefan said before her father could

speak. "I have already placed you and your family at grave risk, Maggie." He turned his attention back to Gabe. "I shall never forget the kindness you have shown me, sir. Please know that I am deeply grateful."

"As my wife has often reminded me, you are a child of God and we are people of deep and abiding faith. Regardless of our political differences, we could not have done otherwise. I accept your gratitude on behalf of my household and Dr. Williams. And I assure you that we will hold you in our prayers as you go forward to whatever God may hold in store for you."

No! Maggie cried silently. But deep in her heart she knew that her father was right. They had done everything they could. The idea that Stefan might simply remain with them and blend into the community was ludicrous and yet . . .

"Margaret Rose, I think you should go back to the inn now. Your patient has recovered. There is no more for you to do here."

Maggie looked at Stefan but he turned away. "I . . ." Her voice broke and she fled the room.

CHAPTER ELEVEN

Maggie stumbled into the kitchen, her eyes and face wet with tears.

"Whatever has happened?" Mama said as she rushed to Maggie's side.

Maggie gulped down her sobs but still could not speak. Instead she just kept shaking her head from side to side. Finally she formed a single word and the word was *Impossible.*

"What's impossible, darling?" Mama crooned as she wrapped Maggie in her embrace and rocked her from side to side. "Tell me what has happened."

By sheer force of will, Maggie controlled her hysteria. "It's Stefan, Mama. If Papa turns him over to the coast guard, then he'll never be able to get his message to the proper authorities. Who will believe him?"

Mama looked surprised. "You doubted him from the beginning, and yet now you believe him?" She held Maggie a little away from her, and when at last Maggie lifted her eyes to meet her mother's, Mama simply whispered, "I see." She led Maggie to a kitchen chair, then handed her a towel. "Wipe your tears away," she said gently as she took the chair opposite her.

"No," Maggie protested even as she scrubbed her face. "You don't see. How can you? I don't understand it myself."

Mama smiled. "Believe it or not, I know a thing or two about two people who appear to be impossibly divided but find common ground. It's perfectly understandable that you have come to care for a patient you have nursed back from the brink," Mama said as she stroked Maggie's disheveled hair away from her face.

"It's worse than that," Maggie whimpered.

"You have nursed him through some very difficult times and spent hours alone with him, hearing the terrible story of the loss of his sister and nephew. The two of you have built a bond that transcends your heritage. You are young people caught in a time of war and disaster. Of course, you have come to care for one another."

"I am in love with him," Maggie said softly.

Mama took a moment. "And does he return your feelings?"

Maggie pushed back the chair and began pacing the large kitchen. "What does that matter? Isn't it enough that I have fallen in love with the enemy, that I have betrayed Michael's love for me in the worst possible way?"

Mama stopped her in midstride, and this time the hands on her shoulders were strong and forceful. "Now, you listen to me, Margaret Rose Hunter. God has taken Michael from us. We don't understand why, but we must move forward with our lives. God has work for you to do in your life — perhaps like me you will raise a beautiful, willful daughter. Or perhaps you will be blessed with many children — sons and daughters — but the idea that you can never love again is preposterous."

"But he is German," Maggie whispered, as if perhaps Mama might have forgotten that little detail.

"Do you love him?"

"I —"

"Yes or no? Listen to your heart, Maggie, for that is the voice of God within you."

"Yes," Maggie admitted, the tears streaming again.

"Then listen to your heart and let God show you the way," Mama said and once again pulled Maggie against her in an embrace that promised everything would be all right.

Later that evening the family was just finishing dinner when they heard the jingle of a harness and the creak of carriage wheels on the drive.

"Ah, perhaps at last you have some paying guests," Jeanne joked, trying as always to lighten the somber mood that had hung over the entire meal.

Gabe went to the bay window that overlooked the porch and drive and lifted the lace curtain. "It's Tom," he said, then added with less enthusiasm, "along with Reverend McAllister and two others from the security watch committee, Gilbert Rowland and Police Chief Anderson."

Maggie gave a little gasp but covered it with a cough as she looked pleadingly from her father to her mother.

"I'll ask Sarah to bring more dessert," Mama said calmly as she headed for the kitchen.

"We'll be in the library," Papa said. "Please excuse us," he added with a nod toward Jeanne and Frederick.

"The police chief?" Jeanne whispered. "Sounds serious. Perhaps they have apprehended someone?" Her eyes were wide with what Maggie could only describe as panic. But why would Jeanne care if someone had been arrested?

"Let's not jump to conclusions," Frederick said, but he seemed every bit as concerned as Jeanne was.

"It's probably nothing." Maggie felt compelled to assure them. "Perhaps a change in schedule, or perhaps one of the volunteers has taken ill and they need to ask Papa to cover the security watch of the beach." She saw her mother take a tray into the library and knew that Sarah had been sent to the cottage to warn Sean — and Stefan.

The library doors slid open, and they all heard Dr. Williams's booming voice. "As long as I'm here," he said, "I may as well check on my patient."

"I'm afraid I need to ask that you stay," Chief Anderson replied as he stepped to the doors, waiting for Mama to exit the room before closing them.

"Has someone come ashore?" Jeanne asked when Maggie's mother returned to the dining room and resumed eating her pie as if nothing unusual had occurred.

"Not that I am aware," she replied. "Now please finish your dessert, everyone."

They did as she asked. The clink of silver on china seemed to reverberate around the room, and the tension was palpable. Finally

Jeanne dropped her fork onto her plate and pushed away from the table. "What can they be doing in there?"

Maggie's mother studied her friend. "It doesn't concern you," she said at the same time that Frederick rose and placed his hand on Jeanne's shoulder.

"Don't," he said softly.

She turned to him, her eyes wild. "But what if . . ."

Just then the pocket doors to the library slid open and Maggie saw her father and Doctor Williams emerge with the police chief followed by the minister and Gilbert Rowland. "I'm sorry, Gabe," the chief was saying. "I just don't see any other way to put this rumor to rest."

"You're only doing your duty, Henry," Gabe assured the man, then turned to the group that had gathered in the foyer. "Chief Anderson has asked to interview our patient. We're going up to the cottage," he explained. "We won't be long."

Maggie saw the look that passed between her parents, saw the love that fairly sparked in the gaze that connected them. She could think of only one thing — one person. Stefan. She had to do something, create some diversion.

"Papa," she said moving forward and then

fell to a heap at his feet.

As she had hoped, everyone rushed to her aid, but Papa got there first. He knelt beside her and lifted her in his arms so that his mouth was close to her ear.

"It will be all right," he whispered. "Have faith, child." Then he gently transferred her to her mother's care. "She's been working too hard, I expect."

"Yes," Mama agreed. "Go. She'll be fine."

"I'll just stay to be sure," the doctor added.

"We won't be long, ma'am," Maggie heard the chief say apologetically. "Sorry to have interrupted your dinner."

As the men escorted Gabe from the inn, Sarah came rushing in from the kitchen. "He's gone," she whispered as she leaned in close as if to assist with Maggie.

Maggie's eyes flew open. "How?" She hardly cared that Jeanne and Frederick were still hovering nearby.

"Through the window. He left this note." She handed the note to Maggie, who read it quickly and then handed it to her mother.

Maggie
These men have come for me and I may well end up in their custody. If so, please make sure the envelope I gave you gets

to the highest possible authority. Please know that I am forever in your family's debt and I am sorry for the trouble I have brought to your door. And Maggie, know that I run not because I am guilty but because I still have hope to reach those I must.

Stefan

"Is someone going to tell me what's going on?" Jeanne asked in a voice that was anything but her usual girlish titter. Her tone demanded an explanation. "What has happened?"

Dr. Williams looked at Lucie and then Sarah. Lucie sighed and pushed herself to her feet. "Let's all sit down," she said.

"I'll make fresh coffee," Sarah volunteered.

It took less than fifteen minutes for Lucie and the doctor to tell Jeanne and Frederick the story of Stefan Witte's stay at the inn. Throughout the telling of it Jeanne kept one fist jammed against her lips, as if at any moment she might cry out, and Frederick sat by her side, one arm around her shoulder. Through it all Maggie sat alone at the far end of the table, silent tears rolling down her cheeks unchecked.

He was out there somewhere in the cold.

272

He would be hunted now by men whose panic at the idea of a German in their midst might make them rash. They would be armed, when Stefan was unarmed. They would label him desperate and dangerous. And she had no doubt that given the high fever pitch of the rhetoric she had often heard from the men of the island, they would not hesitate to shoot him on sight.

Please, God, help him.

The words came as naturally as breathing, and yet Maggie's crying turned from silent tears to sobs that made the others turn to her.

"Oh, my darling girl," Jeanne said, rushing to her side. "Don't worry. He'll be all right. He will be," she said with such certainty that Maggie clung to it. Then the duchess turned to Lucie and Dr. Williams. "This man — this German — he was telling the truth. It was Frederick and I who were to meet him. We were to transport him to New York to meet the former ambassador to Austria-Hungary. He is a friend of ours and a close adviser to President Wilson."

Maggie swallowed the last of her sobs and hiccuped. "Peace be with you?" she whispered, and Jeanne turned to her and smiled.

"And with you and all your countrymen," she replied softly, her gaze never wavering.

"We arrived a day late because of the freeze-up, but we went every day, even after the deadline had passed. We hoped that perhaps he would come. Now we understand why."

"Because he was here," Maggie said. "We must find him. He believes that all is lost, and if the others find him first . . ."

There was a commotion in the foyer, voices raised in anger and protest. "He harbored a German," Gilbert Rowland was shouting. "I never thought I'd see the day that Gabriel Hunter would betray his country."

"Gabe, I'm afraid I'll have to hold you until we can get this all sorted out," Chief Anderson said and Lucie rushed to her husband's side. "You too, Doc," he added. Then he shook his head sadly. "Why didn't you come to me?"

"We should have," Gabe assured him. "I see that now." He kissed Lucie and then got his hat and coat from the hall tree.

"I'll organize a search for the German," the minister volunteered.

"I'll help," Rowland added, and the two of them set off at a near run down the lane toward the church.

"Wait," Jeanne protested, but the men had already headed off, determined in their individual missions and with no patience for further stalling.

As soon as the police chief had driven away with Gabe and the doctor, Frederick went into action. "We must find this German before the others do. Mrs. Chadwick, would you be so kind as to get our wraps from our rooms?"

Sarah nodded and hurried up the stairs. Lucie was getting her own coat when Frederick stopped her. "No, you should stay here. In case Gabe calls or there's other news."

"I'm going with you," Maggie announced and was out the door before there could be any debate.

Outside they could hear the church bell pealing a pre-arranged signal that would have men and women hurry to the church to learn what emergency had arisen and how they could help. Together Maggie, Jeanne and Frederick ran down the path and around the side of the cottage. Maggie caught sight of lace curtains blowing in the open window of Stefan's sickroom.

"There must be tracks," Frederick called and ran to the window. But the evergreen branches had covered anything that might give them a clue as to the direction he had gone.

"Sarah says he had no coat," Jeanne said.

Slippers, Maggie thought. He has no shoes, and Sean was wearing the boots she'd pointed out to him. If his toes freeze again, he might lose them. She quickened her steps.

They searched everywhere, starting with the barn in case he had taken refuge in the loft. But their search turned up nothing, and as they surveyed the horizon — a black-and-white moonlit and shadow tableau of low shrubs and open land — they had to admit they had covered every possibility they could fathom.

Where are you? Maggie repeated the question in rhythm with the pounding of her heart. Just then they heard voices, and turning toward the sound, they saw the torches as dozens of men came up the lane from the direction of the church. Maggie's heart seemed to stop midbeat. Did they intend to set fire to the inn? Was this their way of dealing with those who harbored the enemy — with traitors?

"No," she cried and ran toward them, barely aware that Jeanne and Frederick were running to stop her. But she was faster and her love for Stefan gave wings to her feet. "You must listen," she pleaded, coming to a stop before the minister, who was at the head of the pack of men.

"Please step aside and let us do our duty, young woman." He made a move to go past her, but she blocked his way. Short of pushing her aside, the minister had nowhere to go. He looked down at her, holding his torch to light her face. "You are misguided, Margaret Rose, you and your parents. I have no doubt that you thought you were doing God's work in rescuing this man, but you must see that he has shown his true colors now." His voice was softer, almost kind, as if he were speaking to a small child. "If we are to clear your father's good name, we must find this man and bring him to justice."

"But there are things you do not know. There are reasons why he has come here."

"Yeah," a boy looking no older than fifteen and standing just behind the minister spat out. "He came here to spy on us, to take back information to his officers so they —"

The minister held up a silencing hand. "Brother," he said and the boy fell silent. Behind him the others waited, their flickering torches casting an eerie golden light over the scene. At the same time, Jeanne and Frederick arrived to take their place on either side of Maggie.

"We must find him," the minister said.

"I know," Maggie agreed, "but you don't

have to hurt him." She fixed her eyes on the hunting rifles that several of the men carried. "He is not armed."

The minister hesitated, glancing back at his flock and then down at Maggie once more. "It is as I feared the day I called on the patient," he said. "This man has deceived you, child. He is about the work of the devil and you must . . ."

"He is trying to save his country — and ours," Jeanne said. "He has brought valuable information to us that must be given to the proper authorities as soon as possible. It is urgent, I assure you."

"He is a man of God," Maggie whispered.

"Nevertheless justice will be served," the minister replied and turned to face his followers.

Maggie grasped his sleeve. She had seen his hesitation and realized that he was far less sure of himself than he wanted everyone to believe. "Please," she begged.

Reverend McAllister pulled free of her grip and spoke in his pulpit voice, the words echoing across the landscape. "Stefan Witte! If you can hear me, know that we mean you no harm. We are laying down our weapons, for we believe you to be unarmed." He nodded at the men before him and reluctantly they leaned their rifles against the barn wall.

"If you can hear me, come out. You are in no danger from me or these men."

Everyone waited. Maggie saw that her mother, Sarah and Jeanne's maidservant had come out onto the porch. Beside her Frederick and Jeanne slowly turned to survey the surrounding landscape. The minister and his band of men did the same. But outside the circle of the golden light nothing stirred, and the only sounds were the whisper of the wind in the dried grasses and the distant crash of the waves on the beach below the inn.

"Come, Maggie," Jeanne said as she took her elbow. "There is no more to be done here. Come wait inside with your mother while Frederick and I make some calls."

Maggie paced the length of the foyer as she strained to hear Jeanne's side of the telephone conversation.

"Yes, that's right," followed by an exasperated sigh. "I assure you this is of the utmost importance. If you would just mention my name, the ambassador is expecting my call and I can promise you that he would wish to be interrupted." Another long sigh. "I see, and your name again is? Well, Willard, may I speak to your superior?"

Maggie could stand no more. Either she

must escape or she was in danger of ripping the phone from Jeanne's hand and screaming at the person on the other end until he understood this was a matter of life or death.

"Maggie?"

Mama's quiet voice was more irritating than Jeanne's attempts at diplomacy with the person on the other end of the line.

"What?" she snapped.

"Perhaps if you went up to the cupola," Mama suggested in the same tone she might use to suggest that Maggie lie down for a bit. "It's been a place that has always calmed you before."

Maggie was about to ignore this advice just as she had been prepared to refuse any suggestion other than searching for Stefan. But then she realized what her mother was really suggesting. In the cupola she would be high enough to survey the area from all directions. In the cupola was Papa's telescope. From that vantage point she might see something those searching the grounds would miss.

She bent and kissed Mama's forehead. "Brilliant," she whispered. "Thank you, Mama." She flew up the back stairway without stopping until she had reached the top of the narrow metal staircase and opened the trapdoor.

At first she raced, opening every window, her mouth repeating a single prayer, *Please, God.* But what right had she to ask anything of God, she who had willfully turned her back on her faith?

Outside the windows she heard nothing but the muffled voices of the searchers calling out to one another as they spread out over the property and beyond. She saw torches near the pond and waited for word that someone had fallen through the thin ice but none came. "Thank You, Heavenly Father," she murmured with a sigh of relief.

For an hour she repeated her rhythmic pattern of moving from window to window. Once she tried the telescope but it was useless in the dark. Exhausted, she slumped against the window ledge, listening to the search party call to one another from various parts of the grounds.

She caught a word here and there as gradually the men returned to the front of the house ready to disband. "Too dark," she heard. Then, "Pray we find him, Reverend, before it's too late."

She heard the minister propose that they return to the church to rest, warm up and resume their search at first light.

Before it's too late.

Pray.

The words hummed in Maggie's brain and penetrated her heart and she fell to her knees.

"Father in Heaven," she murmured, "forgive me for doubting You, for turning away in my hour of need. Mama says You are always there even when one of us turns away. Papa says You are patient with us and forgiving. Please help me find him."

She rallied her energy and searched the horizon for some place they might have missed. If only it were closer to dawn than to midnight. If only there were more light.

"Papa, what if the sun wouldn't come up one morning?" she had asked when she was five.

Papa had laughed. "It will come up. We may not see it for the clouds, but the light will be there, telling us the sun is there beyond the clouds."

"But how do you know for sure?" she had demanded.

"It's called faith."

"What's that?"

"The belief in something you can't see," Papa had replied.

"Like God?" she had asked and knew now that it was still true.

Like God. How could she ever have doubted?

"Stefan has never doubted You," she said to the vast blackness of sky and water beyond the land. "His sister and nephew died horrible deaths and he never blamed You. He is trying to do Your work. He has faith — deep and abiding. Please help him. And if it be Your will, keep him safe and bring him back to me. I know that together we could do good work in Your holy name, and I am ready to do that work."

She was on the verge of closing her prayer but realized there was one more promise to be made. "And if it be Your will that Stefan is gone from my life forever, I will accept that as I now accept the loss of Michael and George. I accept that in having known them and having had these few weeks with Stefan, I have been truly blessed."

She was murmuring these last words when something caught her eye. It was not a movement. In fact the landscape had never been so still and quiet. But her eye was drawn to the place where she, Michael and George had played as children and escaped their parents as teens. It was the place where Michael and George had sworn her to secrecy when they confided their intent to volunteer as soon as America declared war. It was the place where Maggie had gone every day after they left to pray for their safe return. Even after they received word that George had been killed in battle, she had prayed there for Michael. Until the day the news came that Michael also had been taken. That day she had gone to the cupola instead.

Her eyes were riveted on that secret place, that hiding place. Had God led her back to the time when her faith had been most fervent, back before the days of denial here in the cupola? Back to the time when she had sat alone under the thicket of grasses and rose vines and prayed for an end to this horrible war? Stefan was out there. She was as sure of that as she was that the sun would rise the following morning.

Ever since she'd heard the news of Michael's death, it seemed as if she'd been running away, chased by the sorrow over what might have been. But as she slipped down the stairway, stopped at her room to retrieve the sealed envelope and some cash she'd saved and hurried out into the night, she knew with clarity that she was running toward something. Stefan certainly, but more. She was running toward the future, a future she had thought would never be. Only now did she understand fully that her life had not ended when Michael had died. She understood that in the time she had left on this earth there were likely to be many new beginnings. Every beginning required an ending but if she focused on the ending, she would surely never know the fullness of the life she had been given.

By the time she reached the arbor, her shoes were soaked and her hair was coming free of its pins. Careless of how she must look, she pressed on, racing against the coming dawn.

Please let him be there, she prayed as she entered the narrow passage beneath the tangle of vines.

He's here, the dried grasses seemed to whisper back as they swayed in the wind.

"Stefan?"

Stefan was shivering violently. Why had he not thought to take the blanket? His slippers were soaked and caked with sand and mud. Torches flickered in the distance, marking the disappointing progress he had made in his journey. His destination was the harbor. His prayer was that there would be a boat there, perhaps a skiff belonging to Sean or the Hunters. But he had barely made it past the inn before he'd heard the angry and excited voices of men on the hunt. Desperately he had sought shelter and found it along a path overgrown with the remnants of tall grasses and wild rose vines that formed a kind of arbor a short distance from the cottage.

He was having trouble thinking straight. His eyes kept closing, and he could no longer feel his toes. Would it end as it had begun, with him freezing to death so close to his destination? *Please God, not yet,* he prayed. *How can I clear my name and theirs if I am imprisoned or worse? I don't know what You want of me.*

He shook himself alert. He could hear the distant calling of his name and was aware of the torches moving in the other direction — away from him, their light fading in the darkness. He fought for consciousness, clinging to the thought that he'd heard Maggie calling his name.

Maggie stood still, listening for any movement, but she heard only the rhythmic sounding of the foghorn at the lighthouse in time with the beating of her heart. Slowly she moved farther into the darkness, toward the faint moonlight at the far end of the arbor.

"Stefan, I'm here," she said softly.

She inched forward and suddenly someone grasped her arm. She swallowed a scream.

"Maggie, go back," Stefan said, his voice hoarse and weak.

She fell to her knees beside him, uncaring of the soft, muddy ground that soaked her clothes. Instinctively she raised her hand to his forehead. He was cold but not feverish. "God has answered my prayers," she told him. He gazed at her in wonder, but she didn't pause for a second.

"Can you walk? We have to hurry." She struggled to rise, but he held her fast.

"No, *liebchen,* you must go back," he said, and he held her face in the palms of his hands, drawing her closer. "I love you too much to —"

To stop the flow of words she did not want to hear, she closed the distance between them and kissed him. In an instant it was as if they had been created for this single moment. Their lips met and there was no war, no danger, no time but this moment.

"If you truly love me," she whispered as Stefan brushed back her wet hair to expose her forehead. He kissed her there.

"No conditions," he murmured as he continued kissing her temple, the tip of her ear, her cheek and jaw and finally covered her lips once more with his own.

But this kiss was different from the first. This was a kiss of farewell.

"No," she protested, pushing away from him. "I'm coming with you. Once we get away, we'll call my Auntie Jeanne and —"

But where would they go? She clung to him, attempting to warm him with her own heat, spreading her shawl over them both as she looked toward either opening of the arbor. One led to the pier and Sean's fishing boat, which would take him to safety. The other led back to the inn and the certainty of help.

Hearing voices, they moved farther into the underbrush. "Sh-h-h," he whispered as he held her close.

"She came this way," Frederick called back toward the inn. "Jeanne saw her from the window."

Maggie judged the distance Frederick had yet to cover to reach the arbor. There was time. "We can make it to the boat. Just lean on me." She couldn't take the chance that Frederick and Jeanne could persuade the others, and she refused to put them in further danger.

In answer, Stefan pushed himself to his knees and wrapped his arm around her shoulders. He struggled to his feet and she turned toward the nearest opening, the one that led to the pier.

"This way," she urged.

The wet, sandy path deadened their foot-steps, and the sheer will to survive made Stefan move in limping strides that Maggie could barely keep up with. "There's a skiff," she told him. "We can . . ."

Suddenly Stefan stopped and gripped her shoulders, forcing her to face him, listen to him. "No. You must go back."

"You can't manage alone — you're too weak and . . ."

"No more, *liebchen*. It's over," he said and embraced her, his mouth finding hers. "I love you," he said when he broke the kiss, and then before she could stop him, he turned and called out, "She is here with me, sir. She has convinced me to surrender."

For an instant there was no sound, and then came a thrashing of the dried vegeta-tion that formed the arbor as Frederick and Sean ran the length of it and Maggie could hear Jeanne calling, "They've found them!"

Stefan was still holding her close when the two men emerged and froze. They looked from Maggie to Stefan.

"Let her go," Sean ordered.

"Now look, young man, it may seem that things are quite desperate at the moment, but the duchess and I can help. You see, Ste-fan, we are your contacts." Frederick was speaking quietly even as he and Sean moved slowly toward Stefan.

"Stefan, listen to him," Maggie pleaded. But suddenly she was standing alone because Stefan had crumpled to the ground.

Sean grabbed her arm and pulled her away as if she'd been in danger of being kidnapped and in need of rescue.

"Stop that," she ordered and rushed to Stefan's side. "He's fainted. We have to get him back to the house."

Both Sean and Frederick seemed rooted in the sand.

"Now," she ordered.

Sean picked up Stefan by the armpits, while Frederick took his feet. "Hurry," Maggie pleaded as she led the way back through the arbor and up the lawn to the inn.

Lucie, Jeanne and Sarah were waiting for them. "Through here," Lucie instructed, indicating the parlor, where the sofa had been dragged closer to the fire.

Everyone began speaking at once.

"Get those socks and wet slippers off him."

"He's shivering. Add a log to the fire."

"Here are more blankets."

"I'll phone for Dr. Williams."

This last from Sarah caused everyone to pause.

"He's been taken to the police station,"

Jeanne reminded them, "with Gabe."

As one they all turned to Maggie, and she realized that they were waiting for her to take charge.

Chapter Twelve

Maggie saw that Stefan was swimming back toward consciousness. He did not seem to be in pain and was actually smiling.

"Ah, the poor lad is dreaming of something good," she heard Sarah whisper.

Something good. The taste of Stefan's kiss lingered, warming Maggie to her core even as she told herself he was still not out of danger. She touched his forehead and cheek and then allowed the tips of her fingers to brush his lips. "You're safe, Stefan. Everything will be all right," she whispered before turning to face the others. "I'll be back," she announced.

"But, Maggie," several others protested almost in unison.

"Keep him covered and calm," she replied. "When he rouses, give him warm liquids. This is going to stop right now."

As she hurried along the road that led from the inn to the church, Maggie regretted the confusion she had created by leaving the others to care for Stefan when she was trained to do just that. But as she had considered all the many forces weighing down on Stefan's future, on her future with him, she had seen only one option.

Jeanne had been unable to persuade the ambassador's top assistant to interrupt his evening and bring him to the phone, so there was no help coming from that quarter. And even if there were, the ambassador was in New York — hours away. Normally Maggie would have looked to her father for guidance, but he had been taken away. Not only was he unavailable to offer the help and advice she needed, but he needed her help, as well.

And looming over it all was the presence of the men at the church. They would return. She had heard their plan to go to the church for some rest and hot coffee and start the search again as the sky lightened. If they found — *when* they found — Stefan, there was no telling what they might do. There were men in the group whose sons had died or returned with life-changing disabilities from the front. There were men, like her father, who regretted that they could not join the fight and would see capturing Stefan as the chance to do their part.

She understood all of that, but she knew that unless she could get them to listen to reason, all of their fears and frustrations would be focused on the one symbol of their hatred: the German. Stefan Witte might pay a terrible price for their zeal to be patriots.

When Maggie reached the church, the men had just donned their coats and gloves. The minister called for all to gather in a circle for prayer. Beyond them, wives and mothers who had answered the call of the church bells and prepared coffee and food to sustain the men of the congregation saw Maggie enter the church hall.

All was silent except the voice of the minister as he uttered the closing words of his prayer. The men raised their bowed heads and glanced at their wives and mothers, who were looking toward Maggie standing alone at the door. The minute they saw her, the men began pelting her with questions. Soon the women joined in as they closed the circle around her. And through it all Maggie stood her ground, her eyes on Reverend McAllister.

"Be at peace," the minister said in his pulpit voice, and the crowd fell silent, yet they eyed Maggie with suspicion and censure. These people who had been her parents' friends, their neighbors and her classmates stared at her with suspicion and wariness as if they had never really known her.

"I have something to say," she began, once again focusing on the minister.

"Very well, sister," the minister replied, and when some in the crowd would have protested, he held up one hand. "We will hear her out."

"Stefan Witte is not what you think," she began, and that set off an outcry that even Reverend McAllister had trouble quelling.

"Please," he entreated. "Let her finish."

"I have come to ask for your help and understanding. I have come to ask that you withhold judgment until you have heard his story. . . ."

"Story indeed," Gilbert Rowland spat out. "Lies — that's the whole of it."

Maggie faced the older man and met him toe-to-toe. "You have known my father all his life, Mr. Rowland. You know Dr. Williams and you know Sean Chadwick. Can you honestly believe that these three men would all be fooled by one lone German?"

It was Rowland who looked away.

"Furthermore," Maggie said, turning to the others, "why would a man, any man, risk his life jumping ship in the middle of winter, clinging to ice floes, fighting his way back from frostbite and pneumonia if his mission was not one of utmost urgency?"

"He's a spy," someone called out from the back of the circle. "A German spy."

Maggie swung round until she found the source. "I thought that at first. But if he is on business for his government, why would they risk putting him out so far from shore? And why on earth would they select Nantucket as the place to . . ."

"The man has blinded you, Maggie dear," Mrs. Pritchard said as she pushed her way through the circle of men and attempted to pull Maggie to her bosom. "He has fought all right, fought to persuade you and your parents that he is an innocent. No doubt he learned of the loss of dear Michael — at the hands of his own people, let us not forget — and he knew you would be vulnerable. He has used the devil's own tools to deceive you."

There was a murmur of agreement, but Maggie only smiled as she pulled free of Mrs. Pritchard's cloying embrace. "He is a man of deep and abiding faith, Mrs. Pritchard. And far from blinding me, he has opened my eyes. He has led me back to God."

There was a communal gasp and all eyes turned to the minister, certain that he would protest such blasphemy.

But Maggie spoke first. "Reverend McAllister, just a few Sundays ago you extolled us all to find forgiveness. Does not forgiving mean opening ourselves to the possibility that there are those within our enemy's borders who hate this war as much as we do? Who have suffered in ways we can only imagine? Is it not possible that God has brought Stefan Witte to these shores?"

"You go too far, Maggie," the minister said but his voice held no reprimand. Instead, Maggie heard a note of uncertainty. "My child, you cannot possibly —"

She pressed her case, speaking directly to the young minister. "The people of Nantucket have always been fair-minded and charitable. It is our nature to listen and make our own decisions, our own choices. My grandparents taught me to understand that living here on an island, removed from the mainland, was both a blessing and a responsibility."

The room had grown so still that Maggie's quiet, determined voice resonated in the hall. "A blessing because God has given us the position of being among the easternmost shores of American soil. A responsibility for that very same reason." She turned slowly until she had looked into the eyes of every person in the room. "Won't you let him speak? Won't you listen with an open heart to what he has to say?"

A beat and then the minister's quiet voice. "Where is he?"

Maggie could hardly believe that she might have persuaded the minister. She squeezed her eyes shut as images of these last weeks flashed through her brain. So much had changed. She felt tears burn the backs of her eyelids, and then the tears exploded in an explosion of grief and sobbing.

She covered her face with her hands as the sobs of weariness and defeat overwhelmed her. And then she felt the circle of church members close in on her, but it was not a move that she found threatening. The circle of fear and blame had changed to one of support and comfort.

She felt the minister's hand on her shoulder as he spoke to the others. "Mr. Rowland will call Chief Anderson, Maggie. Perhaps it would be possible to have Dr. Williams released temporarily to be sure the young man has not suffered further injury."

"I should think we'd make better use of time to notify the military police so they can take this German into custody before he pulls any more escapes," Rowland argued, and Maggie understood that forgiveness would come more easily to some than to others.

"Yes, Gilbert, we must attend to all of that," Mrs. Pritchard boomed. "But for now you go call the chief. Meanwhile, Reverend, with your permission I'd like to bring a few of the ladies and accompany you back up to the inn. Surely a prayer circle would be in order." She pursed her lips. "That is unless you truly believe the man to be a danger to others."

"He's no threat to anyone," Maggie said.

"Perhaps then, Maggie dear, you will join our prayer circle?"

"Excellent idea," Reverend McAllister replied as he led Maggie to the door and the women followed. "And if it be God's will to heal this man, then we will hear what he has to tell us with open hearts and open minds."

Maggie realized that this was not a suggestion. The minister was looking directly at the doubters in the room.

But those who had not been persuaded by either her or Reverend McAllister turned away, finding some task that needed attention. Maggie understood. For several of them there had been terrible losses because of the war — because of the Germans. She knew from her own experience that sometimes it was far easier to hate and blame the forces of evil than to try and find God's will in such madness.

By the time they reached the inn, Maggie had managed to compose herself. She had even found the grace to thank the young minister for his support and willingness to hear Stefan's story.

"I don't wish to give you false hope, Maggie," he said over the low murmur of the women behind them as they hummed "In the Sweet By and By." "You and your family, as well as the Chadwicks, have taken matters into your own hands that you had no right to decide. Your father and the doctor are in grave danger of losing everything they have spent a lifetime building on this island. I will admit to you that I cannot understand that, and I cannot see God's will in any of this. I believe you and your loved ones to be good and caring people — but misguided."

"I understand," Maggie said and she did. Hadn't the minister's opinion of Stefan been exactly her own just a few weeks earlier?

The minister thanked Sarah for taking his

coat and went straight to the parlor, his eyes immediately on Stefan who was half sitting now as Jeanne knelt by his side and fed him broth. Stefan was smiling at something Jeanne had just said as the little band of do-gooders entered the room.

"Well, it appears there has been a speedy recovery," Reverend McAllister said with a smile that seemed forced. The women of the prayer group looked down on Stefan with obvious disapproval, then back at the minister, awaiting his next direction. "Clearly there is no need for your prayers, ladies, at least for the prisoner's recovery. You may wish to entreat God's mercy."

Maggie's emotions swung like the pendulum on the grandfather clock in the lobby. From relief that Stefan was so much better to delight as his eyes filled with love and then back to fearing the danger he was now in because these good people believed him to be a spy and a con man. *Prisoner,* Reverend McAllister had called him.

Maggie was about to speak out when her mother moved forward to take the minister's hand in both of hers. "It is so good of you to come, Reverend," she said. "Circumstances beyond his control have denied our guest the comfort of his faith brought by his own clergyman for far too long." She continued to hold the minister's hand as she led him closer to the sofa. "Stefan Witte, this is Reverend McAllister."

Taking her cue from Mama, Maggie went to stand beside Stefan, one hand resting lightly on his shoulder. The sound of Mrs. Pritchard and the other ladies sucking in shocked breaths made Jeanne smile as she handed the bowl of broth to Sarah and stood next to Maggie. The three women formed a solid front that dared anyone to try and penetrate their line of defense.

"Thank you for coming, Reverend," Stefan said, knowing full well that not an hour earlier, the minister had been at the forefront of the hunt. "Forgive me for not showing the proper respect by rising in your presence and that of the ladies."

"Let us all pray for this man's salvation," Reverend McAllister intoned.

"But first," Maggie interrupted before heads could be bowed, "the reverend has agreed to hear the whole story of how you came to us, why you risked everything to reach these shores. Are you up to this, Stefan?" She handed Stefan the envelope she'd retrieved on her way from the cupola and placed her hand more possessively on his shoulder.

"Perhaps it would be best if we all sat

down," Frederick suggested, drawing side chairs closer to the fire for the church women, who tittered at his courtly attentions. Frederick then indicated that the minister should take Gabe's usual place in the club chair and led Jeanne and Lucie to the love seat. "Would anyone care for coffee or tea?" he asked when everyone was seated except for Maggie and himself.

"This is hardly a social occasion," the minister reminded him tersely.

"Ah, yes. I do tend to forget that you Americans like to keep business separate from socializing." He shrugged and smiled as he leaned against the mantel. "Maggie, why don't you begin? Stefan and the duchess can fill in when needed and so he might reserve his strength."

Maggie cleared her throat, then focused for a moment on the gold cross around Stefan's throat. "To understand Stefan and his mission, you must first know his sister, Uma," she began. For the next hour she gave them every detail that she could recall — the Christmas truce, the deaths of Uma and Klaus, the contacts Stefan had had with the resistance. The details rolled from her tongue as if she herself had lived them. Her passion for the doomed Uma and Klaus brought out the handkerchiefs of the church women. Her description of men on the front from opposite sides coming together on Christmas Eve clearly moved the minister. By the time she unfolded the intricate details of how Stefan had been led to America, how he had jumped ship because it was his only opportunity, how he had placed his fate and the fate of his information in God's hands, her audience was hanging on her every word.

She gathered her strength to continue through the pressure of Stefan's hand grasping hers. She did not know when he had reached out to her, taken her hand and held on, but she realized that for everyone in the room there was no scandal in the act.

Jeanne took up the story, explaining her husband's role in the resistance and her own decision to continue his work with Frederick's help. She gave the details of the comedy of errors that included the famous blue scarf and umbrella, and when she was finished, the crackle of the burning logs and the ticking of the grandfather clock were the only sounds in the room.

"I don't know what comes now," Maggie said. "That is surely in the hands of you and others, but Stefan has always placed his trust in his faith, Reverend. It has carried him this far, and I believe that whatever happens next is for some purpose of God's that we may never fully understand."

The women of the church looked to the minister for direction. But Reverend McAllister's boyish features were in turmoil, his mouth working even as his eyes cast wildly about the room as if looking for some sign to guide his next steps.

"Stefan Witte is in your custody, Reverend," Lucie said, coming to his aid. "Whatever happens next, he is of no danger to this community. You have only to decide if you believe him. Ask yourself, if this were one of our native sons telling this story, would we not do whatever was necessary to see that he had the opportunity to deliver his news to the appropriate authorities?"

Reverend McAllister bowed his head for a long moment.

"Stefan has lost everything to come here," Maggie reminded him. "His family is gone and he has abandoned his country. He can never go home again, Reverend. Think of it — what he knows was important enough to risk everything."

The minister raised his head and walked over to Stefan. "I have never witnessed such courage, such a pure act of faith," he said huskily. "May God bless you. But if you have deceived these good people and placed them in peril of losing their reputation, their livelihood, and indeed the only home they've known, then only God can forgive you."

The phone in the lobby jangled.

"It might be the ambassador," Jeanne cried and ran to answer the telephone, with Frederick close behind.

"The duchess has been trying to reach her friend, the former U.S. ambassador to Austria-Hungary, all evening," Mama explained. "The ambassador has powerful connections in Washington and if we can persuade him to see Stefan, to hear what he has to say, perhaps this will all not have been in vain after all."

"It has not been in vain," Stefan assured her. "For I have met you and your husband. I have known your kindness, witnessed your courage in the face of certain censure from your friends and neighbors. And I have had the rare gift of Maggie's care and comfort for these precious days. I thank you and bless you, Mrs. Hunter. You and your husband and the Chadwicks."

Mama blinked back tears as she turned to Mrs. Pritchard. "Eleanor, I believe you and the ladies here came to pray? Shall we get on with it?"

Eleanor Pritchard bristled as she always

did whenever Lucie Hunter dared speak to her with such authority. After all, Mrs. Pritchard was a member of one of the oldest families on Nantucket, while Lucie Hunter was an Irish immigrant who had been little more than a servant to Gabriel's parents before she'd managed to mesmerize Gabriel into marrying her.

She glared at Lucie and the stony gaze of disapproval told Maggie that the emotional tale of Stefan's journey had not had a lasting effect on her. "Our prayers might better be offered on behalf of your daughter, Lucie, or have you completely abandoned your parental authority where she is concerned?" She turned to Maggie while continuing to address Lucie. "You are aware that she thinks she is in love with this man."

"Maggie is no longer a girl. She is a woman capable of making her own decisions and choices. In this case I believe she has made the right choice, but make no mistake that her father and I would stand by her under any circumstances."

Mrs. Pritchard's mouth worked as if she were chewing something bitter, and she turned her attention to Jeanne, who had just hung up the telephone and returned to the circle gathered around Stefan. "Your Grace," Eleanor exclaimed, "surely you . . ."

Jeanne ignored the woman and went straight to Stefan. "The ambassador is sending his secretary first thing tomorrow accompanied by a military detail. If the secretary believes you, then he'll take you to meet with the ambassador and perhaps on to Washington." She glanced at the others. "Until then, we are all under house arrest, but things could be ever so much worse."

"If need be, I'll go to Washington with you," Maggie assured Stefan.

Mrs. Pritchard fairly exploded before anyone else could say a word. "You are an unmarried woman, Margaret Rose Hunter. Surely you can appreciate that traveling with a man — especially this man — is most unseemly."

"Oh, Eleanor, dear, how caring of you, but should matters come to that, our Maggie will be well chaperoned," Jeanne said with a laugh. "Aside from myself and the duke's nephew, there will be an entire military guard."

"Your Grace, you have spent much time in Europe, where such situations are handled more . . . freely, by all reports. Here in America a woman simply does not travel with a man of eligible age unless they are married."

"Then perhaps they should marry before

we leave," Jeanne replied. "We could make it a double wedding, with Frederick and myself as the other couple. For surely, my dear, if you disapprove of Maggie's behavior, the fact that Frederick and I have been traveling together for several months now must seem an absolute scandal."

Mrs. Pritchard blushed scarlet. Again her mouth was working, this time seeking words that would have her stand her ground without offending the duchess.

"This is hardly the time or place to discuss weddings," Lucie reminded them.

"It will be light in a few hours," Frederick said when the silence became uncomfortable as the church women glanced warily to the minister for guidance. "And the day promises to be one that will demand the highest level of faith and strength each of us can muster. May I suggest we each pass these last few hours in prayer and silent communion?"

"Yes. Very good," Reverend McAllister replied. "Perhaps the ladies might make use of your library to rest, Mrs. Hunter?"

"Of course. Sarah, please make them comfortable."

It was obvious to Maggie that the church women — Mrs. Pritchard in particular — were reluctant to risk missing any further action that might take place in the sitting room. Nevertheless they obediently followed Sarah across the hall. Reverend McAllister took the chair closest to Stefan and leaned forward, his hands folded in prayer, his head bowed, as he murmured verses from scripture.

Mama persuaded Jeanne to go with her to prepare for the arrival of the ambassador's secretary. And Frederick sat down at the piano and began playing a Chopin sonata, the music further dispelling the tension that had filled the room just minutes earlier. Maggie sat on the floor, her head resting on the sofa inches from Stefan's hand. After a moment she felt his hand resting lightly on her hair. It felt like a blessing, and she closed her eyes and let the minister's words and the music lull her to sleep.

But her respite was short-lived. By mid-morning, having traveled overnight by military transport, the secretary arrived and with him what seemed to Maggie an entire regiment of soldiers. Four soldiers immediately surrounded Stefan, who was now up and moving forward to greet the ambassador at Jeanne's insistence.

"Oh, gentlemen, do be at ease," Jeanne insisted, favoring the young men with one of her most radiant smiles. But the soldiers continued to close in on Stefan and seemed prepared to physically take hold of him. Their senior officer muttered a command and they backed away.

The small man dressed in civilian clothing stepped forward. "I am the ambassador's personal secretary, Percy Walls," he announced, and Maggie saw that he was in no mood for socializing, having barely acknowledged Jeanne's assurance that she and the ambassador were dear old friends. He focused his attention on Stefan. "Tell me two things about Germany to demonstrate that whatever information you have is genuine and that the ambassador will not be wasting his time hearing what you have to say," he demanded, ignoring the hand Stefan had extended.

Stefan straightened as he might have if he'd been faced with his own commanding officer. "Last year's crops failed owing to drought, and this was followed by excessive rain," he reported. "By Christmas the citizens of Berlin were completely without bread or potatoes and the same was true of other towns across the country."

Maggie watched Percy Walls closely and saw a flicker of admiration cross his eyes before he turned away. "That's hardly secret information," he challenged. "There are published reports of the shortages."

"The ministers of agriculture ordered reports to the public altered to say that the situation was 'average.' However, a majority of the experts had advised that it was an alarming shortage at best and dire at worst," Stefan added, his voice clipped and precise as it would be were he testifying at a trial.

"What else?" the secretary asked as he moved to the window and pretended an interest in the view of the sea.

Maggie saw a ghost of a smile cross Stefan's lips. "There is much else to be told, sir, but you must understand that I need certain assurances."

"And you must understand that I have no authority to offer such assurances," Walls replied. "When we are done here, you will be in the custody of these soldiers. I will take your information and have it authenticated, if possible. After that . . ." He shrugged and Maggie thought she might actually physically attack the pompous little man.

"You can't do that," Maggie blurted before anyone else could speak.

"Maggie, dear, please," Jeanne pleaded.

"No. Stefan has risked everything to bring our government this information. You can't expect him to trust that you'll do as you say."

"Maggie!"

Walls looked down at her from over the tops of his glasses. "Young woman, I do not know your part in this, but I should be very careful if I were you not to end up identified as an accomplice."

"I am his accomplice," Maggie said, and it was as if all the air had been sucked from the room as everyone fell silent and stared at her with disbelief.

"You are confessing to being a traitor?" The secretary spoke slowly as if he wanted to be sure she understood every word. The soldiers seemed to close in without taking a step.

"Absolutely not," Maggie began. "I am saying that . . ."

"Come now," Frederick interrupted, stepping to Walls's side and clapping him lightly on the back. "It has been a long and exhausting night, sir. No one has slept and understandably emotions are running high. I give you my word that this man's information could be invaluable."

"You know what he has to offer then?"

Frederick swallowed. "Not exactly," he admitted.

Tell him, Maggie thought, casting glances

from Frederick to Jeanne and back again. Tell him that you are with the resistance, that you know Stefan to be exactly what he says he is. Tell him.

"Now, Mr. Walls," Jeanne said, her voice oozing sweetness as she took the man's arm and led him a little away from the others. She spoke to him in such low tones that no one else could make out a word of what she said. Not that Mrs. Pritchard didn't try.

"Speak up, your Grace," she said when the secrecy became unbearable. "We are all at sixes and sevens here with this matter."

Jeanne escorted the secretary back to the center of the room, where he once again ignored everyone but Stefan.

"The duchess has suggested what might be a workable plan. Write out the information you have, seal the envelope so there can be no question of tampering and I will carry it to Washington myself."

Maggie was confused. Nothing had changed. She looked imploringly at Jeanne, who actually winked at her and held up one finger as if to say, *Wait for the rest.*

"In the meantime," Walls continued, still addressing Stefan, "you — and the rest of you — will remain here under house arrest and under the constant guard of Captain Swann's force."

"Thank you, sir," Stefan said and pushed himself to a standing position to once again offer the secretary his hand. This time Percy Walls accepted it.

"No tricks," he warned. "It is my understanding that you have used up all of the goodwill these people have freely offered and then some."

"Yes, sir," Stefan replied. "You have my word."

A snort from the corner of the room stated more clearly than any words what Mrs. Pritchard thought of that.

"Ma'am?" Captain Swann stepped forward and addressed Lucie. "I wonder if I might have a look around the premises. My men and I will need to set up a campsite and choose the best accommodations for keeping watch over our prisoner."

Sean stepped forward. "I'll show you around, Captain."

When they were gone, Lucie pulled out the chair next to her small secretary and lowered the writing surface. "Sit here, Stefan."

"That won't be necessary," Stefan assured her as he handed the envelope to Percy. "The information is here, sir."

Maggie glanced around the room. The scene before her was like some stage setting. There was Stefan, standing by her mother's desk, calmly waiting for the captain to complete his tour and decide where to hold him. Sean was explaining the various entrances and exits to the inn, while Mama and Sarah had headed for the kitchen to prepare food for the soldiers. The aforementioned soldiers had stationed themselves around the entrance to the parlor and the front door, obviously prepared to go into immediate action should Stefan decide to make a break for it. Jeanne and Frederick were cornered with the secretary around the telephone at the end of the hall as he called Washington to give his report. And then there was the minister and the women of the church, who seemed unsure of what their new roles might be.

It was almost comical, and Maggie felt a wave of hysteria threaten — when suddenly Mrs. Pritchard stepped to her side.

"Seriously, Margaret Rose," she said, "I know that your poor mother has been ill and your father is such a busy man, but really we must discuss your future. I am quite fearful that your grief has gotten the better of you and you are making rash decisions."

Maggie had been on edge all night — searching for Stefan, coming so close to escape, facing the people at the church and now what? She wasn't sure how much more she could take. It was her last thought before the room went black and blessedly silent. And this time she wasn't faking.

CHAPTER THIRTEEN

"Maggie, wake up."

Mama's voice came through the blackness, accompanied by the hum of a concerned chorus of others. She fought her way back to consciousness and opened her eyes a slit to find herself reclining on the same sofa Stefan had recently vacated. She smiled and turned her face to the cushion, certain that she could still smell the essence of him as she allowed her eyelids to flutter closed.

"Maggie." It was the distant echo of Stefan's voice, the last thing she had heard before fainting. She opened her eyes and waited for him to come into focus. But he was gone.

"She's coming around," Mama said and was immediately interrupted by Mrs. Pritchard's wail.

"I was afraid of this. She's exhausted and distraught. It's all been too much for her. She's completely overcome, and who can

318

blame the poor child? That horrible man — that *German* . . ." She ground out the last word as if it were a bitter taste in her mouth.

Maggie was sorely tempted to surrender to the pleasant netherworld of unconsciousness, where she could at least imagine Stefan being there, touching her cheek, speaking her name. "Stay with me, *liebchen,*" he would murmur. "All will be well."

Eyes closed, she reached for his hand and felt instead the flush of her own skin. "I'm fine," she said, turning over so that she was facing her mother and the others. If they had taken Stefan away, then she must go to him.

"You are not fine, Margaret Rose," Mrs. Pritchard protested. "Lucie, I think it would be best if she went to her room."

Maggie forced herself to a sitting position. "I am fine," she repeated firmly.

"Perhaps what would be best for all concerned, ladies," suggested the minister, "is if we turn our thoughts to the return of our brothers Gabriel and Thomas now that this man is in custody."

"Yes, excellent idea, Reverend," Mama said and waited while the women followed the minister across to the library before turning her attention back to Maggie. "Eleanor is right, Maggie. Enough is enough. Go upstairs now."

"But Stefan . . ."

". . . has been taken back to the cottage for questioning, and trying to go to him will only make the authorities more suspicious," Mama said in a low voice as she wiped Maggie's brow with a cool, damp cloth. "Can you think of no one but him? What about your father and Tom?"

The anxiety that Maggie saw in her mother's eyes brought her back to the full reality of the mess Stefan had created for everyone. Her mother was right. As much as she wanted to go to Stefan and assure herself that he was not being mistreated, she had to think of her father. "An hour," she bargained in a teasing attempt to lighten the mood by reminding her mother of how as a girl she had bargained for shortened nap times.

"Until I come for you," her mother countered and she did not smile.

Despite Maggie's every attempt to fight her weariness, sleep won out; the sun was waning when she woke. The day was almost gone. What had she missed? What were they doing to Stefan? She ran to the window and looked across the yard to the cottage. She could see a few of the soldiers milling about, setting up their campsite near the barn. The captain and Sean were smoking their pipes and talking as if they were old friends.

She opened the door to her room and leaned over the banister. There was a soldier stationed on the landing between the foyer and the second floor. She eased down the hall to the back stairway and jumped when another soldier leaped to his feet at the sight of her.

"Miss," he said with a polite nod as he made room for her to pass.

"Why are you here?"

"Orders, miss."

"Yes, yes. But why here on this stairway?"

He glanced behind him at the spiral stairs that led to the cupola, and Maggie's eyes widened in horror. "Surely you aren't holding Stefan up there. The man will freeze. He's already fought his way back from a serious case of frostbite and —"

"Captain Swann thought the cupola the safest place to hold the prisoner while the cottage is being readied for his incarceration," the soldier explained, then shut his lips tight as if he'd already said too much.

A thousand questions ran simultaneously through Maggie's brain. Incarcerate? What happened to house arrest? Were they taking him away after all? And above the fray rose the single question uppermost in her mind: How can I get to him?

"Have you had anything to eat, Private?" Maggie asked, keeping her voice calm and chatty. She'd heard Jeanne use this same tactic dozens of times when she wanted something.

"No, miss. The others are making camp and having their supper, and then I'll be relieved. Thank you," he added.

She fingered the afghan she kept on the railing for those times when she had stayed in the cupola reading or just staring out at the Atlantic. "Private, it's very damp today, and with the sun going down, the temperatures are sure to drop. As the prisoner's nurse, I really must insist that he have this extra protection." She cradled the afghan in her arms. "I could take it up to him, make sure he's all right. You know just last night he suffered a setback and well, we —"

"Sorry, miss. Orders," he reminded her. He held out his hand. "I'll give him the cover, miss."

Maggie was just about to pass him the afghan when there was a crash on the stairway below and the soldier turned his attention away. He was distracted just long enough for Maggie to dash up the stairway and slip inside the cupola.

Stefan pulled her to her feet as she bent to trip the latch on the trapdoor. "Maggie, what's happened now?"

His questions were answered with the private's knock at the trapdoor.

"Please, miss," the soldier pleaded, keeping his voice low. "You'll get me in trouble with the captain."

Maggie glanced at Stefan, torn by her wish to be with him versus the fate of the poor soldier below. "Five minutes," she said softly. "They all think I'm still asleep. Just five minutes, please."

"Not a second more," the young man replied, and they heard him move back to his post.

"Maggie, what are you thinking?" Stefan chastised her even as he pulled her to his side and wrapped the wool afghan around them both.

"I am thinking that since you came into my life, I have been unable to think straight, and in spite of believing I was running in the opposite direction, I have moved steadily along a path that has brought me to my senses."

Stefan held her close and kissed her hair. "How so?"

"I have survived the valley of the shadow of death, and despite all my doubt and denial, God was with me for every step."

"And now?"

Maggie lifted her face to his. "I know now that God has led me to you."

Instead of embracing her fully, sweeping her away with the power of his kiss, Stefan released her. "Do not think of me as your salvation, Maggie."

"I don't. That's not what I meant."

"Ours is an impossible love, *liebchen.* You know that. We have had these few moments in time, but now we must understand that each of us will move forward on a new path, one that cannot include the other."

"No! The ambassador will read your letter and send word that you are to be freed immediately. We will go forward from there."

"Even so, I have nothing to give you, Maggie. What kind of life would we have with people always wondering, speculating? I will be a man without family, without country, without a home to call my own."

"Do you love me? You said you loved me. Was that nothing?"

He held her close, rocking her from side to side as he murmured against her ear, "I love you more than I can ever express."

"Then that's all I need," Maggie said and cupped his face in her palms as she stood on tiptoe to kiss him.

"Miss? Time's up." The latch on the trapdoor rattled. "They're coming to change the guard, miss. Please."

Stefan set her away and reached up to remove the gold cross from around his neck. "Take this," he said. "Know every time you look at it that I am thinking of you — only you."

He bent and released the latch, and the soldier pushed the trapdoor aside as Stefan helped Maggie through it. Below them they could hear the new guard coming down the hall.

"Go," Stefan and the soldier begged in unison, and Maggie hurried down the back stairway that led to the kitchen, clutching the gold cross so tightly that when she finally opened her fist, the imprint of it was clear in her palm.

Stefan waited until he was sure that Maggie was safely on her way down the back stairs to the kitchen. Then he went back to the window and waited, alert to the changing of the guard below.

"Private, call for the prisoner." The voice was that of the captain, a middle-aged man who reminded Stefan of the Belgian resistance fighter who'd given him his first assignment and then helped orchestrate his plan to bring word to the Americans.

The private climbed the spiral stair, and his eyes begged Stefan not to reveal Maggie's visit.

"Danke," Stefan said quietly as he followed the young man to the landing and faced the captain.

"This way," the captain instructed but there was no malice in his tone, only weariness.

Stefan followed the man down the back stairway and into the kitchen. He heard Maggie's breath catch at his unexpected appearance and caught the glint of the gold cross around her neck as he passed her.

But the captain neither paused nor spoke as he traversed the kitchen and exited by the back door. Stefan had no choice but to follow his lead, since the young private was right on his heels.

He gave Maggie a smile as he passed but did not dare risk touching her face or hand, as he so longed to do.

Outside the captain slowed his stride and fell into step alongside Stefan. "You understand English, right?"

"Some," Stefan replied warily.

The captain laughed — heartily as if Stefan had just shared a good joke — then pulled a cigarette from his pocket and offered it to Stefan.

"No, thank you."

Captain Swann shrugged. "Suit yourself." He paused to light his cigarette and took a long draw on it as he studied Stefan. "Dismissed, Private," he muttered. "I'll take it from here." The relieved private saluted and scampered off toward the campsite. Captain Swann hitched one booted foot onto a stump and leaned on his knee as he exhaled smoke.

Stefan stood straight and tall but not quite at attention and waited for what might come next.

"You have some powerful friends," Swann said. "What exactly is the connection between you and the duchess and her British companion?"

"I met them last night for the first time." He saw by the tensing of the captain's body that he preferred to hear the answers he expected rather than the truth.

"So you expect me to believe that they called the ambassador and summoned us all the way out here because they liked you so much after meeting you for the first time last night?" He took another draw on the cigarette. "Do I look like a fool?"

"No, sir."

"Or perhaps it's your lady friend and her

parents who've staged this whole thing," he muttered more to himself than to Stefan.

"Maggie — the Hunter family — only cared for me after they found me on their beach. It was the Christian thing to do. They would have done the same for anyone."

"Even a German?"

"They did not know that I was German when first they brought me here. That came later." He did not add that the family was well aware of his nationality within an hour of rescuing him.

"You and the daughter have something going between you." It was not a question, so Stefan did not respond.

The captain crushed out his cigarette with the toe of his boot and started in the direction of the cottage. "Well, let's get you in and settled," he said.

"Where's Aunt Jeanne?" Maggie asked the following morning as she helped her mother prepare food for the soldiers.

"She's in her room writing the ambassador and others who might help."

"And has there been any word about Papa?"

Lucie backhanded a tear and continued peeling peaches. "Chief Anderson sent word that we are free to visit this afternoon —

with an escort of the guard, of course. I thought I'd take along some of my peach cobbler. It's your father's favorite."

The paring knife trembled and then fell from Lucie's fingers as she burst into tears. She covered her face with her apron as Maggie led her to a kitchen chair and knelt beside her.

"Mama, it's all going to work out. Once they read Stefan's letter — once they understand what . . ."

Lucie dropped her apron and stood up. "We should never have allowed the man to stay so long. The minute he was able to travel, we should have . . ." She turned and faced Maggie. "Your father is in jail, Maggie. And so is Tom. These are our family, our dear friends. Who is Stefan Witte to us?"

Maggie swallowed hard but did not back down in the face of her mother's anger. "He is the man I love and he is a man who has had the courage to do what is right. He is so like Papa — and you — in that, Mama."

As Lucie stared at her, Maggie realized that in many ways they were less mother and daughter than they were two strong-willed women in that moment. They were equals in that they were each determined to protect the man they loved.

Finally Lucie's expression softened. "Oh,

Maggie, you cannot imagine the life you are bargaining for in loving this man. He is German, and despite his noble intentions there will always be those who see him as their enemy."

Maggie smiled. "He won me over," she reminded her mother.

This time Lucie smiled, as well. "So he did," she said. "Go tell Jeanne we will go into town just after lunch. She can post her letters."

But as it turned out there was no need to go into town, for shortly before lunch there was a commotion in the yard.

"It's Gabe," Mama cried, racing to the door and throwing it open. She ignored the police chief and the several additional soldiers that accompanied him and threw herself into her husband's arms.

"I'll have to get myself arrested more often if this is to be my welcome home," Papa joked as Lucie clung to him.

"Papa, what's happening?" Maggie asked, taking a count of the men with him.

"There's been a change of mind," Papa replied with a tight smile. "Captain Swann has decided that it's in the best interest of the government to hold all detainees in one place."

"I don't understand." Lucie looked at the

police chief for an explanation.

"Gabe and Tom are being detained by the military, Lucie," Anderson explained. "Just until this whole business can be cleared up, you understand. Just a formality to keep folks from getting their noses out of joint."

"We aided the enemy," Gabe translated. "It's a federal matter, not a local one. The chief has no jurisdiction."

"But where is Tom?"

"He's at the hospital. Captain Swann agreed that he was needed there and could be guarded while he attended his patients."

The arrival of the captain interrupted further conversation. "This way, if you please," he said, indicating that Gabe should go with two of the soldiers.

"Where are you taking my husband?" Lucie demanded, and Maggie saw the captain blink in surprise.

"Well, ma'am, as Chief Anderson explained, he's being detained along with the German. It's best to hold them in the same place."

"That's ridiculous," Mama argued. "Surely he can be detained with me in our own home. He's right here should you need him for questioning or such."

"Now, ma'am, you've got a point. It's true that you are all under house arrest, but frankly it makes my job easier to have separate accommodations — the men in the cottage there and you ladies in the house."

Lucie straightened to her full height, which was not more than an inch taller than Maggie but impressive nonetheless. "Now see here, young man,"

"Lucie, love," Gabe interrupted, "the captain is simply following orders. Don't make this any more difficult than it already must be for him."

"Well, maybe that's the problem. Maybe that's the thing about this entire war business — people blindly following orders instead of considering what makes good sense," she huffed.

"I'm sure President Wilson would agree, my dear," Gabe said, stepping forward to kiss her on her forehead and pull her into a long embrace, "but unfortunately he never asked you, now did he?"

Maggie saw a whisper of a smile cross her mother's lips. It was a long-standing joke in their family that when Lucie got riled up about something, she would rant for several minutes and then take a deep breath and mutter, "But they didn't ask me, did they?"

Papa held out his free arm to Maggie, pulling her into the circle of the family embrace. "Keep strong and keep faith."

Gabe broke away from his two women, but he paused one minute longer as his gaze settled on the gold cross around Maggie's throat. She saw the confusion that passed over his weary features — was she wearing it because of the romantic connection or, as he had hoped for months, because —

"I will pray for all of us, Papa," she said, fingering the cross. And when she saw the relief and happiness that lit her father's smile, she knew that she had told him what he needed to know. Further, she realized that it was the truth, for whatever the outcome of this situation, she had started down a new path and would never again start a journey without God as her guide.

As the day wore on, Maggie had never seen her mother so agitated and out of sorts. She eyed the soldiers on duty in the house with disapproval, as if each had personally affronted her in some way. For their part they tried hard to stay out of her way, accepting the food that Sarah dished up for them with a murmured thanks and downcast eyes before hurrying back to their post as they made their escape from Lucie's accusing stare. It might have been comical had the situation not been so serious.

"Maggie, go choose some reading materials from your father's library," Lucie ordered the following afternoon. "And change into something besides your uniform. We are going calling."

"But Lucie, dear," Jeanne protested.

Lucie cut her off with a statement directed just as much to the guard at the front door as to Jeanne. "If we had permission to go all the way into town to visit, then surely we can make the trek across the yard without causing undue harm."

Thirty minutes later the three women marched down the path to the cottage. Mama was dressed in her best: a pony-skin coat that featured an impressive fox collar and cuffs, a matching hat and taupe leather gloves. Underneath she wore her celery-green silk afternoon dress trimmed with a deep forest-green stain at the neckline and at each of its three tiered skirt panels. Maggie was dressed in a red wool broadcloth walking suit, with its offset row of self-covered buttons marching the length of the jacket and aligning with the straight, ankle-length skirt and its high, narrow collar, which showed off her long neck. Her hat was wide-brimmed felt and the velvet trim matched the cuffs of her suit jacket. And Jeanne topped them both in her flamboyant lime-green satin kimono coat and matching turban hat by the famous Paris designer

Paul Poiret.

Maggie could not help thinking what a sight they must make as they walked in matched strides, their fashionable but serviceable leather boots hitting the shell-strewn path in unison. She saw the young soldier on duty at the front door of the cottage hurry inside. A moment later Captain Swann appeared on the porch. "Good afternoon, ladies," he said with a cordial smile and wary eyes.

"Good afternoon, Captain," Mama replied. "I have come to visit my husband."

"And you?" The captain's smile bordered on a smirk as he shifted his gaze to Maggie.

"I have come to see my father," Maggie said.

"I'll have to check your parcels," Swann said, eyeing the basket of food Mama carried and the armful of books that Maggie clutched to her chest.

"Of course," Mama agreed and waited for the captain to step aside. "There's a nice table in the front hall where we can set everything for you to inspect."

The captain held open the door and then followed them inside. Maggie followed her mother's example and set the stack of books next to the basket on the table, then Lucie pulled off her gloves and removed her hat as if preparing for a long stay. Maggie and Jeanne followed her example.

Maggie glanced toward the first-floor bedroom where she had nursed Stefan. The door was open and the room unoccupied. A footstep above drew her attention up the stairway, where she saw a guard seated outside George's former room.

"Twin beds in that room plus a cot. A bit crowded perhaps but secure. Also it's on the second floor," the captain said quietly, following her gaze as he fanned each book to make sure there were no hidden weapons or messages.

"Very wise," Mama said and went directly into the parlor. "Maggie, perhaps you could light the fire here while I make us some tea and lay out the cookies Sarah made."

Jeanne indicated a chair near the fireplace. "Captain, you will be joining us, I assume."

Swann seemed momentarily nonplussed. "I had thought a few moments would suffice, ladies."

"Surely matters are not so dire that we can't make use of the parlor," Jeanne replied as Maggie bent to light the fire.

Jeanne relieved the captain of the books he still held. "Perhaps you would enjoy reading one of these in the evenings, Captain. After all, your prisoners can hardly read more than one at a time and it must be, well, a bit boring just sitting here for hours on end."

"That's very kind of you, ma'am."

Maggie replaced the bellows and turned her most radiant smile on the captain. "It is you who have shown kindness, Captain, by allowing our visit. Shall I call for the guard to bring my father and Mr. Witte?"

"I thought you came to see your father?"

"Indeed, but it seems cruel to sit here with him when Mr. Witte has no family to visit him. Surely the Christian thing to do would be to include him?"

Swann scowled at her but stepped to the door and signaled to the guard at the top of the stairs. "Get them down here," he ordered. "Half an hour," he told Maggie and Jeanne, "and I'll be right here."

"We wouldn't have it any other way," Maggie assured him as her mother arrived with a tray set with tea for seven. "Shall I pour, Mama?"

Maggie heard multiple footfalls coming down the stairs. She resisted the urge to run to Stefan, to examine his face for any signs of mistreatment, but instead forced herself to take a seat near the tea tray, prepared to serve the others.

Mama had no such reservations as she ran

to Papa the moment she saw him and wrapped herself in his embrace as if it had been months, not hours, since she last saw him. "Are you all right?" she asked.

Papa laughed and kissed her. "Other than missing you, I am fine. Our young friend here, however, may be a bit worse for the time he's spent sharing a room with me." He kept his arm around Lucie's waist as he led her to the settee. Maggie couldn't help feeling envious that the others had such freedom to express their true feelings.

She risked a glance at Stefan and looked just as quickly away when she saw Captain Swann watching her. But oh, how Stefan's eyes had glowed with his love for her. "Sugar, Captain?" she asked as she poured the first cup of tea.

"Three," he replied and declined both milk and lemon as he accepted the cup and saucer from her. "Well, sit down, Witte," he commanded as he took the chair across from Maggie, leaving only a straight-backed side chair next to her for Stefan.

He was so near that she could have moved her knee no more than six inches and touched his. Her hand shook as she poured another cup of tea and prepared it for her father.

"We brought you reading materials,"

Mama told him as she relieved Maggie of the teacup and passed it to her husband. "Maggie, get the books, please. We didn't know what to choose, so if there's anything you'd rather have, we can bring that when we visit this evening."

Swann's eyebrows shot up. "Now, ma'am," he began.

"Oh, come now, Captain," Mama replied. "The situation we all find ourselves in is unique. Surely there is no need to make matters worse than they already are — for my husband or for you. Have a cookie, Captain." She passed him the plate while Maggie handed her father the stack of books.

"Ah, Tennyson," Papa said, cradling the slim leather volume. "My favorite. Have you read the poet, Captain?"

Swann chewed the cookie slowly as he considered the situation. "Yes, sir," he replied. " 'The Charge of the Light Brigade' inspired me to join the military when I was still in school."

"Really?" Gabe leaned forward as he continued to pepper the captain with questions about the poem, about his schooling and about his family.

When the clock chimed three, Swann looked up in surprise. The cookies were gone, and he had lost all track of the time. He leaped to his feet and cleared his throat. "That's enough," he said sternly. "Private," he called in the direction of the hall, "escort the prisoners to their quarters."

Once again Gabe embraced Lucie and then held out his arms to Maggie. "You may want to look at the book by Morse," he said as he released her. "I think you would enjoy it."

Maggie was mystified at this strange parting message. "I'll look for it," she replied, searching her father's expression for any further clue. But Papa only smiled. "Gentlemen," he said, as if he were in his own house and inviting his special guests to retire to his study and join him in a cigar.

"We'll see you this evening," Mama promised, clasping Stefan's hand between hers as he passed.

"Tomorrow," Swann corrected her. "I'm not running a social club here, ma'am."

"Let the man do his duty, Lucie," Papa said as he caressed Mama's cheek.

Mama's lips thinned but she nodded. "Tomorrow. I'll ask Sarah to make that chocolate cake you love so much."

The minute Maggie got back to the house, she ran to her father's library and scanned the shelves for books by Morse. The only volume she found was an instructional guide to learning Morse code. What is he thinking? she wondered and took the book to her mother.

To her surprise Mama laughed.

"Your father has always been a romantic," she said. "He inherited it from his father. Your grandfather served in the Union Navy during the Civil War."

"I know," Maggie said, "but —"

"When he was courting your grandmother, her parents, especially her father, did not approve. There were bitter feelings as you can imagine between her family, who were Southern plantation owners, and your father, who had been assigned the task of securing Charleston harbor."

"Yes, but what has that to do with this?" Maggie waved the book.

"When your grandmother's father forbade her to see your grandfather, she found this book in her father's library. Your grandfather had promised to come every evening and signal his presence with a light. One night Grandma signaled back, and they communicated that way until her mother finally persuaded her father that love could not be denied."

Maggie tried hard to picture the frail, elderly couple she had known as a child as young and so much in love that they would defy her grandmother's parents and society to be together. "It's like my love for Stefan," she whispered and then realized she had spoken aloud.

"Exactly," Mama said softly. "I think your father is giving you the tool you need to speak with Stefan."

"And his blessing," Jeanne added.

"Yes, our blessing," Lucie murmured. The magnitude of what her mother was saying left Maggie speechless. Gratitude and joy grabbed her heart and squeezed it so tight that for a moment she could not catch her breath. "Truly?" she finally managed.

Mama laughed and hugged her. "Truly," she assured her. But then she held Maggie by the shoulders and her expression turned serious. "We will not stand in your way, Maggie, even though we will always worry . . ."

"I know."

Jeanne joined them, wrapping her arms around them both. "Listen to your heart, child, for it will be your guide in what is best for you and for Stefan — even if that turns out to be letting him go. Do you understand?"

Maggie nodded. "But for now," she said as she clutched the book to her heart. "For now, we are together and I will not take one hour of that time for granted." And with that she ran up to her room to compose and practice the message she would send Stefan that night.

CHAPTER FOURTEEN

Stefan had just heard the clock chime midnight when he turned to find Maggie's father bending over him, shaking him gently. "I'm awake, sir," he said as he sat up. "What's happening?" Surely the old man wasn't planning an escape.

"Look out the window," Gabe whispered as he crawled back under the covers of his bed and turned his back to Stefan. "There's a message for you."

Baffled by the older man's instructions, Stefan sat up and glanced out the window. At first there was only the blackness of the night, but then there was a blink of light followed by dark and then another blink.

He moved closer. The light came not from the direction of the lighthouse, as he might have expected, but from the inn. More specifically from the room in the tower — Maggie's room. He waited. And there it was again.

"I'm hoping you know Morse code," Gabe said.

"Yes, sir."

"Good, then you won't need me to translate and you and my daughter can speak freely. I'm going back to sleep." He rolled over to face the wall and pulled the blanket over his head to shut out the lamp. "You'll have to give her some time," he mumbled. "Remember, she's just learning, so keep it simple."

"Yes, sir." Stefan hoped *I love you* was simple enough.

With each passing day the weather would promise to improve, and then deteriorate again. Fortunately, Captain Swann expanded the visiting hours to include a visit after lunch and another shorter one after dinner. He accepted the books that Maggie chose for him and seemed to look forward to the afternoon tea, which moved out onto the porch when the weather improved. It was only a short leap from that to including Stefan in the pickup baseball game the guards played when they were a man short.

One evening, at Jeanne's suggestion, Maggie and Stefan took turns reading poetry aloud during the visit. No one doubted that the selections they chose were meant to send the secret messages of their growing love.

"I wonder, Stefan," the captain mused after the ladies had returned to the inn, "if you might not spend a part of your time tutoring my men in the practice of Morse code."

"Excellent idea, Captain," Gabe said and returned to reading his newspaper. Stefan glanced at Gabe but Maggie's father ignored him.

"Of course, if you aren't interested," the captain continued, "I could always ask Miss Hunter. She seems to have been a quick student, judging from the communications I've noticed flashing across the compound here lately after lights-out."

Stefan felt his face flush, but then the captain smiled. "Might want to save the more private stuff for the poetry readings, son," he muttered as he patted Stefan's shoulder on his way out.

Gabe lowered his newspaper just enough for Stefan to see the frown that furrowed his brow.

"I assure you, sir, there has been nothing said that I would not say in front of you and Mrs. Hunter."

Gabe grunted and went back to reading his paper. After a while he folded the paper and tapped it lightly against his knee as he stared at Stefan. "Do you truly love my daughter, Stefan?"

"I believe you know that I do, sir."

"Enough to give her up should that be in her best interests?"

"You mean if I go to prison."

"Or are deported back to Germany, in which case I expect you would face an even harsher punishment."

"I would not permit Maggie to suffer," Stefan said.

"That doesn't exactly answer my question. Whatever your fate, she will want to be with you."

"I will see to it that Maggie is never in danger and never has cause to suffer because of me."

"She's already suffered a great deal. Women take these things harder than we do."

"I don't agree with that, sir, but I do agree that she has been through enough. I assure you that I will do everything in my power to ensure she suffers no more."

"That's all I ask," Gabe replied as he passed Stefan the newspaper and then stretched. "It's been another long, boring day. I think I'll turn in."

Stefan considered the moment and decided the timing was right. "I wonder, sir, if I might ask you a question."

Clearly Gabe heard something in Stefan's tone that made him give the younger man his full attention. "What is your question?"

"Well, sir, if God should see fit to show the American leadership that my information can be believed and if in return for that I am able to find sanctuary here in your country, then I would ask permission to marry your daughter."

"Let's not get ahead of ourselves here," Gabe replied with a frown. "There's a lot that needs to happen before you can even begin to . . ."

Stefan shrugged. "We are speaking hypothetically this evening, sir. I appreciate that. You have asked what happens if I am imprisoned or deported. I am simply asking what happens if I am not."

"What kind of work were you in before you joined the war?"

Stefan smiled at what only appeared to be an abrupt change in subject. "I was studying for the law, sir. My father and grandfather were both in that field." Stefan saw that Maggie's father was surprised and impressed.

"Would your desire be to complete those studies here in this country?"

"I would very much hope to do that."

"Then, hypothetically speaking, you would have my blessing to marry Margaret Rose — and her mother's, I'm sure."

"Thank you, sir. With your blessing all we need is God's."

"Can't help you there, son," Gabe replied as he started for the door. "Also can't help you make up Maggie's mind, either."

On Sundays the women were permitted to attend church services, with the guards driving and standing watch outside the small church. The women took their place in the Hunters' usual pew and ignored the whispers of speculation that accompanied their entrance and exit from the church. But on the second Sunday after they'd returned from church, Maggie was surprised to see the minister and his wife drive into the yard in midafternoon.

"We've come to pray with the prisoners," Reverend McAllister informed the captain. "If they cannot be permitted to come to the church for prayer and worship, then my wife and I shall bring them the word of God here."

Captain Swann invited the McAllisters inside the cottage and kept watch while they prayed. The following Sunday, he met the minister in the yard and made the suggestion that perhaps Reverend McAllister might want to minister to his men. "They won't have duty like this forever," he said. "In time — and sooner rather than later — they will be assigned to units overseas. Some of them won't make it back, Pastor."

Yet even as the pattern of their days and evenings took on a kind of routine normalcy, Maggie could not shake the feeling that they were all waiting for something — the other shoe to drop, her mother had once said. This was not real life. That would come only once they had gotten the decision from Washington. Every day Maggie waited for the phone call that would decide their fate.

"It's surely a good sign that they are taking so long," Jeanne said, but after two long weeks even she had trouble sounding positive.

Maggie returned to her habit of spending time alone in the inn's cupola. The difference was that now she spent that time in prayer. She had heard her mother telling Sarah of Stefan's conversation with Gabe. She knew what he had promised, and she had no doubt that he would never ask her to marry him unless good news arrived from Washington.

She no longer doubted that God would

hear her prayers. It was waiting for some sign that He had decided to grant or deny her prayer that was the torment. Surely God would touch the hearts and minds of those strangers in Washington who unwittingly held her fate in their hands. Surely soon there would be word. But she was torn between wanting desperately to know Stefan's fate and her fear that he would be taken from her.

Well, whatever the outcome, I will go with him, she thought defiantly and was immediately contrite. *If that be Your will,* she added.

The party line telephone was signaling a call when the women returned from their nightly visit to the cottage. With Easter just a few weeks away, they had shared a wonderful evening filled with songs and stories. Maggie's parents had done their best to raise everyone's spirits with reminders of happier times. Although it was very late for any call that was not one of distress, Maggie paid no mind as she ran to the phone. "Hello?"

"This is the office of Ambassador Clarence Tisdale calling. To whom am I speaking, please?"

"Maggie — Margaret Rose Hunter," Maggie replied, her voice barely a whisper. She cleared her throat. "Would you like to speak with the duchess?"

"Indeed."

Maggie held the receiver out to Jeanne. "It's the ambassador's secretary," she whispered.

"Hello?" Jeanne shouted as if she needed to make herself heard without benefit of a telephone. "Clarence? Is that you?" She pressed the receiver tighter to her ear. "I'm having trouble hearing you," she shouted.

Maggie and Lucie pressed closer as Jeanne held up one finger and concentrated on listening. "What has happened? Is there news?" Her expression crumpled with disappointment as she replaced the receiver on the hooks. "The line went dead."

"But what did he say? Is Stefan to be cleared? And Papa?"

"I don't know. The connection was bad, and all I got was something about arriving tomorrow."

"I'm going to tell them," Maggie said and took off at a run before either of the other women could stop her.

"Whoa, little lady," Swann said, intercepting her before she could reach the cottage. "Visiting hours are over for today."

"But there's been news."

"Yes, ma'am, there has." Swann looked toward his command post, where one of the soldiers was scribbling furiously as he listened to someone on the other end of a field telephone.

"Then it's true." Maggie thought her heart would quite literally burst with relief and happiness.

Swann scratched his head. "Tell me what you know."

"The ambassador telephoned. It was a terrible connection, but we think that the decision has been reached and he's . . ."

"Now, miss, I think it would be best if you wait until the ambassador and his party arrive before we say anything to your — to the prisoners. It wouldn't do to raise false hope, now would it?"

False hope?

"If I could just see my father for a minute," she pleaded.

"Now, miss, we both know it's not your father you're wanting to see. Please go on back to the house and wait for the ambassador to get here tomorrow." He signaled to two of his men, and they immediately came to stand at either side of Maggie. "Please, miss. It's for the best."

Maggie took one last glance at the upstairs window of the cottage. "Very well," she agreed, knowing there was more than one way she could talk to Stefan.

But when she went to her room and sent her news, the room at the cottage remained dark and there was no reply. She tried again with the same result. Grabbing her father's binoculars from the side table where they'd been since she'd first begun signaling Stefan, she focused on the window across the way.

It was dark because it had been covered with a heavy black drape. As Maggie lowered the binoculars, she saw Captain Swann standing in the yard and looking up at her. When he saw her looking, he tipped his hat and returned to the cottage.

A fierce storm reminiscent of the night when Stefan had first come to them delayed the ambassador's arrival for three long days. During that time the afternoon and evening visits were more like vigils than social gatherings. Finally, on the third day, the sky cleared and early that afternoon Maggie spotted a carriage coming up the lane.

"Mama! Jeanne!" She ran down the stairs from the cupola, along the hallway, past the open doors of the inn's guest rooms and down the main stairway to the front hallway. "Someone's coming," she shouted even as she tore open the front door and ran across the yard to meet the approaching carriage. Behind her she could hear her mother, Jeanne and Sarah, their voices entreating her to wait for them as they ran to catch up with her.

"Whoa," the driver ordered his team and pulled the carriage to a halt at the entrance to the circular drive.

The carriage door swung open and Maggie paused as she watched the ambassador's secretary emerge and then hold out his hand to assist another passenger. An elderly man dressed in a business suit with matching bowler climbed down from the carriage. "Pay the good man, Percy," he declared. "We can walk from here."

"Clarence!" Jeanne shrieked as she ran to the older man and embraced him. "It is so wonderful to see you. Come, let me introduce you." She hooked her arm through his and led him toward Lucie.

"This is Mrs. Gabriel Hunter and her daughter, Margaret Rose. The woman there on the porch is Sarah Chadwick, and the men, as you no doubt know, are being held prisoner in that cottage there."

"Now, Duchess," the ambassador said in a voice that was raspy and thin, "you know as well as I that matters of this sort must be allowed to run their course."

"And have they run their course?" Jeanne asked as she paused next to Maggie and her mother so that all three women were surrounding the ambassador.

He smiled. "My secretary and I have had quite a long journey," he replied. "Perhaps, Mrs. Hunter, I might impose upon you to permit us a place to freshen up and have a small glass of water?"

"Of course," Lucie replied and led the way up the drive to the inn.

Maggie watched them go, thinking she would have driven a harder bargain. Tell me he's free, she would have demanded. Tell me you believe him and you may drink your fill.

"Percy," the ambassador called, "be so kind as to send for Captain Swann and the . . . the others."

He hadn't said *prisoners,* although he'd come close. Maggie felt the knot in her heart loosen just slightly.

By the time everyone was gathered in the parlor of the inn, Maggie thought she would surely go mad. It seemed to have taken forever for the ambassador to refresh himself, for Captain Swann to bring Papa, Frederick and Stefan down to the inn and for the endless offering of tea and food to run its course. Finally the ambassador cleared his throat and took from his pocket the letter Stefan had written.

Maggie drew in her breath and forgot all about releasing it as she leaned forward, her hand itching to clasp Stefan's.

"Young man," the ambassador began, then cleared his throat, a habit Maggie was beginning to find annoying. "Young man," he repeated, "we have perused your information, and admittedly it has some validity."

"Some validity? It's the truth," Maggie said. "He has risked everything to . . ."

"Seems to have validity, but what?" Jeanne asked as she placed her hands firmly on Maggie's shoulders.

The ambassador kept his attention fixed on Stefan. "The offensive you have described began two days ago. The new tactics for attacking are exactly as you wrote about them. But, as you surely must realize, the news has come too late to really do anything to prevent what has already begun."

Maggie thought her heart would hammer right out of her chest. "He's told you all he knows," Maggie argued. "Surely the timing . . ."

"Perhaps. Perhaps there is more to tell — details you do not even realize that you know. That is the hope."

"And if I cannot provide such further detail?" Stefan asked.

The ambassador shrugged and picked up his teacup. "Then there is a question of whether or not you were well aware of the timing, knew the attacks would take place this week and deliberately withheld the information so that they could not be stopped."

"He was ill — near death several times. He delivered this news as soon as he could," Maggie protested.

The ambassador studied Maggie for a long moment. "Did he? Or did he only give up the information when it was necessary for him to do so in order to save himself?"

Maggie glanced around the room looking for reinforcements, but all she saw was that the others, her parents included, were actually considering this possibility.

Maggie twisted around to look up at Jeanne. "Tell him. You know better. You and Frederick were to meet . . ."

"A German seaman who had certain information. How do we know for certain that the seaman was Stefan?"

"He knew the pass code."

Jeanne shrugged. "So what happens now, Clarence?"

"I should like some time alone with Mr. Witte," he replied.

"May I ask what is to become of my husband in the meantime?" Lucie asked, having held her tongue for her daughter's sake, knowing that Stefan was in the greater danger.

"I apologize, madam," the ambassador replied. "I should have told you and the duchess immediately that a decision there has already been made. There will be no charges against your husband, the good doctor or Mr. Chadwick. Their actions were not political but were offered purely in the spirit of common decency in caring for someone in need. Your husband and the doctor will be relieved of their responsibilities as part of the island patrol, but beyond that there will be no repercussion."

Maggie saw her mother bow her head for a moment and then look up with tears gleaming. "Thank you."

"And Sir Groton?" Jeanne asked.

The ambassador took some time to sip his tea, wipe his lips and clear his throat. "I am sorry, dear Jeanne. I fought against it, but the times being what they are, certain members of the government's inner circle seemed quite alarmed that you and Sir Groton — residing outside this country and all . . ."

"We are to be deported?" Jeanne seemed to barely be able to get her breath and Frederick moved immediately to her side.

"I'm sure it's temporary, my dear. Once this whole awful business is . . ."

"No," Maggie declared in a calm, steady voice as she stood to face the ambassador. "You have said yourself that you do not yet have the entire story. Then the decision is not yet finalized?"

"Well, no, but . . ."

"Then surely where whole lives are about to be changed forever, there is room for further consideration?"

"I have said I will question Mr. Witte, young woman," the ambassador replied, his voice gaining in strength. "Quite frankly it is my opinion that we are going well beyond what would be considered the norm in such circumstances."

"And his information? It has no value at all?" Gabe asked, coming to stand alongside his daughter.

"Well, of course, it has value. Just knowing the tactics to be used . . ."

"You tell me the offensive has begun," Stefan said. "If you show me a map of where the attacks were launched, I can help you

360

track the most likely progression of the front. It would be only a guess, but it would be based on the conversation I overheard that evening."

"And if you are wrong?"

"But why not think he might be right?" Maggie asked. "What is there to lose?" She hurried from the room and returned a moment later with a large atlas from her father's study. "Here," she said, pressing the oversized book into Stefan's hands. "Show him."

Gabe and Frederick cleared a table and Stefan set the book on it, turning the large, brittle pages until he came to a map of western Europe. "The attacks began here?" he asked and the ambassador nodded.

Stefan's finger hovered over the map. "Here," he said. "And then on to here," he added, tracing a line across the page with his forefinger. "If they are not stopped . . ." He drew his finger across the landscape all the way to Paris.

"No," Jeanne whispered. "Not Paris."

"Is there no stopping them?" the ambassador murmured as much to himself as to Stefan or anyone else surrounding the atlas.

"Are your American soldiers battle ready?" Stefan asked.

The ambassador shrugged. "Who can say

for certain? They are there."

"Unless he changed his mind, it was the general's intention to concentrate his force here," Stefan said. "I am no strategic planner, sir, but it would appear that in that case . . ."

"This entire area would be undefended," the ambassador replied, sweeping his hand over an entire stretch of the terrain.

"The resistance is very strong in that region," Frederick said. "They could be quite helpful."

"Indeed," the ambassador replied. He focused his gaze on Stefan. "Why would you do this? Betray your own countrymen?"

"I am not, sir. I love my country as you love yours. It is that love of country that has driven me here. This war must end if humanity is to have any hope of finding a lasting peace."

"And if the Germans are victorious?" Gabe asked quietly.

"If the regime currently in power in my homeland is victorious, then may God have mercy on us all," Stefan replied.

Maggie thought that she could not possibly love him more than she did in that moment. To admit such a thing was so clearly heartbreaking for him that she wanted desperately to reach out to him, to reassure him that he was doing the right thing, not only for his country but also for any hope of a future that she and Stefan might have. "You must believe him, sir," she said, watching the ambassador as he studied Stefan closely.

For one endless moment it seemed as if everyone in the room had stopped breathing. Finally the ambassador drew in a long sigh. "This is not my decision to make," he said, addressing Stefan directly. "But because the information you provided has proved truthful and because this new information gives me a thread of hope that it is not too late, you, the duchess and Sir Groton will return with me to Washington and speak to President Wilson."

Maggie suppressed the flare of hope that threatened to burst forth. "And in the meantime?" she asked, ignoring the warning glances her parents and Jeanne flashed in her direction.

"In the meantime, young lady," the ambassador replied, "I should think that you and your family and friends here have some decisions to make. Mr. Witte has involved all of you in his actions — whether intentionally or not, that is the reality. In spite of his apparent courage and heroism, he might yet be deported back to Germany." He widened his attention to include everyone. "I would respectfully suggest that you all use the time it will take for me to go to Washington and meet with the president to prepare yourselves for the worst."

"I cannot ask this of you," Stefan said later that evening when the ambassador had agreed to give Stefan and Maggie a few minutes alone on the porch of the cottage.

"You aren't asking anything. If you are sent back to Germany, then I am going," Maggie said. She folded her arms tightly over her chest and pushed the porch swing into motion with her feet. "I have learned my lesson, and I will never again be separated from the man I love."

Stefan forced the swing to a halt by planting his feet firmly on the floor. "Not even if I ask that you give me the time to see this through?"

When Maggie ducked her head, stubbornly refusing to look at him, he lifted her chin with his forefinger. "Look at me," he pleaded. "I am not Michael. This is not like that. If it's God's will, then I will come back to you."

"And if not? If they put you on trial? If you have no one to speak on your behalf?"

"Ah, *liebchen,* we both know now that

364

God has His reasons for everything. If it is meant to be that we had this time, that we touched each other's lives deeply and irrevocably, isn't that enough?"

"But I want so much more," Maggie admitted.

Stefan kissed her. "So do I, Maggie."

She snuggled against him as he rocked the swing and held her. "For tonight we know nothing of my fate, so can we not simply pretend that it could as easily go well for me, that one day we will be married?"

Maggie pushed a little away from him. " '. . . we will be married,' " she mimicked. "That is hardly my idea of a proper proposal, Stefan Witte." His eyes grew so wide with alarm that she couldn't help but laugh. "Oh, Stefan, I am teasing you. Of course, I will marry you. I would marry you tonight."

"And if things go badly in Washington?"

"We will be together whatever happens," she assured him.

Stefan sighed heavily and took her by the shoulders. "I cannot allow you to leave your home and family," he argued.

That was the final straw. Maggie stood and placed her hands on her hips. "You cannot allow? Well, I cannot allow the man I love to face this alone. If you go, then I am coming with you and that is that."

"You are very stubborn," Stefan grumbled. "Fortunately your parents are more sensible."

But once Maggie told her parents that Stefan had proposed and that she intended to marry him as soon as possible, her mother took her side. "A wedding in the midst of all this heartache," she said, "would be such a blessing — like the coming of spring, a new beginning."

"Now, Lucie, love . . ." Gabe said.

"It's perfect. A kind of confirmation of life continuing along its normal course," Jeanne announced, and the women in the room immediately began making lists and time-tables, while the men watched, each wondering how it had happened that these three women had taken charge of the situation and their lives.

CHAPTER FIFTEEN

On Good Friday it not only rained, it poured. The sky was gray, the sea was gray and the harbor was lost under a thick gray drizzle and fog. And as Maggie retreated to the cupola for perhaps the last time for months to come, her mood was definitely somber. How ever would Stefan make it in such a storm?

He had gone to Washington to present his incredible story to the president. Captain Swann and a detail of his men had accompanied them. Maggie had pleaded to go as well, but Stefan had smiled and cupped her cheek.

"But, *liebchen,* you have a wedding to plan," he'd said.

It was true. If the outcome of the visit with President Wilson was that Stefan was to be deported, then there would be no time to waste. And if it wasn't? If by the grace of God his story touched the president's heart and Stefan was granted asylum?

"Please let it be so," Maggie prayed aloud as she pressed her palms against the glass of the cupola window and listened to the distant mournful wail of the foghorn. She closed her eyes and tried to imagine herself in her bridal suit walking down the aisle of the church with her father. She imagined Stefan waiting for her, his gaze a beacon she would seek the rest of her life.

War bride, Mrs. Pritchard had called her with a disapproving curl of her lips that left no doubt she believed Maggie had chosen the wrong side in the war. Of course, it was true. She was to be a war bride. The plans were in place as far as possible, meaning she had decided what she would wear, who would be in attendance, assuming the ceremony took place on the island, and what flowers she might carry. The day and time — and place — had yet to be determined. If all went as planned, she and Stefan would be married on Easter Sunday afternoon in a simple ceremony at the church. But if not, if he was to be deported immediately without being allowed to return to Nantucket, then she would go to him and they would be married by the ship's captain or chaplain as they made their way toward an unknown future in a country that would view them both as enemies.

"Maggie, come down!" Her mother's voice was strong and filled with an urgency that made Maggie run for the trapdoor and down the spiral stairs.

"What is it?" she cried, leaning over the banister so she could see her mother. Lucie was standing in the lobby holding a distinctive yellow sheet of paper. "You have a telegram."

Maggie had no idea how she made it from the upstairs hall to the lobby so quickly, but she accepted the envelope her mother handed her. With her hand trembling as her heart threatened to hammer out of her chest, she opened it and took out the single sheet of paper. "It's from Auntie Jeanne," she whispered and saw that her father, Sarah and Sean had gathered behind the front desk to hear the news. Terrified at what news she might yet have to share with them all, Maggie scanned the contents of the message.

Stefan granted sanctuary STOP
F and I as well STOP
Will work for our government here
    STOP
Back soon STOP

                                    Jeanne

Sanctuary. The word resounded through Maggie's brain as she read the telegram through twice more to be sure she wasn't missing anything.

"Well?" her mother demanded, unable to stem the tide of her curiosity a moment longer.

Maggie handed her the telegram and listened as Lucie read it aloud. There was a moment of stunned silence, and then Sarah began to laugh and cry at the same moment. "Ah, Margaret Rose, it's over," she said, hugging Maggie tightly.

"You'll be living in Washington from the sound of this." Gabe frowned at the words on the telegram as if by sheer will he might change that fact and keep Maggie safe on Nantucket.

"It's not the end of the world, Papa," Maggie said. "It's not Germany."

"Oh my, we have a great deal to accomplish," Lucie said and ran to get her collection of notes from under the front desk. "We no longer need this — or this or that," she chanted as she tore pages from the notebook she had called her "just in case" lists.

Early the next morning Maggie slipped back up to the cupola. The steamer that would bring Stefan back to her would arrive in a matter of hours, and she found it fitting to be in the place where so many of the seminal moments of her young life had occurred when he came up the lane. She opened the window and breathed in the scent of nature coming into bloom as the soft drizzle washed her face clean of all the heartache and worries she'd suffered ever since Stefan had gone away. She closed her eyes and fantasized about her wedding — her Nantucket wedding.

Maggie rested her head on her hands and dozed. She and Mama had stayed up late going over the details of the wedding and although she fought to stay alert lest Stefan arrive and she not know it, she could not help being lulled by the sound of the waves rushing onto the shore, then retreating again. The wind became the murmur of guests gathered on a sunny spring afternoon. The foghorn became the church bell calling everyone inside. The rain was the traditional rice pelting her and Stefan as they left the church, and the garden was the perfume of her bridal bouquet. Maggie smiled at the vision of her perfect wedding day.

But what was that squawking sound?

Impatient with anything that might interrupt her revelry, she opened her eyes and peered out into the gray mist. Again came the squawking, like a goose in distress, followed by laughter that carried through the gloom and up to the cupola. And then she heard the undeniable putter of a car engine.

"Auntie Jeanne," she shouted as the car pulled up to the front of the inn. "Up here," she called when Frederick stepped down from the driver's seat and glanced around. He waved and then opened an umbrella as he ran around the car to the passenger side to open the door for Jeanne.

Maggie held her breath, peering through the rain and fog to see a third person exit the car.

Stefan!

Every prayer of thanks that she knew flew straight from her heart toward Heaven as she ran to meet him. She had listened for God's answer, and now Stefan was here, standing at the foot of the stairs, his arms outstretched to catch her.

"You're here, truly, really here," she said as she buried her fingers in the silk of his hair and covered his face with kisses.

"I'm here," he assured her as he swung her round in a circle so that her feet left the ground.

"As are we," Jeanne reminded them.

"Oh, Auntie Jeanne, thank you a thousand times," Maggie gushed. "And you as well, Frederick."

"While we'd be happy to take credit, the truth is that Stefan here was the one who insisted we traverse the high seas during an electrical storm," Jeanne said with a dramatic sigh.

"We were never actually on the high seas, my dear," Frederick reminded her.

"And then the automobile got stuck. I really do need to speak with Gabe about the roads on this island," Jeanne insisted. "Now come with me, young lady. Frederick, could you get me that box from the car?"

"I'll bring it," Stefan offered.

"Now, Maggie, do forgive me, but you and Stefan will have a lifetime to catch up. We really must plan this ceremony properly."

"Oh, Auntie Jeanne, everything's arranged. Reverend McAllister will perform the ceremony Sunday afternoon, and Mama has invited him and his wife to join us all here for the wedding supper. Sarah's making a cake."

"But what are you to wear?"

"I have a new dress," Maggie assured her.

"A wedding dress?"

"A dress," Maggie said firmly. "It will do."

"Oh, my dear Margaret Rose, for your wedding day, one cannot simply make do."

Stefan brought the box and seemed somewhat confused when Frederick ushered him into the library, leaving the women alone in the lobby. Maggie opened the large box, and among layers of tissue she found the most beautiful cream-colored silk suit she had ever seen. "I couldn't," she whispered.

"Well of course, you could and you will," her mother replied looking over her shoulder as Maggie lifted the jacket and held it to her. "Thank you, Jeanne," Lucie said and hugged the duchess. "It's perfect."

"Well, I had visions of her wearing that starched apron and ridiculous nurse's cap. Are you aware, Maggie, that Stefan abhors that hat?"

"He's mentioned that," Maggie admitted.

"This will do much better," Jeanne announced as she opened a hatbox that Stefan had brought along with the box. She held up a cream straw hat with a wide brim trimmed in delicate silk roses and a wide satin ribbon. "Ever so much better than that white thing," she announced.

In a whirlwind of activity, Jeanne took charge. By midafternoon the lobby was filled with a parade of vendors summoned by the duchess and more than willing to offer their services in spite of the fact that the groom was known to be a German.

As the evening wore on, it became increasingly apparent that Stefan was confused and frustrated by all the activity that seemed specifically designed to keep Maggie and him apart until the ceremony. But Frederick assured him that such was the American way when it came to women and weddings. "It's a bit as if they are planning their own nuptials," he said with a chuckle. "Stefan, you will need someone to stand with you at the ceremony. I would be honored to serve."

"Thank you," Stefan replied. "It is you who honor me."

"And I shall walk my daughter down the aisle," Gabe said with a yawn. "Seems to me we men have sorted this entire business out in the span of a few minutes. Why can't the ladies learn to simplify?"

All three men burst into laughter at the foolishness of such an idea.

On Saturday, Stefan was finally able to catch Maggie alone. She was in the garden, gathering herbs for the wedding supper that Sarah would help the caterer prepare.

"Come walk with me," he pleaded. "We've hardly had a moment alone."

She laughed. "Oh, Stefan, we have the rest

of our lives. It's been so long since I've seen Mama so happy and excited. It's almost as if she's reliving her wedding."

Stefan took the basket she carried and set it on the path. "Come."

They headed for the beach. The overnight storm had left the air clear, the skies a brilliant blue and the surf light and foamy.

"Give me your shoes," Stefan said as he paused to remove his shoes and socks and roll the cuffs of his trousers above his ankles.

"Turn your back," Maggie instructed.

"We're to be husband and wife," he reminded her.

"That's tomorrow. Turn your back," she repeated, and when he did, she pulled off her shoes and stockings and dropped them on the sand. Then she tagged him on the shoulder and took off at a run.

"Not fair," Stefan called as he gave chase. He caught up with her easily, grabbing her round the waist and lifting her high over the waves as he stepped into the water up to his knees.

"Put me down," she squealed. "Not here," she amended when he pretended to lower her into the water.

Laughing, he swung her up and into his arms and walked out of the waves and onto the beach. "How about here?" he asked.

"Better," she said, her face a hair's breath from his, her eyes on his laughing mouth. They kissed with no thought of who first reached for the other. They were in love, deeply and without reservation. Finally they parted and Stefan allowed her to slide to a standing position. Hand in hand they walked slowly along the shore toward the lighthouse at the very end of Great Point, to a place where the harbor was on one side and the ocean on the other.

"Maggie, think of it. The waters of your Nantucket flow into the sea, as do the waters of the great rivers of my homeland. Those waters that brought me here to you are connected as we are connected. We come from different worlds, different cultures, and yet we have found each other."

"Perhaps this is the covenant that God intended for us, Stefan. A common ground where I come as myself and you come as yourself, but together we walk side by side and hand in hand in love and faith that erases all doubt."

They were silent for several moments as they stood with arms intertwined and looked out to a horizon beyond which they knew the world was in chaos and pain.

Maggie rested her head against Stefan's

shoulder. "I can't wait to start our life together."

"Even though it means leaving your home?"

"My home is wherever you are," she said and tweaked his nose. "Whither thou goest . . ." And as they retraced their steps along the beach and back up to the inn, Maggie could not remember a time when she had felt more certain of the path her life had taken.

Maggie's wedding suit featured a jacket with a single offset button closing, a wide shawl collar and three-quarter sleeves with deep cuffs lined in satin. Her ankle-length skirt flared at the hem and was edged with a row of satin French knots over cream-colored stockings and matching leather shoes with silver buckles. Her bouquet was a traditional nosegay of purple hyacinth, pink tulips and golden daffodils that had miraculously blossomed just in time for the ceremony.

She stood nervously at the back of the church, thinking how ridiculous it was that she should walk down the aisle when only her parents and the Chadwicks would be in the pews. Jeanne was her only attendant, as Frederick was Stefan's. The minister and his wife, of course, were there, he to pronounce the words and she to play the music, but that was a given.

"Ready, Maggie?" Her father offered her his arm as Jeanne took her place just ahead of them in front of the closed sanctuary doors.

"Yes, Papa," Maggie said and drew in a deep breath as Jeanne tapped lightly at the double doors and magically they opened. Maggie gasped as Dr. Williams and Sean held open the doors. Beyond them the pews of the small church were packed with townspeople, school chums and neighbors all standing and smiling as Maggie and Papa made their way down the center aisle.

"They came," she murmured as she nodded and smiled.

"They wouldn't have missed it. You and Stefan have given them something to celebrate," Papa said.

Stefan!

Maggie forgot everything and everyone else as Stefan stepped forward before she and Papa could reach the altar. Papa kissed Maggie's cheek and then placed her hands in Stefan's as they turned together to face Reverend McAllister.

And to the background of the time-honored vows, Maggie saw that on this Easter Sunday, God had resurrected so much more than her faith. Through her union with Stefan God had given the people of Nantucket hope. Whatever storms might come their way, they would weather them. Maggie would love Stefan every day of their lives together, be that time short or long, and she would thank God for every challenge and every blessing and every precious hour they would share.

Dear Reader,

It's always a writer's joy to revisit characters from a previous book, so this opportunity to bring back Gabe and Lucie Hunter from *SEASIDE CINDERELLA* and tell the tale of their spirited daughter, Maggie, was a special treat for me. The World War I setting also gave me a chance to explore an era of history that has long fascinated me, and it was indeed an eye-opening experience to research how frostbite might have been treated in 1918! I hope you enjoyed returning with me to Nantucket to consider the challenges of opening one's heart to finding the way to forgiveness and acceptance in a time of war. And as always, be in touch via my Web site at www.booksbyanna.com or through regular mail at P.O. Box 161, Thiensville, WI 53092.

All best,
Anna Schmidt

QUESTIONS FOR DISCUSSION

1. In what ways was Stefan able to hold fast to his faith in spite of the losses and challenges he suffered?

2. Stefan tells Maggie that if she questions and doubts, then she has faith. Agree? Why or why not?

3. What preconceived ideas about Germans in general did Maggie have?

4. How were those prejudices changed so she was freed to love Stefan?

5. What is your definition of prejudice?

6. Have you or someone close to you ever experienced prejudice firsthand? If so, how was that incident unfair to you or your loved one?

7. Can you think of a time when you were guilty of prejudice against another person or group of people — even if you did not openly express those feelings? If so, how did God help you come to terms with that?

8. Scripture tells us to love our neighbor. Who are our neighbors?

9. Was Stefan a traitor or a patriot for Germany? Why?

10. What challenges might Stefan and Maggie face once they marry?

11. What does the Bible teach about forgiveness?

12. In today's world, how important is it for us to open our hearts and minds to a better understanding of cultures and peoples that differ from our own? How might we accomplish that?

ABOUT THE AUTHOR

Anna Schmidt is a two-time finalist for the coveted RITA® Award from Romance Writers of America, as well as twice a finalist for the *Romantic Times BOOKreviews* Reviewers' Choice Award. The most recent nomination was for her 2006 novel, *Matchmaker, Matchmaker . . .* The sequel, *Lasso Her Heart,* inspired readers to write to Anna via her Web site (www.booksbyanna.com) and declare that its theme of recovery from tragedy brought them comfort in their own lives. Her novel *The Doctor's Miracle* was the 2002 *Romantic Times BOOKreviews* Reviewers' Choice Inspirational Category Winner. A transplant from Virginia, she now calls Wisconsin home and escapes the tough winters in Florida.